"Lijena Farleigh,
I have come for you!"

Securely astride the horse, the Faceless One wrenched forth a sword of crystalline flame. Crackling sparks of blue-white licked along the blade's cutting edges, dimming the afternoon sun's brightness with their unholy glare.

Not waiting for the demon to attack, Lijena took the offensive. A battle cry tearing from her throat, she once more hefted the Sword of Kwerin Bloodhawk above her head and charged the demon foe.

Magic-forged steel met sword of crystalline fire in a shower of sizzling green sparks. From fingertips to arms, the bone-jarring impact of clashing magicks raced through Lijena's slender body until her knees buckled beneath her own weight, throwing her to the deck.

The Faceless One's mount reared, its burning hooves hovering over the fallen woman for a heartbeat before descending. . . .

Ace Fantasy Books by Robert E. Vardeman and Geo. W. Proctor

THE SWORDS OF RAEMLLYN SERIES

TO DEMONS BOUND
A YOKE OF MAGIC
BLOOD FOUNTAIN
DEATH'S ACOLYTE
THE BEASTS OF THE MIST
FOR CROWN AND KINGDOM

Ace Fantasy Books by Robert E. Vardeman

THE CENOTAPH ROAD SERIES

CENOTAPH ROAD
THE SORCERER'S SKULL
WORLD OF MAZES
IRON TONGUE
FIRE AND FOG
PILLAR OF NIGHT

Ace Science Fiction Books by Geo. W. Proctor

STARWINGS

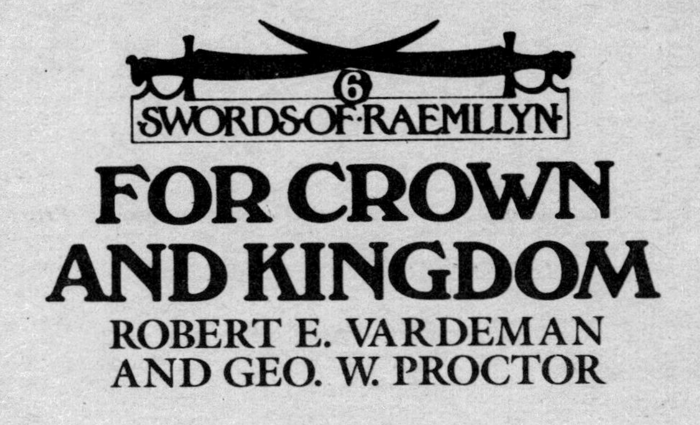

FOR CROWN AND KINGDOM

ROBERT E. VARDEMAN
AND GEO. W. PROCTOR

ACE FANTASY BOOKS
NEW YORK

This book is an Ace Fantasy original
edition, and has never been
previously published.

FOR CROWN AND KINGDOM

An Ace Fantasy Book/published by arrangement with
the authors

PRINTING HISTORY
Ace Fantasy edition/January 1987

Cover art by Luis Royo.

ISBN: 0-441-24565-X

Ace Fantasy Books are published by The Berkley Publishing Group,
200 Madison Avenue, New York, New York, 10016.
PRINTED IN THE UNITED STATES OF AMERICA

For Lana—thank you for being

...GWP

For a spectrum of Karens, from legal to leptonic

...REV

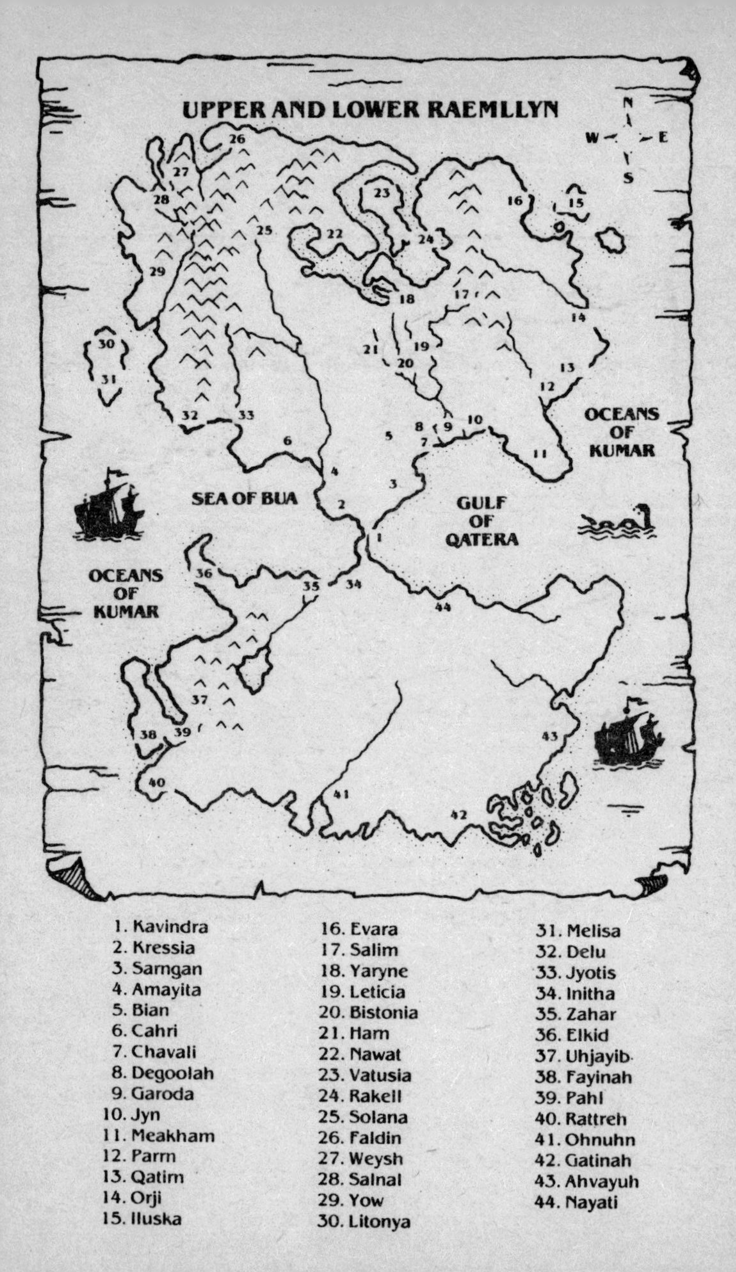
UPPER AND LOWER RAEMLLYN
N
W
E
S
OCEANS OF KUMAR
SEA OF BUA
GULF OF QATERA
OCEANS OF KUMAR
1. Kavindra
2. Kressia
3. Samgan
4. Amayita
5. Bian
6. Cahri
7. Chavali
8. Degoolah
9. Garoda
10. Jyn
11. Meakham
12. Parm
13. Qatim
14. Orji
15. Iluska
16. Evara
17. Salim
18. Yaryne
19. Leticia
20. Bistonia
21. Ham
22. Nawat
23. Vatusia
24. Rakell
25. Solana
26. Faldin
27. Weysh
28. Salnal
29. Yow
30. Litonya
31. Melisa
32. Delu
33. Jyotis
34. Initha
35. Zahar
36. Elkid
37. Uhjayib
38. Fayinah
39. Pahl
40. Rattreh
41. Ohnuhn
42. Gatinah
43. Ahvayuh
44. Nayati

1. Wynae Mountains
2. Plain of Kismor
3. Nawat
4. Bay of Pilisi
5. Yaryne
6. Rakell
7. Isle of Loieter
8. Vatusia
9. Bay of Zaid
10. Muu-Kou Mountains
11. Evara

chapter 1

DEATH, EYES ABLAZE like burning rubies set amid the black void of nothingness, riveted Neith Rigmar with its gaze. The Bistonian bargemaster's pulse tripled in a runaway pace. A cold sweat trickled down the river man's body in spite of the cool afternoon spring breeze.

To be certain, this was not the *Death* whom Raemllyn's denizens deified and gave the name Black Qar, but it was death just the same. In a coarse-woven, black, cowled robe, this death came riding astride a glistening, ebon battle stallion, with flaming hooves and fire streaming from its quivering nostrils.

A Faceless One! Neither giving a name to the demonic apparition nor the twenty feet of muddy water separating Neith's craft from the hell-rider on the bank of the River Stane quelled the bargemaster's terror. When he had accepted the pouch of golden bists from High King Zarek Yannis' emissary in payment for the betrayal of the two passengers aboard his *River Runner,* he had not bargained to commerce with hell creatures—with the legendary death horde from the shadowy dawn of Raemllyn's history!

May Jajhana visit the usurper Yannis with a plague of misfortune for this! Neith silently invoked the Goddess of Chance and Fortune to deliver the ill will that he, a mere mortal, could never hope to repay the would-be ruler of Upper and Lower Raemllyn for binding him to such hellish beings.

"A half-league ahead, Neith Rigmar."

A cold, flat voice that betrayed no hint of human tone or emotion called to the bargemaster. Neith was uncertain whether those words were born in the center of his mind or carried on the breeze from the Faceless One's unseen lips to his ears.

"I will await your boat half a league upstream where the river turns sharply eastward."

Unable to drag his gaze from the demon rider, Neith watched the Faceless One lift a skeletal talon and point one yellowed, boney finger northward. In the batting of an eye, a long, broad tail flicked from beneath the hem of the hell-rider's black cloak. Silver scales flashed as that unearthly appendage writhed. Then the mounted demon and its unholy steed were gone.

Neith Rigmar blinked as an icy finger of fear ran up his spine, then worked its way back down. Had the Faceless One vanished into the air, or merely hidden behind a copse of *morda* trees that grew near the Stane's bank? The bargemaster shook his head; when mortal man dealt with supernatural beings torn from another realm of existence, one could never be certain.

A half-league more. Neith glanced at the team of six oxen, and their driver, who pulled his barge up river. *A half-league more and I can wash my hands of these damnable matters!*

A smile touched the corners of the man's thin lips at the thought of the gold-laden pouch safely hidden within his quarters on the barge's stern. Remembering Zarek Yannis' generosity, he added a postscript to his thoughts: *at a handsome profit!*

Lijena Farleigh rose from a pallet of sleeping furs within the tent raised on the barge's deck. Listlessly, she stretched and yawned, her aquamarine eyes shifting to a second mound of furs piled across the tent. There Count luBonfil sat cross-legged, busying himself with quill and scroll.

"How long since I drifted off?" Lijena asked, edging aside a stray strand of frosty-blonde hair that tumbled across her forehead.

"Slept, Lijena," luBonfil corrected with a thin, dark eyebrow arched in reprimand. "You did not drift, but were soundly asleep. You spend far too much time in sleep, my lady. It's as though you seek to lose yourself in dreams."

"What else is there to do aboard this damnably slow barge?" Irritation crept into Lijena's voice.

Count luBonfil was right. Since leaving Bistonia two weeks past, a rootless lethargy had cloaked her mind and body, leaving her like one lost in the narcotic daze brought by inhaling the fumes of smoldering *calokin* buds.

Rootless? A wry, bitter smile twisted the young woman's lips. She lied to herself, and luBonfil was correct once more. She slept to escape the agony of the memories haunting her mind. Only there was no surcease. Even in her dreams, Chal's fair face beamed that smile her eyes would never again behold.

"Will you accompany me in a walk around the barge?" Lijena asked her traveling companion as she reached for the sheathed sword lying beside her pallet. "Oh!"

Her fingers jerked back the instant they brushed the weapon's hilt. A preternatural heat coursed through the blade.

"What?" Count luBonfil's head straightened. His eyes went round when he saw the source of his weaponswoman's distress. "The sword's fire is returned?"

Lijena nodded as she firmly grasped the magic-forged Sword of Kwerin Bloodhawk in both hands and lifted it by hilt and scabbard. "It pulses with heat!"

"Wait here!" The count tossed scroll and writing utensils aside, pushed from his piled furs, and darted from the tent ere Lijena could strap the ancient blade about her slender waist.

"Nothing," luBonfil said with a perplexed shake of his head when the blonde-tressed woman opened the tent's flaps. "I like this not. Give me a moment with our bargemaster. Perhaps he can provide a hint to the mysterious forces that stir the Bloodhawk's sword."

While Count luBonfil strode toward Neith Rigmar, who stood near the barge's prow, Lijena turned and walked to a rail on the craft's portside.

"Master Neith!" called Count luBonfil. "Are we nearing our evening's port?"

"Nay, Lord, not for another hour. Maybe more. The oxen're tiring quicker'n I ever seen. The bags of bones! Heavy spring runoff makes the river run fast and deep, dragging us backward. Harder for them to pull. Slippery mud on yon bank path adds to the beasts' burden."

"And all remains quiet?" luBonfil eyed the burly master of the river craft.

Neith Rigmar, the Bistonian bargemaster, spat thick and black into the River Stane and watched the swift currents seize the gobbet and absorb it into the muddy murk of the river. "The Stane is an old river, my lord. Except for drought or flooding, little changes it. Quiet is another name for the Stane."

Neith turned slightly and, out of the corner of his eye, caught sight of the lovely blonde wench dressed in gray doeskin. The sheathed, old longsword dangled from the shapely flare of her hip as it had for the whole journey.

The bargemaster's attention returned to the ferret-faced lord clothed in fine, embroidered silks. "All is quiet on the River Stane, my lord."

Neith spat again, his full contempt for this blue-blooded peacock in the gesture.

A needle of doubt pricked the bargemaster's scorn. Was Count luBonfil's suspicion aroused? Should he give a more detailed explanation for their slow progress upriver?

No, probably not, Neith decided. This fancy-dressed dandy gave no indication that he knew spit about river travel. Count luBonfil's arse looked like it'd be more at home in a fancy, gilded carriage drawn by white, prancing horses with jewel-studded harnesses. Neith's chapped lips pulled back in a smile that rapidly turned to a sneer, revealing black, *mylo*-weed-stained teeth.

For the Count, Neith had nothing but contempt. For the woman he had nothing but lust. Yet he knew better than to kill the Count outright and have his way with the wench, especially when Zerek Yannis' minister had promised additional rewards when these two were delivered.

But the wench! Even the man's clothing she wore could not disguise her trim figure, the upthrust of high, firm breasts, and the womanly flared hips. *Aye, a temptation in that beauty! By the gods, I bet she would scratch and claw like a she-devil! Might be worth defying High King Yannis' dictum.*

The grizzled sailor rejected the idea as quickly as it was born in his mind. He knew well the whispered rumors about Zarek Yannis' Hall of Screams and the punishments meted out to those who disobeyed the usurper's orders. Neith doubted none of those grisly tales of torture. Nor did he deny the reality of the Faceless Ones.

The hell-riders had returned to Raemllyn after ten thousand generations, summoned by the High King to enforce his rule across the face of the world. Twice a day since leaving Bistonia's docks, the demonic riders and their hellish mounts had appeared on the Stane's bank to remind the bargemaster of the powers Zarek Yannis wielded.

'Tis no time to think with my gonads! Neith decided as he watched luBonfil scan the river's bank, then turn to rejoin the enticing blonde.

Neith would remain loyal to the Velvet Throne. It mattered naught if Zarek Yannis had deposed and killed Bedrich the Fair, that many called Yannis a usurper and believed Prince Felrad the rightful heir and high king. The bargemaster simply plied his trade on the River Stane, made a decent wage and tried to ignore all the political intrigues emanating from Kavindra.

Go north, Yannis' emissary had said. Keep those who watched apprised of the count's movements. Do not let the two leave your vessel.

Neith decided that the count and his concubine—for what else could so lovely a wench be?—were criminals fleeing and, at some time to be determined by Zarek Yannis, they would be arrested. Neith saw his duty. He took the gold offered for his services just as he had accepted the count's money for safe passage to the headwaters of the Stane.

Neith spat out the last of his *mylo* weed and looked back at the oxen pulling the barge upriver. Occasionally, he shouted at the teamster to hasten the sluggish beasts, but mostly Neith watched for the Faceless One.

Count luBonfil leaned indolently against the barge's rail beside Lijena. He opened a multicolored cloth pouch strung from his jeweled belt, dipped his fingers inside, and popped a candied fruit into his thin-lipped mouth.

The man's words vibrated with an energy and urgency that belied his pampered pose. "The bargemaster hides something! I feel it. We must prepare for the worst."

"How can you be so certain?" Lijena Farleigh glanced over a shoulder and stared at Neith's broad back. "Old Pen said the man was reliable."

"Pen," spat luBonfil. "I do not trust that one. Even if he once served as a captain in Bedrich's guard, I do not trust him. Is he loyal to Prince Felrad? Who can say? Trust me, Lady. This bargemaster schemes!"

Lijena tossed her head and let the gentle breeze from upriver catch the shoulder-length, lustrous, frosty-blonde hair and pull it away from her face. She tired of the intrigue, of the constant suspicion of even devoted companions.

A tear came to her aquamarine eyes, and she unashamedly let it spill down her cheek without brushing it away. *Chal!* How she longed for his gentleness, his truth, his love.

No more would she rejoice in the Elyshah's touch, both physical and emotional. How her heart and soul ached from the emptiness left by Chal's death! The gentle poet-minstrel had given his life to save her from the dark mage Aerisan and his unholy summoning of the Death God's life-consuming aspects.*

Black Qar had feasted on countless souls while Aerisan's magicks had held the city-state of Bistonia in their grip. Armed with the mystical Sword of Kwerin Bloodhawk, Raemllyn's first high king, Lijena had defeated Zarek Yannis' murderous wizard and her old enemy Jun, emperor of Bistonia's thieves, but not before her beloved Chal offered his life to the Dark God in her stead.

The morning she had walked from Aerisan's black tower with the magician's blood running from her sword, Bistonia's citizens had hailed her as their savior and placed the city-state's crown in her hands. Lijena had refused to rule her home city, appointing the old soldier Pen to serve as a regent until Bistonia's exiled lord returned to his throne.

"We might be able to take the skiff and drift back downstream." LuBonfil's words intruded upon Lijena's silent grief. "But I fear that any who might follow would see us—or Neith would alert them."

"Pen assured us Neith Rigmar was an honorable man."

*Swords of Raemllyn, Book Four, *Death's Acolyte*.

Lijena cast another glance at the bargemaster.

The sailor's dark eyes met her gaze, then nervously darted back to the river's bank. A shiver ran down the young woman's spine. She let luBonfil and his constant worrying sway her.

"And what of the sword's fire?" LuBonfil arched an eyebrow. "You admit Kwerin's blade can sense the presence of spells."

Lijena's fingers drifted to the sword forged in antiquity. The blade was no ordinary weapon of tempered steel and fine balance. Lijena carried the Sword of Kwerin Bloodhawk. Once before, when the Faceless Ones had blighted the lands of Raemllyn, Kwerin Bloodhawk's master mage, Edan, had fashioned this sword so that a mortal might stand against the accursed demons.

Twice Lijena had faced and defeated the Faceless Ones that Zarek Yannis had sent against her. Without the sword, its sheath, and the magicks forged within both, she would now be dead. A single hell-rider easily equaled a hundred—more!—human fighters!

"Many spells are woven across the lands," Lijena finally answered the count. "The Bloodhawk's sword merely reacts to errant magicks."

LuBonfil snorted and shook his head. In truth, the answer did not satisfy Lijena either, but there was no other explanation for the tingling warmth that suddenly awoke within the sword. Neither she nor the count had seen any evidence of mages, magicks, or demons since leaving Bistonia. Nor did she yet fully grasp the source from whence flowed the powers within Kwerin's blade. Perhaps the sword did react to errant spells; she simply didn't know.

Lijena took a deep breath and slowly released it. The stench of the river had long since numbed her nostrils to its odors, and the gentle lapping of waves against the barge hull faded into the background. Her quick eyes fixed on the teamster who clucked to the oxen on shore. The man jerked and twitched at every small sound. His nervousness struck her as strange, as did the way Neith stared at the land rather than studied the river for potential snags and sandbars.

Mayhaps Count luBonfil's eyes see more than mine.

If they were being watched, why hadn't Zarek Yannis' troops

struck the instant they had been drawn out of sight of Bistonia's lofty spires? Why play a game of seek-and-hide?

Nor did she doubt that the usurper sought her. Of all the men and women in Raemllyn's far realms, only she possessed the key to toppling Zarek Yannis from the Velvet Throne in Kavindra. That key was the legendary sword she wore—a blade she would soon deliver into the hands of Prince Felrad, rightful heir to the crown.

A mirthless smile touched Lijena's lips. The befuddling fog that clouded her thoughts cleared. The usurper sought Prince Felrad throughout all Upper Raemllyn. The prince's movements had become bolder and his victories more impressive—until the Faceless turned the tide of battle against him. Lijena touched the Sword of Kwerin again.

The sword, in Prince Felrad's hand, would do more than turn the tide in the rightful heir's favor. It would vanquish Zarek Yannis once and for all time. His most potent weapon, the Faceless Ones, would fall under the sword's magical edges.

If Count luBonfil was correct and Yannis' henchmen followed them, they did so to retrieve the fabled sword.

But they wanted more. They wanted Prince Felrad himself! In one treacherous act they might capture the only weapon capable of dethroning Zarek Yannis, and slay Felrad.

Yannis' minions wanted it all!

Do they believe Count luBonfil and me stupid enough to blindly lead them to the prince? She snorted in disgust at such a naive scheme.

Not even luBonfil knew Prince Felrad's whereabouts. Rumors had been rife in Bistonia that the prince fortified the city of Rakell on the Isle of Loieter, but that did not mean the prince himself supervised the building. Felrad might be anywhere in Raemllyn. Hadn't she heard that Prince Felrad had climbed the Tower of Lost Mornings in Kavindra and shouted his challenge to the usurper? Zarek Yannis could not allow such a formal and humiliating challenge to go unheeded.

Zarek Yannis wanted Prince Felrad, and his minions no doubt thought that she would lead them directly to him. Lijena laughed harshly. The trap would have to be cleverer than that to ensnare her!

"What amuses you, Lady?" came luBonfil's soft question.

She studied the royal-born lord while he tossed another candied fruit into his mouth. His exaggerated courtly manners, his stylish dress, and his precise speech all seemed so decadent, so weak and vulnerable. The count's outward appearance was deceptive, a master performance by a master actor carefully designed to befuddle his enemies into underestimating his true abilities.

Lijena had seen luBonfil with sword in hand during the rebellion against Jun in Bistonia. The man was no fop. He was a trained leader with a core of tempered steel and nerves to match. Prince Felrad had chosen wisely in naming luBonfil an emissary.

A bellow from an ox on shore and a startled yelp from the animal's driver jerked Lijena's head around. Her heart leaped to lodge in the sudden dryness of her throat.

Brush and bramble set ablaze by flaming hooves, a black stallion burst from the underbrush lining the river's bank. With fire and greasy black smoke snorting from its flared nostrils, the demonic horse reared, forehooves pawing the air.

Astride the beast's back sat one of Zarek Yannis' hellish servants—a Faceless One. The demon-spawn stretched an arm toward the barge, and its burning, coallike eyes focused on the daughter of Bistonia. A voice like the spitting hiss of a thousand serpents resounded, "Lijena Farleigh, I have come for you!"

chapter 2

WITH THE RAMPANT beat of pulsing temples pounding in her ears, Lijena Farleigh saw and assessed the scene in a single glance: the Faceless One; the shouting teamster with his cracking whip, urging the oxen to draw the barge to the shore; Neith Rigmar's well-muscled back, tensed by the strain of what he saw—everything flowed to form a coherent picture before the swordswoman.

Nor did Lijena pause for the blink of an eye. Five quick strides brought her directly behind the treacherous bargemaster. With all her might, she lashed out with her right leg. A booted foot caught Neith in the backside.

The sailor yelped in surprise, then found himself tumbling headlong over the barge's rail and into the muddy Stane.

Before Neith hit the water, Lijena wrenched the Sword of Kwerin from its sheath. She raised the ancient blade high above her head and brought it down in a flashing arc that severed the barge's towline.

The oxen bellowed when their burden abruptly vanished from their wooden yokes. One stumbled to its knees; the others trampled over the fallen beast, causing enough confusion to halt the Faceless One's attack.

A humorless smile slid across Lijena's red lips as the barge drifted away from the shore and into the swift current at the center of the river.

"Quick and certain work, my lady." Count luBonfil dipped in a mock bow when he joined Lijena near the barge's prow.

The frosty-tressed swordswoman arched an eyebrow in question when she noted the bloodied sword in the lord's hand.

LuBonfil smiled, white teeth gleaming like a hungry direwolf. "The three other crewmembers no longer find this craft to their liking."

A bestial snort, and the sizzle of flaming hooves in mud, returned the pair's attention to the river bank. There the Faceless One sat, still astride his jet steed. The demon betrayed no sign of emotion, no irritation at being robbed of its prey. Instead, it lifted black booted legs and drove spikelike spurs into the hell-horse's flanks.

"By great Yehseen, *no!*" Lijena railed in shock. What she saw couldn't be!

The instant the Faceless One's spurs touched the demon mount's sleek, black coat, fiery hooves cut into the muddy bank and the horse leaped. With the ease of a bird launching itself from a limb, the massive animal hurled itself and hell-rider in an impossible arc that covered the hundred strides from shore to barge.

The craft listed heavily to one side as those flaming hooves slammed onto the deck!

Snorting fire, the hellish beast pawed at the deck, then twisted about to face Lijena and luBonfil. Still securely astride the horse, the Faceless One wrenched forth a sword of crystalline flame. Crackling sparks of blue-white licked along the blade's cutting edges, dimming the afternoon sun's brightness with their unholy glare.

"The Sitala casts strange fate in our direction." LuBonfil blanched at the sight of the hell-rider but did not retreat.

Instead, he darted over the deck, positioning himself on the left side of the demonic horse, opposite the Faceless One's sword. When facing a right-handed human warrior, the count's tactic might prove valuable. Against a demon with a sword of flame, it would give only a moment's diversion.

Not waiting for the Faceless to attack, Lijena took the offensive. A battle cry tearing from her throat, she once more hefted the Sword of Kwerin Bloodhawk above her head and charged the demon foe.

Magic-forged steel met sword of crystalline fire in a shower of sizzling green sparks. From fingertips to arms, the bone-jarring impact of clashing magicks raced through Lijena's slender body until her knees buckled beneath her own weight, throwing her to the deck.

Spiked spurs flashed, digging deep into bestial flesh. The Faceless One's mount reared, its burning hooves hovering over the fallen woman for a heartbeat before descending.

Lijena rolled to the left to escape a fiery death, then crawled to her knees. In a two-handed grip, she swung the Bloodhawk's blade, imitating a maneuver that had saved her when first she faced these hell-born demons.

White sparks erupted and sputtered the instant the ensorcelled sword touched the horse's left hindleg, just above its smoldering hoof. There was a moment of resistance before the magic-tempered steel sliced through meat and bone.

The black stallion tried to rear once again. Hoof and balance lost, the demon horse toppled.

But not its rider!

As if floating on wings hidden beneath its midnight cloak, the Faceless One leaped from the back of the crippled beast and alighted on the deck. Crouched in an inhuman stoop, the hell-rider advanced on Lijena in gliding strides.

A blur of brightly colored silks flashed behind the Faceless One.

"No! Don't!" she shouted to Count luBonfil.

The count sought a rear attack on the demon while its attention lay locked on the weaponswoman. Lijena doubted a single thrust, no matter how strong or well-targeted, could harm one of Zarek Yannis' demons. Legends told of as many as a hundred human warriors perishing as they vainly attempted to kill a single Faceless One.

Pushing to her feet, Lijena swung her sword in a wide circle above her head and brought it down with all her might. Again the magicks of the Sword of Kwerin Bloodhawk exploded against crystal fire as the Faceless One's blade jerked up to parry the blow.

The demon's coal-red eyes doubled in their intensity, and a serpentine hiss spat from unseen lips. The creature leaped back as the fiery blade fell from its grip and struck the deck with a high-pitched ringing.

Lijena had no moment to rejoice or even strike a killing blow—if death could ever come to such a supernatural being as this. The Faceless One's bony fingers snaked out to seize her slender wrist.

Lijena cried out in pain as those inhuman fingers tightened with the strength of a steel vise. Her own hand numbed beneath the pressure of those biting talons; the Sword of Kwerin Bloodhawk slipped from her grasp!

"You die!" came the demon's cracked words.

The Faceless One slowly drew her toward that empty black cowl—empty except for red-burning, hellish eyes afloat in nothingness. The stench of brimstone invaded her nostrils, choking her, threatening to rob her of life's breath.

"For the glory of Prince Felrad!" luBonfil cried as he drove a razor-edged sword into the Faceless One's back.

The hard-swung steel rent the hell-rider's black cape, but seemed to do naught else.

However, the well-timed attack did divert the monster's attention. Releasing Lijena, the Faceless One spun, and with a contemptuous backhanded slap sent luBonfil sprawling to the barge's deck.

"Worm!" the demon spat in a voice of hissing serpents. "You will die soon!"

Lijena dropped to her knees and clutched the hilt of her fallen sword. She sensed rather than saw the Faceless One whirl back to her. Fingers locked around the sword, she rolled to her side and brought the blade up. As the demon lunged, so did Lijena. The tip of the spell-endowed sword skewered half its length into the Faceless One's chest.

Hideous death cries echoed up and down the River Stane. Lijena watched in mute fascination as the creature's eyes burned ever brighter, flared, and then faded like the embers of a camp fire. The skeletal hands clutching at the sword blade turned to dust. The robe once worn by the hell-creature fell shapelessly to the deck, and gray fingers of smoke escaped from its weave. Of the Faceless One, she found no trace. Gone, too, in wisps of smoke, was its crippled steed.

Lijena sucked in a steadying breath that refused to quell the trembling of her hands. The strain of fighting still another of Zarek Yannis' hell-spawn wore at her—and at the same time it strengthened her resolve to deliver this marvelous weapon into Prince Felrad's hands.

"We're free of it," she weakly called to Count luBonfil.

When the man failed to answer, fear constricted her throat. She had seen the Faceless One strike the lord. Had the demon killed him with a single blow?

Lijena rose to shaky legs and staggered to luBonfil's side. The man lay with eyes staring wide and sightless.

"Count!" She knelt and cradled his head in her lap as she pressed fingertips into his throat seeking a pulse. A thready beat reassured her that, in spite of his deathly pallor, the man still lived.

The rigidity slowly faded from the lord's muscles, and his eyes blinked. A wan smile crossed his thin lips.

"You are both lovely and a skilled fighter," he said. "Prince Felrad does well having you in his camp."

"What happened? The Faceless One appeared merely to slap you with the backside of its hand."

"I . . . I think I can sit up. Yes, let me try." Count luBonfil weaved, but with Lijena's aid, managed to sit straight. "Such power in that 'mere slap.' Never have I felt such stunning force in a blow! Truly, Zarek Yannis' demons must be feared by even the gods themselves!"

Leaving luBonfil to shake off the daze of that blow, Lijena stood and looked about them. The barge now drifted in the center of the river, caught in strong currents that sent it back downriver toward Bistonia. If there had been any others waiting for them in ambush, Lijena felt certain that they had been left far behind.

But she and the count would still have to pass them. Loieterland and fortified Rakell and Prince Felrad lay to the north.

"We must reach shore," said Lijena. "Does this miserable boat have a rudder, or do we have to wait for a sandbar to ground us?"

"A rudder?" asked luBonfil as he rose and steadied himself with a hand on the rail. The lord shook himself and looked around, as if seeing the barge for the first time. "No, there is no rudder, but there might be a centerboard."

"A what?"

"Help me below. It's easier to show you than explain."

Lijena supported luBonfil with an arm about his waist as they made their way down a crude hatchway. In the leaking cargo hold, Lijena discovered what the man meant. A board dropped down through a narrow slit cut almost the entire length of the bottom.

"What an odd arrangement," she said, seeing how it worked. The poor fit between a crude gasket and the centerboard accounted for most of the bilge.

"A rudder cannot be constructed strong enough to turn a fully laden barge," the count explained. "Help me lower the centerboard. That will keep us heading with the current and prevent the barge from spinning."

"What's the difference?" asked Lijena. "I just want dry land beneath my boots once more. I've had enough of this river."

Lijena's motives for returning to the riverbank encompassed more than weariness with their mode of travel. If they succeeded in reaching the far bank, that put the width of the Stane between them and potential ambushers.

The pair succeeded in lowering the centerboard to its full extent. Immediately Lijena felt the difference in the way the barge rode in the water. Back on deck she squinted into the sun. The barge gradually slipped across the river. She estimated that it would run aground when the river flowed around a tight bend, scarcely a bowshot distant.

Lijena called below. "Dry land's but a few minutes ahead!"

It came quicker!

The stern of the barge slammed into an ancient tree trunk half submerged beneath the muddy water. The craft swung wildly to the left, crashing bow-first into the bank, wedging itself between land and trunk.

Lijena reeled under the impact, clutching at the barge's rail to save herself from a muddy bath. The crack of splintering wood sounded to her right.

The mounts and pack animals that Pen had provided for their journey skidded across the deck, shattered the wooden fence of the pen, and then crashed through the rail into the river. In a panic, the animals swam with the current until they gained purchase on the muddy bank. Once out of the water, they shook themselves, and ran southward with ears perked high and tails streaming behind them.

"Jajhana be damned!" Lijena cursed in frustration. Not only had she been robbed of the barge, she now found herself afoot. She called down into the hold. "Count luBonfil, hurry! We've leagues to travel, and unless we find horses it'll take us forever to reach Prince Felrad."

The count wobbled to the deck like a drunken beggar. His hands flailed the air, and he collapsed face down.

Lijena ran to the count and rolled him to his back. "What happened?"

The man's face turned a sickly yellow, as if a creeping jaundice seized his features. He seemed to whither before Lijena's eyes. A startled gasp escaped her trembling lips as his thin moustache, eyebrows, and hair turned snowy white in the space of five heartbeats.

"The Faceless One," he muttered. "I have been touched by evil. Find Prince Felrad. Give him the sword. You must. You—by the gods! The *pain!*"

The count's thin body arched in Lijena's arms. Bone cracked beneath the intensity of that convulsion, snapping the man's spine. He twitched once, then lay still—another soul sent to Peyneeha for Black Qar to hoarde.

Lijena pushed his still body from her and backed away, shaking her head. She stared at her hands, as if they might have been tainted. The cold, sinking feeling deep in her stomach reminded her that she, too, had grappled with the Faceless One. It had touched her. Her wrist still trickled blood from its lacerating grip.

Yet she felt no weakness. Her fair skin showed no sickly, jaundiced tint. Lijena's hand rested on the Sword of Kwerin. Had the weapon's magicks protected her?

"Jajhana!" she prayed to the Goddess of Chance and Fortune. "Give me the strength to deliver this sword to its rightful owner!"

Forcing herself to perform the odious task, Lijena cut a grave in the river bank and placed Count luBonfil in it. Again and again her fingers crept back to the Sword of Kwerin Blood-hawk. Whether it protected her from the evil magicks of the Faceless One, Lijena Farleigh didn't know. But there was security in having it so close at hand.

chapter 3

"I'LL CUT YOUR damned ears off, you thieving whoreson!" roared Goran One-Eye.

The huge, barrel-chested, red-bearded Challing in human form upended a heavy wooden table to send cards and coins scattering across the room. Half the patrons of the Inn of the Singing Nymph scurried back, removing themselves from the giant's path.

"Cheat me, will you?" Goran stood to his full height and drew a breath that expanded his chest until it threatened to pop the buttons on his gaudy, green-and-orange-hued shirt.

Across the inn, Davin Anane watched, an amused smile curling his lips. He held out an arm to restrain the two women sitting with him.

"Davin, he's enraged!" cried Kulonna, daughter of Duke Tun of the Isle of Prillae. "He's more than a man, but he can't fight six of them. They'll kill him!"

"Kulonna, be at ease," Davin reassured the honey-haired young woman and eased her back to her chair.

The Jyotian thief had seen his friend Goran gamble and rob for almost six years. In that time, the only person Davin thought a better thief was himself. The Challing's hulking size worked against him when it came to smash-and-run thefts, and for those requiring delicacy of touch, Goran was a complete loss. But in other techniques, the one-eyed giant was a master.

"You don't think they'll hurt him?" asked the woman. She placed a slender-fingered hand on Davin's forearm and squeezed in obvious concern for the red-maned Goran.

"Awendala, dearest." Davin's gaze lingering on the young woman's full form, her own red tresses, and darting, intelligent emerald eyes. "Goran faces only a half-dozen of those Evara street rats. Did we not rescue you and Kulonna from a mage? From a man infinitely more cunning and evil than these bits of gutter refuse?"*

"I doubt not your courage," Awendala replied, "but think it foolish to risk so much."

She glanced around the public room of the inn and nodded toward several of Zarek Yannis' soldiers, who lounged near the fireplace, more drunk than alert. The red-haired beauty shuddered and pressed close to Davin. "We've come to the usurper's stronghold, gold filling our purses, and Goran dares attract attention."

"Sometimes those in full view are less conspicuous than those who scurry about trying to hide," the raven-haired Jyotian answered. "Consider this: Zarek Yannis is a man of intrigue, always seeking out the most intricate and devious of plots. Who would notice a drunken brawl and think it anything more? Not the usurper."

Davin leaned back, propped himself against a wall, and hiked his boots to the table top. Thusly situated, he saw Awendala's beautiful profile in the dim light from the fireplace and managed to watch both drunken soldiers and Goran's progress in the brawl all at the same time. The soldiers ignored the fight, too deep in their cups to do more than moan.

Davin lifted a flagon of ale and quenched his own thirst with a healthy gulp. His attention shifted to Awendala. To be certain, Kulonna was pretty; nay, beautiful—with her golden hair and cornflower-blue eyes. Yet the noble-born young woman lacked the spark, the inner fire, that elevated Awendala above other women.

Davin Anane stumbled over that last thought, weighing it over and over in his mind. A smile touched his lips when he realized the truth held in that idle comparison. He cared not that Awendala was common-born. Let Goran dally with his

*Swords of Raemllyn, Book Five, *Beasts of the Mist*.

duchess. During their long weeks together as crewmembers aboard the merchanter *The Twisted Cross,* Awendala had conquered his heart, and he hers.

Not that either had planned it that way. These times were not meant for matters of the heart. But the Sitala, Raemllyn's five deities who cast the fates of men and women, cared little for human times and suffering when they capriciously interwove lives for their amusement.

Davin's gaze traced Awendala's features. The mouth that his critical eyes had once found a bit too wide, a nose slightly too angular, and the chin a tad too square, now seemed to blend in a perfection he had failed to notice when Goran and he had rescued the two women from the beasts of the mists.

Beautiful. And so unlike Lijena.

A knot formed in his throat when the frosty-tressed daughter of Bistonia wedged into his thoughts.

For Lijena Farleigh, he had sacrificed much. A full year had been spent chasing her across the length of Raemllyn to free her from the demon bound to her mind and body by the magicks of the sorceror Lorennion.* Davin grunted. Her gratitude had been less than he'd anticipated from the woman he'd come to love.

Thought I loved! Davin downed another swig of ale. Did he lie to himself? Were there still open wounds left by that woman who swore to have his head when they again met?

Lijena Farleigh had robbed Goran and him of their horses and belongings in the Forest of Agda, outside the coastal city of Weysh. From there, they'd made their way along the northern coast of Upper Raemllyn, encountering hideous beasts creeping from a rent in space, a would-be sorcerer—and that sorcerer's isle of captive women.

Davin and Goran One-Eye had rescued Awendala and Kulonna and scores more. The others had continued on with Captain Iuonx and Prince Felrad's mage, Bertam, to the port of Iluska. Davin had been content to avoid Yannis' port blockade and had been put ashore with his friends, just north of Evara.

Not that Evara proved any less infested with Zarek Yannis' swine. The arrogant soldiers strutted about and held sway over

*Swords of Raemllyn, Book Three, *Blook Fountain.*

the populace with quick swords and no hint of mercy.

It was that danger that sent the sweetness of life coursing through Davin's veins with tingling excitement the moment he entered the city the night before. Ten thousand traps lurked within Evara for men of his chosen profession, ready to rob him of life should his wit and quick fingers falter for an instant. Yet, by Raemllyn's gods, how he savored it!

And with Awendala at my side, that savoring is all the sweeter! Davin drained the flagon with a greedy swallow. With the new, rich clothing and weapons they had purchased during the day and the bustle of a city around him, he felt like himself—Davin Anane, master thief of Raemllyn realms—again! It was something he had forgotten during the long months plodding through the wilderness or standing on the decks of *The Twisted Cross*.

A startled gasp from Kulonna and a pained, masculine cry tugged the Jyotian's gaze back to the center of the inn.

Goran One-Eye's meaty fist smashed into a smaller man's face and sent the unfortunate Evaran tumbling across the floor head over heels. Goran's laughter roared from belly and chest, as he ducked a flying stool meant for the side of his head and kicked out to fell another of his opponents.

And, while he fought, the red-bearded giant's thick fingers scooped silver and gold coins from the floor and filched money pouches dangling from belts.

Davin kicked away from the table and motioned for Awendala and Kulonna to leave the moment he saw Goran's single eye aglow with the smoldering green of witch-fire.

Magicks! Davin silently cursed his friend's true nature while he escorted their companions toward the inn's door. In spite of his muscular, manly appearance, Goran One-Eye was no man at all! He was a Challing, a changeling creature nine parts mystical to one part physical. It was those nine parts that now worried Davin; they often exerted themselves without warning or control!

Goran One-Eye had been ripped from another space and time and imprisoned in this world by the mage Roan-Jafar. For this heinous act, the Challing had killed the mage—and found himself trapped in human form.

Day by day, the Challing regained portions of his lost powers, although often without the ability to control them. Shape altering was one; this, Davin Anane had experienced firsthand. Of the others he wasn't certain, especially since Goran preferred to brag outrageously about his Challing abilities rather than tell the truth.

"Goran will join us in a moment," Davin said, gaze darting up and down the deserted night street, seeking the best escape route.

After the inn recovered from the altercation, only a few minutes would pass before the patrons discovered their heavily laden purses missing. Their angry shouts would rouse the soldiers, demanding the thief be apprehended.

"We should find a carriage. I grow weary of this endless search for good gaming tables. I'd prefer that Goran rest." This from Kulonna. A deliciously wicked smile uplifted the corners of the lovely blonde duchess' full lips. "If I can't interest him more than a game of chance, I'll walk back to the Isle of Prillae—on the water!"

Davin chuckled. He had no doubt that Kulonna could interest Goran for tonight—and longer. His own arm snaked around Awendala's trim waist and hugged her close. She replied with flashing green eyes and a kiss filled with enticing promises.

Black Qar take Goran! Davin returned Awendala's kiss with mounting passion. If the Challing didn't want what these fine ladies offered this night, he wasn't going to refuse!

"Davin, run! The soldiers!" Goran's voice bellowed with urgency as the changeling in human form charged from the tavern's door like a bull tricorn. He skidded to a halt atop the night-mist slickened, cobblestone street. His shaggy head jerked to the left and right. He lifted an arm the size of a tree limb and jabbed a finger into the night. "There!"

Davin sucked in his breath; his pulse doubled, pounding in his temples. Apparently, Goran's thievery had inflamed the ire of at least one of the inn's patrons.

An entire patrol of guards trotted down the street, filling the night with the clank of armor and the pounding of horses' hooves. Avoiding a few drunk soldiers provided sport. But this patrol was an entirely different matter. The soldiers were both mounted and armed with lances.

Davin glanced at the low-hanging roofs and cursed the Goddess Jajhana as he discarded the idea that popped into his head. Taking to his wonted aerial escape route over rooftops wouldn't work now. Although Goran and he might vanish easily across the roofs or through the sewers, he had Awendala and Kulonna to consider. Less dangerous paths must be followed.

"Damn your eyes! Run!" Goran urged when his head swung around to his companions. "We've got to get away before they ride us down!"

The nearness of the approaching hooves announced that the time for a swift retreat had passed. Only cleverness would avail them now, Davin realized. He shot out an arm, snared Goran's brilliant orange-and-green blouse, and jerked hard enough to spin the Challing about.

The Challing's mouth opened in protest, then clamped shut. Behind the fiery-haired giant, the sergeant of the guard drew his mount to a halt and prodded Goran's backside with his spear.

"Good Captain," cried Davin, intentionally promoting the soldier's rank. "Inside! The spies are inside!"

"Spies? What spies are these?" The soldier's face twisted with puzzlement. "We're summoned to stop a fight. Nothing was mentioned about spies!"

"They plot to betray our glorious High King Zarek Yannis." Davin answered with all the fearful desperation he could muster in his voice.

"Yes, inside. Five of them," added Awendala, obviously discerning the Jyotian's ploy.

"No, there're six. All are still inside, Captain. Hurry!" Kulonna urged.

She elbowed Goran, who nodded so vigorously his fox-fur eyepatch came loose, so that the Challing had to hold it in place with one hand while he pointed with the other.

"You two, stay here while I check this out." The sergeant and four others dismounted.

Their booted feet barely crossed the tavern's threshold when Davin and Goran acted. In unison, the thieves grabbed the bridles of the two remaining guards' mounts and snatched them sharply. The horses whinnied and reared. In the next instant, their riders tumbled from saddle to street. Davin's and Goran's fists assured that neither would rise again for several minutes.

"Up you go, my lovely lady." Goran lifted Kulonna by the waist and swung her high into a saddle. The Challing mounted another horse while Davin helped Awendala onto a mare and selected the sergeant's steed as his own.

"Hurry," Davin shouted as he scattered the remaining animals with waving arms. "They do not take kindly to thieves in Evara."

"Especially horse thieves," Awendala laughed.

"Who steal from the guard!" added Kulonna.

Their laughter ringing down the night-cloaked street, the two thieves and their enchanting companions laid heels to flanks and raced into the freedom of the city's darkness. Across avenues, down alleys, along tree-lined boulevards they rode, slowing only when they had placed half of Evara between themselves and the soldiers at the inn.

"To our quarters," Awendala suggested when they stopped beneath the flickering, orange glow of a brazier hung from the front of a building whose sign named it the Inn of the Dancing Dolphins. "I've had enough excitement for the night."

"Oh?" Davin arched an eyebrow, then glanced at the inn's second story where their bedroom was. "I had hoped that this would only whet your appetite."

Awendala grinned broadly and winked. "Aye, it has. But a saddle is not the place for such adventures as those of which you speak." She stood in the stirrups and rubbed a palm over her backside. "Months at sea have ill-prepared me for a night of riding."

Davin watched the woman's every movement, suppressing the desire to sweep her in his arms and carry her to their waiting bed. Shared pleasures would have to wait until the business at hand was concluded. "Goran and I will return when we've gotten rid of the horses."

"Get rid of the horses?" Kulonna glanced at Davin. "Why not stable them here at the inn?"

"I think the innkeeper would frown on having stolen horses in his stalls, my dove," Goran replied. "I would hate to have our night disturbed by the rudeness of city soldiers come to drag us away to Evara's dungeons."

"Oh!" Kulonna gasped as though the thought that they might

be caught had never entered her mind. She reached out a hand and stroked her fingers across Goran's cheek to tug at his fierce red beard. "Don't be long, my love."

The Challing took her delicate hand in his meaty paw and kissed it. "Fear naught, lovely one. This worrisome Jyotian and I will be back before you can toss back the sleeping silks."

When the two beauties dismounted, Davin and Goran took the reins of their stolen mounts and left the women in front of the Dancing Dolphins. It was the heir to the House of Anane who spoke as they turned onto a broad avenue. "Good fortune has indeed ridden at our side since we found them."

"I am pleased to hear you admit such wondrous truth, friend Davin." Goran answered with obvious surprise. "You had me worried with the way you carried on about that skinny wench."

"Lijena," Davin Anane said softly, trying to deny the feelings that stirred within his breast.

"There—down the street to your right." Goran tilted his head toward two torches ablaze a block away. "Those stables should do nicely."

"What? Have you lost all your senses?" Davin reined beside the Challing as Goran turned toward the livery stable. "We can't board them. The soldiers will find them before . . ."

His voice trailed off when Goran boomed out a hearty greeting to a sleepy-eyed stablehand sitting beneath the torches.

"There, my good lad," Goran continued, ignoring Davin's questioning stare. "We have fine horses for sale."

"For sale? At this hour?" The stablehand rubbed his eyes, then looked around to assure himself that the two riders were alone. When his gaze returned to Goran, he said, "Master, those horses carry the High King's mark. And the tack is military."

"Good eye, lad! Yes, you have quite an eye. What can you offer us for these fine horses?" Goran replied.

"Nothing!" the youth blurted. "You stole them!"

"Stole? How dare you make such groundless accusations? We came by them honestly enough. We are surplusers." The Challing's chest puffed in mock indignation.

"What?" the stablehand asked suspiciously. "What's a surpluser?"

"We take the extra horses," Goran said, as if explaining to

a halfwit, "and we find markets for them. Do you not think that our gracious High King has more horses than he needs?"

"I've heard it said that he does," the lad admitted with a nod.

"So it is our proud duty to take those surplus horses and see that they are put into capable hands—for a decent price, of course." Goran dismounted and waved for Davin to do the same.

"But I can't buy horses," the youth said. "I'm not the stable owner."

"But you are an enterprising youth, and you can aid us." Goran moved closer and lowered his voice to a conspiratorial whisper so that the stablehand strained hard to hear. "We fall behind on our schedule. If we don't sell a specific number of horses every day, High King Zarek himself becomes wroth. And we know what that means, don't we?"

Davin shook his head in disbelief. Goran played the youth like a fisherman pulling in his netted catch. Gullible didn't describe the lad! The Jyotian had rarely seen anyone more eager to please than this youth. The stablehand seemed willing to do anything to aid the High King. From either devotion or fear, Davin couldn't say. It didn't matter, except to set Goran's hook deeper into his fish's mouth.

"Surely, you see that these steeds are fine creatures and worth much," the Challing artfully worked his scam. "Easily, say, fifty bists apiece."

"That much?" The stablehand marveled at such expensive animals.

"Easily that," Goran assured him. "But we are patriots and will part with the horses for only sixty bists, since we can't expect you to have two hundred on hand at this time of night. How much coin *is* available?"

"Less than that in silver," the youth admitted.

"Yes," said Goran, trying to keep from grinning too much, "We'll accept fifty silver eagles as deposit on these four."

"You want me to keep the horses and give you only fifty silver coins?" The youth scratched his head, obviously weighing the amounts in his head. The animals were worth ten gold pieces each and no more, but Goran had asked for only a small part of their real value.

"The fifty silver coins," said Goran, "and two of your scraggliest horses as good faith trade."

"What? Why would you want two more?" the stablehand asked. "I thought you wanted to get rid of these surplus animals."

Goran sighed and shook his head. "Lad, you have the look of an honest boy about you, but we know nothing of your master. We agree to leave these fine steeds in your care as a show of good faith that he will do right by us. But we'd be fools not to accept some small token to insure that he won't cheat us: your two worst horses and fifty pieces of silver as collateral until we can return and get the High King's due for these animals."

Davin saw the greed play across the youth's face. He could foist off swayback nags for fine, well-kept and well-fed horses.

"My master will be here at dawn. You can speak to him then."

"Lad, I thought you'd been listening. We need to report our success in selling the horses this night, not in the morning. *This night!* The silver and the horses are only tokens of our trust. We need to report, and you hold it within your capable hands to aid us—and the king."

"Done." The lad smirked.

Goran and Davin appeared as businesslike as possible when they accepted the fifty silver eagles and two horses well past the days of their youth. Both animals were sway-backed and showed more ribs than flesh on their sides.

"My master will be here at dawn," the stablehand repeated.

"Never fear. We'll be back," Goran assured the youth while he and Davin mounted. "On morrow's morn, lad." He then waved and reined back into the night.

When they were out of earshot, Davin said, "Well done, you scoundrel. Not only did you get fifty silver pieces for animals easily identified, you got us transportation back to Awendala and Kulonna."

"If the youth works quickly enough, he can cheat his master and find buyers for the horses before every soldier in Evara is on the lookout for those animals. If not. . . ." Goran shrugged his massive shoulders.

Davin smiled; the night had gone well. The youth thought

he cheated them. If they returned at dawn, how could they prove they'd left any horses at all? They had been given no receipt. The lad hoped to sell the horses, replace the fifty silver eagles, perhaps tell his master some fool had purchased the two nags for a few more coins—and then pocket the remainder of the money, leaving the High King's "surplusers" the losers.

"Here we are," Goran said when they approached the Inn of the Dancing Dolphins. "And about time. This creature's belly sags so much that it rubs the ground as she walks." Goran dismounted and shooed the horse away.

Davin did the same with his pathetic mount. "I hope we haven't been gone too long. Would be a wasted night were Awendala and Kulonna fast asleep."

"There's but one way to find out."

Goran motioned his friend into the inn. Together they climbed the stairs to the back rooms they had rented. Goran managed a wink with his good eye before he vanished into the room where his lovely Kulonna awaited. Davin lingered no longer and went to Awendala.

"Awendala," Davin called softly into the room's darkness.

"Here, my love," came the woman's voice. "I thought you had forgotten me."

"Forget you? Impossible!" Davin shed his weapons and clothing as he made his way across the room. By the time his knees touched the edge of the bed, he had divested himself of all encumberances.

He never reached the warmth of Awendala's tantalizing embrace. The muffled scuffle of boots sounded behind him. He jerked around just as an invisible sledgehammer slammed into the side of his skull. Then the world was aswim in swirling blackness.

chapter 4

"It's a crime, I say!" Goran One-Eye held his throbbing head in his hands and growled. "Those brigands robbed us. Robbed us! *Us!* We—the ones who robbed the Harnish Spring Fair but a year gone by!"

"Three of them," Kulonna said for the hundredth time that morning, "were waiting in the room. Two men and a woman. They bound and gagged me, blew out the candles and lamps, and waited for Goran to enter in the dark."

Davin Anane merely sighed when Awendala gingerly placed a cool, moist cloth atop a swollen, pulsing knot on the side of his head. Three thieves, another pair of men and a woman, had lain in wait inside his own room. He had put up no more struggle than Goran when they struck the blow to his head.

"It feels as big as a *kelii's* egg." Awendala lightly kissed the bruised bump.

"Robbed us of every bist, eagle, and copper to our names!" Goran continued to growl. "Didn't they realize who they dealt with? The greatest thieves in all Raemllyn, that's who! By Nyuria's scorched arse, how could they be so brazen!"

"Quiet, Goran." Davin's gray eyes darted around the inn to see if the Challing's outbursts attracted attention. The still-somnolent innkeeper worked at the far side of the room, attempting to start a fire in the hearth.

"I'll get the city guard!" Goran shoved to his feet and shook a fist in the air. "Those thieves won't get away with this!"

"Sit down, shut up!" Davin made no attempt to hide his irritation both with himself and his friend. They had been careless and had been picked like two plump pigeons. "Draw attention and Yannis' troops will have our heads on pikes. We've no one but ourselves to blame."

"Ourselves? Why . . ." Goran's protest faded as did the anger on his face, leaving him with an expression reminiscent of a lost puppy. "Aye, you're right. 'Tis our fault. We were careless. Besides, what have we lost—mere gold and silver. I have been robbed of worse."

"Uh, we should go. . . ." Davin spoke with haste and a feeling of dread. His words came too late.

He groaned when Awendala asked. "You have been robbed of worse than gold and silver?"

"Aye!" The Challing ignored Davin when the Jyotian cleared his throat rudely. "My very eye was stolen from me." Goran touched the new, plush fox-fur patch that covered the socket that once had held his left eye. "'Twas a terrible and a moral lesson I learned that day."

"Moral lesson?" Kulonna questioned.

"We can find food elsewhere," Davin attempted to intercede again. "It doesn't look as if the landlord will be ready any time soon."

"Davin, wait. I haven't heard how Goran lost his eye. What do you mean losing it was a moral lesson?" Awendala's emerald eyes narrowed when she turned back to the Challing.

Davin Anane groaned a second time and settled into his chair. There'd be no stopping Goran until the tale had run its course, now that he had two willing—and gullible—listeners.

"Gatinah, it was," said Goran, naming the southernmost port in Lower Raemllyn. "I had been washed ashore less than a league from that fine city. Not a pair of coins left to rub together. Awful storm, an even worse wreck that killed all aboard, save me."

"What a pity the storm wasn't more thorough," Davin grumbled.

"I entered Gatinah thinking to ply my trade." Goran flexed his meaty fingers before his face. "Surely, thought I, a careless merchant would give up a few bists or a mouthful of moldy bread. But the city!"

"What was wrong with it?" Kulonna asked, obviously mesmerized by the Challing's telling. "I've heard it is a prosperous city, though I have never seen it with my own eyes."

"Prosperous? Now it might be, but not then. Then," Goran said with drama in his every syllable and gesture, "it was almost a deserted city. Black Qar himself stalked the people. Why the Death God had chosen this particular city at that particular time to fill his Death Rota, none can say."

"And so ends the story," Davin interrupted. "Let's eat."

"Get us the food, Davin, my love," said Awendala. "We'll listen to Goran."

The Challing's chest swelled with pride at having won the full attention of two such beautiful women. He gave a toss of his head in Davin's direction, indicating the Jyotian should fall silent and do as he was told. With ill grace, Davin pushed from the table to barter with the innkeeper for breakfast.

"Black Qar stalked the people of Gatinah," Kulonna said in a breathless tone. "Why?"

"That I cannot say, but the effect of his icy touch was apparent. Nahtahl, known to mortals as Plague, stole lives—the ones not taken by Nyuria."

"Black Qar's chief demon!" Kulonna gasped. "The city must have done something terrible!"

"Aye, so it seemed to me. I wanted only to escape when I saw so many dead and dying from Death's touch. Caring naught for food when I witnessed a dark cloud drifting down the street, I sought to flee, but couldn't."

"Why not?" Awendala silently accepted the platter of sausage and bread Davin handed her and began to munch as she listened to Goran's tale.

"A small child, barely seven summers old," the Challing said with a gusty sigh. "There came the Death God's cold black breath down the street, and this small urchin stood between me and certain death."

In spite of himself, Davin Anane listened. This tale took a different turning from countless others he had heard Goran spin. Why?

"I knew that Qar wanted only a soul—the Death God cared

not whose he stole and bore off to Peyneeha. Half-drowned and weak though I was, I knew my retreat was certain. But not the boy's. He would die, and I would live."

"You saved him!" squealed Kulonna. "But how? None cheats Qar when he hunts."

"Nor did I, though I admit that I tried. Staggering forward, I scooped up the boy and held him close in my arms. The black mist whirled around me, and I heard Qar call the boy's name."

Goran cupped hands around his mouth and resonantly called, "'Wernoan, I seek your soul, Wernoan.'"

"Wernoan, that's the boy?" asked Awendala.

Goran nodded, his shaggy red hair flopping forward. He hastily brushed it from his single good eye and stroked his bushy red beard. "I held my hand over the boy's mouth to prevent him from answering and drawing Qar's attention. In his stead, I volunteered to journey to Peyneeha."

"Goran, no!" Kulonna clung to the Challing's arm.

He smiled slightly, then forced a stern expression to his face to complement the mood of his tale.

"I had lived life well, and Wernoan was but a child. He had everything worth experiencing in front of him: the taste of fine *phorra* brandy, the exhilaration of freedom, salt air blowing through his hair, the love of a good woman."

"So Qar took you, you died, and that's the end," Davin interjected.

"Silence, friend Davin." Goran solemnly shook his fire-maned head. "It did not happen that way, much to my surprise. Black Qar called *my* name, which did not surprise me since Death knows all names, even a Challing's. But when he did not immediately steal my soul, I dared hope."

Goran gnawed at the sausage and bread, downed half a tankard of ale, and said, "After I dared hope, I decided to act. I bartered with Qar."

"Goran," warned Davin, "you tempt the gods."

The Challing motioned him to silence. "For Wernoan, I said, I will give myself. To this Qar answered, 'I do not call you this day—if you grant my wish.'"

"Qar asked? He did not simply take?" Kulonna blinked in awe.

"What the Black One required astounded me. Qar told of

his concubine—I forget her name—and of her affliction," Goran continued.

"What affliction could a god's concubine have?" asked Davin, again fascinated in spite of himself.

"She lacked an eye. Incredible, I know, but true. Qar's very own concubine had only one eye and desired two."

"You mean . . ." began Kulonna.

"Yes, my lovely, I traded my eye to Qar for the life of that boy—and my own!"

"The innkeeper will require more than your remaining eye unless we pay for our lodging and this meal," Davin said. "I've convinced him that we will stay one more night, but he obviously suspects our ability to pay."

"A pox on him!" Goran spat. "It was under his leaking roof that we were robbed!"

"Not so loud. The city guard, Yannis' soldiers," cautioned Davin. "They both seek us now."

"Then let us give them reason to seek us all the harder." Goran leaned back and popped a sausage in his mouth.

Davin Anane had to smile at his friend. This Goran was no less the braggart and teller of tall tales designed to impress the ladies, but the light in his good eye told of mischief, of the desire to commit a theft at least equal to stealing the prize money at Harn's Spring Fair.

"Jewels," Goran suggested. "We need jewels, even though we have the two loveliest in all Raemllyn."

He patted Kulonna on the backside as she rose to fill the Challing's tankard. She squealed but offered no serious objection.

"Where might we find jewels, but at a jeweler's?" finished Davin.

He remembered only too well their last attempt at theft. Goran had assured him that Parvan Weeselik of Weysh was a doddering old man too arthritic and nearsighted to stand against agile thieves making off with his finest stones.

Weeselik had proven to be young, a master swordsman, and quick to anger. They had snared the jewels, but had barely escaped Weysh with their lives. Davin didn't want to repeat such a sorry performance, not in a city teeming with Zarek Yannis' troops.

"It will take days searching out the best jeweler. We haven't that much time." He glanced in the innkeeper's direction. They could always leave and keep going, but without supplies their journey would be difficult, if not impossible.

"You mean the richest jeweler?" asked Kulonna. "Or the one most easily robbed?"

"They are one and the same to me at this moment," Davin answered. "Why? Do you know of one?"

"I might." The blonde duchess nodded. "My father has often sent to this city for special pieces. Once he ordered a *drenn* jewel mounted in an ethium ring setting for my mother."

"Lucky woman," said Davin.

"A rich one," Goran added. "Which merchant did your father employ? And should we even consider robbing someone who has dealt fairly with Duke Tun?"

"Your consideration is touching." Kulonna smiled, obviously impressed with Goran.

Davin snorted in disgust. He knew his friend's habits. Most of what Goran said was meant to sway Kulonna—and the Challing succeeded!

"But," Kulonna went on, "my father learned that Eznoh-Fadey cheated him on price, quality and workmanship. Eznoh-Fadey refused to make good the outrageous behavior. He thought, and rightly as it turned out, that the distance separating Evara and Litonya was too great for my father to do anything but simmer at the perfidy."

"So this Eznoh-Fadey is our target!" Goran said with relish. He looked around the table, put his powerful hands in front of him, and leaned forward to ask, "Why do we hesitate? There are jewels to be stolen. We go to get the refund due Duke Tun!"

"Too many guards." The Jyotian thief shook his head as he surveyed Eznoh-Fadey's jewelry shop.

Two burly guards, armed with swords and spears, stood just inside the door, barring entry to all who did not appear to be prospective customers. In the short time they had watched the shop, Davin had seen several prosperous businessmen turned away.

"This Eznoh-Fadey definitely caters to an exclusive clientele. Certainly, the likes of a Jyotian and a Challing in human form are not going to easily pass those doors just to eye the merchandise." Goran stroked his bushy beard, then smiled. "But one of noble birth would be admitted without question."

Davin looked up, suddenly suspicious. He was the last of the Jyotis House of Anane, but no longer considered himself of royal blood—not since Zarek Yannis had ascended the Velvet Throne and many of the old-line nobility had been put to death. Nor since Davin had been driven from his homeland, branded as a murderer by his bitter foe, Berenicis, called the Blackheart because of his tyrannical rule over Jyotis.

Davin spat at the thought of Berenicis, who now aligned with Prince Felrad. That he served the same cause as that whoreson was almost enough to drive him into Yannis' camp. Almost, but not enough. For the usurper had foully slain King Bedrich the Fair, and no man had ever lived who Davin loved more.

"If you mean me, they wouldn't let me near the door." Davin glanced at his friend.

"You?" Goran replied. "I meant the Duchess Kulonna and her serving wench Awendala."

"Too risky," Davin said. "We're the thieves. We shouldn't involve them."

"They will not steal the gems," protested Goran. "I merely ask them to look around, to remember where the choicest items are, to see if other guards might be posted in a side gallery. It is purest folly rushing in to steal if you cannot find anything worth stealing. What if Eznoh-Fadey locks up his gems in a vault of special complexity? Ward spells? Who knows the power of a mage's devotion to such a rich merchant."

"All right, you've made your point. But I still don't like it." Davin had no fear when it came to his own life. To his surprise, it troubled him thinking of Awendala entering a shop with criminal intent.

The women eagerly accepted the challenge. To them, this presented another adventure. Davin worried the more. Thieving was no game lightly undertaken. The slightest mistake spelled death, sometimes by torture for the unlucky thief who was captured rather than slain on the spot.

"All we require is for you to note the location of the choicest gems," Davin said sternly to Awendala and Kulonna. "Nothing more."

"Except," Goran cut in, "that you should distract the guards after you have been in the store for a few minutes. Davin and I need to examine the roof. It would not do to have attention paid to muffled footfalls, should we grow careless."

"Goran," Davin said in reprimand, only to relent to the Challing's wishes.

What Goran suggested was no riskier for Kulonna and Awendala than simply entering the shop. Without knowledge of the building, robbing it would be impossible. Since time pressured them, Davin saw no other choice.

Davin swallowed and said, "Goran should have told you to keep the guards occupied for at least five minutes. That might be hard." Davin peered around the corner at the two visible guards. Neither looked as if he had the intelligence of a mud louse.

"Oh?" Awendala slipped to Davin's side and seductively rubbed a hip against his thigh. "Are you implying that Kulonna and I cannot interest *any* man?"

Davin grinned. "You interest me—and don't you dare interest either of those guards a hundredth as much!"

Awendala kissed him, then spun, straightened her clothing, and said to Kulonna, "My lady, surely this cannot be the shop where you seek to buy a new *drenn* jewel?"

"Quiet, girl. Of course it is!" Kulonna assumed a haughty tone. She made an impatient gesture for Awendala to follow. Together they crossed the street, Kulonna berating her incompetent lady-in-waiting.

"The guards," whispered Davin. "They're not going to let Kulonna inside."

"Doesn't that strike you as odd?" Goran frowned. "There is more happening here than meets the eye. No merchant, even the most prosperous, turns away such a customer." His single eye fixed on Kulonna with obvious appreciation.

"There," said Davin. "Kulonna's gotten them inside. Tarry not. The sooner we learn what we need, the better I will like it."

The two thieves hastened around the rear of the shop. A

posh carriage, outfitted in Kavindra-style gilt and leatherwork, awaited its occupant.

"A royal customer?" asked Davin. "Do you suppose the High King himself orders through Eznoh-Fadey's shop?"

"We owe it to Prince Felrad to find out," Goran answered. "And who is to deny us a few coppers for our trouble, eh?"

The Challing rummaged through trash bins until he found tattered rags. He selected a large bundle for himself and tossed the remainder to his fellow adventurer. Both tied the rags about their boots, covering the soles but leaving the toes bare. Silently, they clambered up the uneven brickwork of the building adjoining Eznoh-Fadey's shop. On padded feet and in a crouch, they crossed the roof, keeping low to avoid being seen from street or alley.

"Is it time for Kulonna to create the diversion?" Goran asked. "How I long to see what that wench does! I'd wager a hundred gold bists that the guards will be so bewitched that we could drive in an ox cart to loot the store and they'd not notice."

"Not even if you gave me odds would I take that bet." Davin's gray eyes studied the roof stretching before them.

The front of the store provided no possible entry point, but a heavily barred skylight in the rear looked promising. He pointed. On silenced feet, they moved to the skylight and peered down. In an office below sat two men.

Davin cupped his hand and whispered to Goran, "Can you raise the glass so that we can listen?"

Goran's strong fingers lifted the glass, but the iron bars prevented him gaining more height than the thickness of a knuckle. Davin dropped belly down on the roof and pressed an ear to the opening.

". . . immediately. King Zarek requires as much as ten thousand bists to mount the campaign against Rakell."

"Your Lordship knows that it will take me a day or two to raise that much."

Davin and Goran exchanged looks. Ten thousand gold pieces was an immense fortune, and this man—Eznoh-Fadey?—claimed to be able to produce the kingly sum in only a day?

"Your work as Zarek Yannis' comptroller for northeastern Raemllyn will not be forgotten, Eznoh-Fadey."

"Comptroller of the Realm is a position of greater importance," Eznoh-Fadey said, leaning back in his cushioned chair and steepling pudgy fingers under his multiple chins. "The current holder of that position is loyal, I am sure, but . . ."

"But might be persuaded to retire," Zarek Yannis' emissary finished smoothly. "In light of your noble service, it will be done."

"And in light of the fact that you skim a full one-part-in-ten of everything going to Yannis," Eznoh-Fadey said in a cold voice.

"I protest!"

"Is it more?" Eznoh-Fadey asked, his tone brooking no argument. "We are not children. I know how the realm finances are managed—or mismanaged."

"You admit to stealing from the king?" demanded the emissary.

"As I said, we are not children. And I believe we understand one another well. Comptroller of the Realm is such a fine title, and I yearn to be of even greater service to King Zarek than I am now."

The emissary chuckled. "It shall come to pass. I must go now. The campaign develops quickly and other matters need my immediate attention."

"The funds will be ready tomorrow at noon," said Eznoh-Fadey.

Zarek Yannis' emissary left. Davin and Goran heard the clatter of the carriage fade and finally mingle with other Evaran street sounds.

When Eznoh-Fadey looked up to see where the unwanted breeze came from, he saw nothing. Davin Anane and Goran One-Eye had long left the rooftop, their minds churning with new schemes.

What was to have been a simple theft had turned into something much more!

chapter 5

AS WITH MISERY, evil loves company. So it was that the two wayfarers who wound their way out of the Wynae Mountains onto the Plain of Kismor had much in common.

The dethroned Lord of Jyotis, Berenicis the Blackheart, rode easily, outwardly relaxed, his body flowing with his mount's rhythmic strides. A slight smile of amusement touched his thin lips, and his sandy-colored hair stirred in the cool spring breeze. He would have been a portrait of contentment, were it not for a glint of inner tension within his cold gray eyes. That flash of light bespoke a man ready to explode into action at the slightest provocation.

Beside him, cloaked entirely in black, rode a woman whose beauty would be undiminished by any of Raemllyn's enticing sirens. Had the promise of power not lured her to the black arts, she might have been called Valora the Beautiful. Instead, she was simply Valora. Formerly High King Zarek Yannis' master mage, she had plotted once too often against the usurper. Now she held no title, although she still possessed her life—a thing with which few wizards who served Yannis managed to escape his employment.

The wind blowing from the east off the Bay of Pilisi caught the sorceress' long, raven-wing-dark hair and turned it into a wild, fluttering war banner. The spring wind blew cold, but not as cold as Valora's jet black eyes when she turned to Berenicis and asked:

"How much longer until we reach Nawat? I grow weary of this endless travel."

The former Jyotian lord chuckled without humor and shook his head. "Your impatience will be the death of you. When you oppose tyrants as powerful as Zarek Yannis, nothing must be rushed. We will bide our time and strike only when well-prepared."

"I did not ask for a lecture in philosophy," the sorceress snapped, unable to contain her irritation. "I seek only a hot bath and decent food. This has turned wormy on the trail." She thumped her saddle bags to indicate the jerky within.

The Blackheart's anger steamed. He had withstood Valora's taunts and sneering remarks for too long, through an icy winter stranded in a mountain village while snow blocked the eastward passes.

Worse was his anger at himself, which increased with each stride of his mount. It pained him to return to Prince Felrad bearing news of failure—his failure. Although, had he succeeded, he would not now be returning to the heir to the Velvet Throne. He would have sought the High King's crown for himself.

He had lost the sheath to the Sword of Kwerin Bloodhawk—and the sword itself! He had no idea where that ancient weapon of power was now, but he knew the thief responsible for its disappearance.

Davin Anane! Of all those in Raemllyn to have stolen blade and sheath, it had to be the last son of the House of Anane! Berenicis' perfect white teeth ground together, and his gray eyes burned with hatred. When their paths crossed, he should have taken Davin's head.

Berenicis twisted in his saddle, anger growing to towering black heights. Valora annoyed him; Davin Anane transformed him into a vindictive creature with instincts only for hatred and killing. If he had not been entrusted by Prince Felrad to retrieve the sheath for the Sword of Kwerin Bloodhawk from the mage Lorennion, he would never have agreed to even a brief alliance with the Anane.

"His victory galls you, doesn't it?" taunted Valora. "Davin

Anane bested you, robbed you of the weapon you needed to gain the Velvet Throne."

"For Prince Felrad to regain his throne," Berenicis smoothly corrected without the bat of an eye.

"Fool, there is no need for lies between us. I know what binds you to Felrad," Valora answered. "It is not loyalty that stirs in your breast. It is hatred and greed for power. You see Felrad as an easier target for your own ambitions than Yannis."

"And you? Are your motives so lily white, my dear?" Berenicis snorted his contempt. "You conspired against Yannis and were caught."

"There is something odd about the High King," Valora said, sidestepping Berenicis' accusation. "His mages are strong. Payat'Morve was truly a master among masters, yet he died by Zarek Yannis' hand."

"With your aid," Berenicis added with a smirk.

"With my aid, yes," agreed Valora. "But Morve's usefulness to Yannis had just begun. There was no reason for the usurper to dispose of him. Morve was still a powerful pawn in Yannis' game of intrique."

"Yannis saw you as the lesser of two evils. He thought you were less likely to succeed in a conspiracy against the Velvet Throne," Berenicis smirked.

"He knew my plans. I see that now." Valora didn't hear the Jyotian's insult. She was lost in her own ponderings as she gave voice to her thoughts. "He knew of my liaisons with the captain of his personal guard. He knew it all. No, there is something else—something more—to Yannis' removal of his most powerful mages."

"What?" Berenicis' right eyebrow arched in interest.

"I don't know. I can't puzzle it out." Valora's shoulders sagged as though bent by an invisible weight, and she slumped forward, deep in thought, her argument with Berenicis forgotten.

What *did* the usurper gain from this never-endiing parade of sorcerous power? It was as if Zarek Yannis drank the lifeforce from his wizards, then discarded the husks that had once been master mages.

Valora bit at her lower lip, then sat straight in the saddle with a toss of her head.

Ridiculous! Zarek Yannis was no mage, at least not one of great ability. He held no magical powers of his own. All he controlled was derived from the work of others. And she had failed to find the wellspring of that knowledge.

Yet, the usurper did summon and command the Faceless Ones. No man, common or sorcerer, had wielded that power since Nnamdi first called them from their realm to battle against Kwerin Bloodhawk.

"In another day's time," said Berenicis.

"Eh, what's that?" asked Valora, coming out of her deep reverie.

"We'll reach Nawat in another day at most. From there we ship to the Isle of Loieter and Rakell."

"And Prince Felrad," finished Valora, a wicked smile marring the perfection of her features.

She had no love for the pretender to the throne any more than she did for the usurper. But Zarek Yannis had turned her out and Prince Felrad offered asylum—and an opportunity to regain lost power.

She felt the stirrings of vast unrest about her. The sensation stemmed not from paltry physical battles, where armored men clashed with sword and spear, but from magicks astir. Never had she sensed such power, raw force just waiting to be tapped and directed, and Valora intended to be the one to command it!

But what source? Valora closed her jet eyes, concentrated and reached out with her mind. Repeatedly she—almost, not quite—touched it, only to taste hollow failure.

In time, the dark-haired sorceress vowed, *I will touch and hold the elusive energies aswirl in the air!* When she did, all Raemllyn would bend a knee to her! Like pesky flies she would brush aside Zarek Yannis and Prince Felrad and all the others to reign supreme!

"Your ambitions are too obvious, Valora," Berenicis warned. "Think not that the prince is an easy mark. In spite of his reputation for meting out fair-handed justice, there is a hard center to the man. He is no decadent noble-born, play-acting at rebellion. He wants to regain the Velvet Throne and will, or die trying."

"You think he will triumph? That is why you support him

over Yannis?" Valora closely studied her companion of long months.

"That, yes," admitted Blackheart, "but there are other reasons. Yannis and I have not seen eye-to-eye since he ordered me deposed from my throne in Jyotis."

Before Valora could reply, Berenicis Blackheart held up a hand, warning her to silence. Valora strained to hear, her head cocking to one side then the other. A peculiar snapping crackle, like burning leaves, sounded in the distance. She sniffed the crisp spring air, delicately at first then with deeper draughts.

"Do you sense them?" came Berenicis' quick words. "The Faceless?"

"Their horses' hooves!" Valora exclaimed. "That is the burning odor!"

"Is there anything you can do against the Faceless demons?" Berenicis' cold gray eyes shifted to his voluptuous companion.

"Yes!"

With that Valora put heels to the flanks of her mount. The frightened horse neighed, bucked slightly, then bolted, the sorceress' rowels digging bloody tracks in the animal's hide.

Berenicis Blackheart drew a deep breath as he urged his own horse after the fleeing mage. He had hoped his ally of convenience wielded some arcane spell to ward off Yannis' hell-riders. That she so feared the unearthly demons told Berenicis much. He cursed as he rode hunched forward, the wind tugging at his cloak. Valora might not be able to provide as great a service as he'd hoped.

Once more unleashing his contempt, Berenicis called out when his mount edged beside Valora, "Why do you flee so, my lady? Surely, you have powers great enough to ward off even the Faceless Ones."

The dethroned lord of Jyotis delighted in the dark rage that stormed across Valora's lovely pale face. She tugged at the reins, slowing her horse to a tired walk. The animal's lathered sides heaved heavily, as did those of the Blackheart's mount.

"Unless you have a renewing spell, we must rest them," Berenicis said when he slid to the ground, inhaled, and looked about, neither smelling nor seeing a trace of the Faceless Ones. "A nice spot to dally. Trees, a small brook running swift, clear, and clean, the first of the green and blue spring flowers. An excellent spot for a romantic assignation, wouldn't you say?"

"I see no whores for you." Valora sneered.

"Oh? And what else can we call ourselves? Mercenaries? Does that term suit you better, dear lady?"

"Name yourself as you see fit, Blackheart. And seek another to sate your lusts!" Valora's dark eyes narrowed. "Perhaps you might find another wench like the pimply-faced girl you left with child in the mountain village!"

Berenicis laughed and began rubbing down his horse with clumps of dried grasses. The horse tugged at its reins, wanting to drink from the brook until it exploded, but Berenicis held it tight. Only when the animal cooled did the man allow its head to dip to the stream. And then, for only small amounts of the water at a time.

"I don't think my steed likes me, either," Berenicis taunted Valora.

"It shows good taste." Valora dismounted, dropped heavily under a tree, and bent her head forward, trying to calm her seething emotions.

She realized that Berenicis baited her with his every word. Yet she could not control her anger, betraying herself and giving the Blackheart advantage. Valora began a low chant, a weave of magic designed to aid her in focusing her energies. The spell took form as though sparking a life of its own. Valora's head lifted, and her eyes grew wide and round.

"The Faceless Ones," she whispered as though from the depths of a heavy dream. "So many. Dozens of them—and all moving northward. From all parts of Raemllyn, they come like a deadly tidal wave."

Berenicis frowned; the witch worked herself into a trance and saw beyond the physical limits of her eyes. She sat lost in a vision of the usurper's demon horde marching to the north, a movement that meant Zarek Yannis had decided to allow Prince Felrad to go no further in his attempts to fortify Rakell.

"What of conventional troops?" he probed. "Can you sense them between here and Nawat?"

"Only the magicks released by movement of the Faceless are revealed." Valora shuddered, shaking free of the vision. She collapsed against the gnarled bole, her face drained of color.

Such power within the army of hell-riders! Can Felrad withstand such?

She doubted it.

"It is imperative we reach Felrad and warn him of this." Not for the first time, Berenicis cursed his carelessness in allowing Davin Anane to steal the Sword of Kwerin and the mystical sheath from whence the blade drew its power. A single man, even Felrad, could not hope to turn aside an entire army of the demons from another realm of existence. Only with the ancient, magical sword might it be possible.

"We can continue toward Nawat." Valora's voice intruded on his reflections. "The Faceless ahead have passed. The way is safe again, but more come soon."

"I applaud your magicks," said Berenicis, executing a mocking bow. He left it to the mage to determine if he chided her lack of skill in warding off the hell-riders, or congratulated her for detecting their movement.

Two hours past dusk, they rode into Nawat.

"It is good to be in a city again," said Valors. She bit her lower lip even as she spoke.

It did not bolster her position to thusly reveal weakness to Berenicis Blackheart. The man's every word contained a barb, a trap, an invitation she dared not accept. But Valora could use such as Berenicis the Blackheart once she gained Prince Felrad's trust. No contender for the Velvet Throne would allow a willing mage to go unused—and in that use would lie her power.

"The activity is unusual," said Berenicis. He pulled his cloak tighter around his slender frame. "Nawat is a seaport, but Zarek Yannis controls much of the sea lanes in Upper Raemllyn. I trust he has not taken full possession of Nawat."

"How long must we wait for transport?" asked Valora. Her dark eyes penetrated shadows and saw lounging ranks of soldiers—all Yannis'.

"That I cannot say. Prince Felrad agreed to send a vessel here now-and-again to check on my return from his quest."

"Our wait may be *long*," Valora made no attempt to conceal her disgust with the Jyotian.

They had ridden to the dock area. Zarek Yannis' troops

patrolled in strength, and every docked vessel sported a banner emblazoned with the royal sigil.

"Troop ships." Berenicis turned cold inside as he perused the docks. Zarek Yannis openly mustered his troops for a full-scale invasion of Loieterland and Rakell. "Seven, eight, nine, I count. If each ran fully laden on smooth sea from Pilisi to the Bay of Zaid, Yannis could transport a thousand men."

"Magicks are awork here, too. Two mages other than myself are within Nawat's walls. They practice their spells." Valora sneered. "Inept, both of them. They think to summon fire spells. All they do is create smoldering balls. Both are little more than apprentices."

"Valora!" snapped Berenicis. "Stop that."

The sorceress' fingers ceased the magical pattern she traced in the air before her. The dazzling sparks from the spell guttered out and fell darkly to the pavement.

Too late; the damage had been done. This small show of her contempt drew unwanted attention from a passing squad.

"You there, halt!" called the sergeant of the guard. "Show your passes or give reason."

"Good evening, Sergeant," greeted Berenicis, as if the entire dock area was his personal domain. "I see all proceeds according to schedule."

"Ahead," the guardsman said, then realized he had lost advantage and demanded again: "Your papers."

"You do not recognize me?" Valora pulled herself straight in the saddle and stared arrogantly at the guardsman. Heads up and down the dock turned toward her. "I am High King Yannis' master mage. I should have you taken to the Hall of Screams for such an insult."

To both Berenicis' and Valora's surprise, the guard sergeant did not cower or show any indication this threat held terror for him.

"Seize them," the sergeant ordered his squad. "Just this morning I was told that our lord, King Zarek Yannis, and his master mage would leave Kavindra soon. There is no way for them to have arrived in Nawat with such speed—even if they rode with the Faceless demons!"

Berenicis twisted slightly in his saddle, freeing his sword. The long blade arced up and then plunged downward, catching the sergeant where neck joins shoulder. The fountain of blood that spewed forth gave pause to those he had commanded—and provided the time needed for the Jyotian lord and Valora to wheel their mounts about and spur them to a full run.

"We cannot stay here," Valora cried as she clung low to her horse's neck. "The entire city will be alerted!"

"No thanks to your clumsy lie."

"How was I to know that Yannis informed his troops of his every movement? Seldom have I found a soldier who didn't crumble and fall to his knees at the mere threat of a mage."

"Your magnificent spells will have to work better against Zarek Yannis than his troops, if you're to prove any worth to Felrad." Berenicis sneered in contempt.

Valora's anger erupted but was given no vent. The deposed ruler of Jyotis pointed to a stable ahead. "There. We must rest the horses."

"But the entire city's after us!" the sorceress protested.

"Then," said Berenicis, grinning broadly, "let us confuse them and do the unexpected. If they seek us beyond Nawat, let us hide here. A lesson in tactics, lady mage: never do what the enemy expects of you."

Valora controlled her anger as she followed Berenicis into the deserted stable.

"It appears as though Zarek Yannis' men have stripped this fine establishment of anything of worth," the Blackheart said. "That makes it even better for us. They are not likely to routinely bring their own horses by, having bivouacked elsewhere in the city."

Valora dismounted and put her horse into an empty, unclean stall. She closed her jet eyes and turned inward, a scrying spell on her lips. Everywhere around her came signs of activity, troops moving, mages practicing, ships sailing in and out of harbor.

She and Berenicis Blackheart were in the eye of Zarek Yannis' hurricane—a storm that would soon break, spreading havoc and chaos across the face of Raemllyn. How long must they await Prince Felrad's promised rescue? Valora feared that the answer was . . . forever!

chapter 6

LIJENA FARLEIGH PRESSED belly down in the bottom of a sluggishly flowing drainage ditch. The sucking ooze caked her skin and clothing with foul-smelling slime. She neither noticed nor cared. Her right hand crept to her waist, fingers encircling the tingling hot hilt of the Sword of Kwerin Bloodhawk. There they remained, afraid to free the blade from its enchanted sheath lest the weapon's magicks be detected, yet ready to do just that if required.

Above the pounding in her temples, she heard the sizzling hiss draw closer. Lijena willed herself deeper into the mud until the water lapped over her back. She worried not that her once-shining blonde hair would catch a vagrant beam of sunlight. The past week's travel had turned her tresses a dull brown with grit and filth. Lijena kept nose and mouth above muddy water but, other than this small concession, she wished she could simply sink out of sight entirely.

The hissing grew louder. She heard the snorting of horses. Daring a glance, she craned her head and peered over the low embankment. She bit her lower lip to stifle a startled gasp half-born in her throat. She ducked back.

Riding in single file came not one, or two, but a full score of the Faceless Ones. Their horses' burning hooves sputtered and hissed in the mud, sending dark plumes of smoke into the air with each step; tongues of fire flared from equine nostrils;

sunlight vied with the sheen of the Faceless Ones' crystalline swords dangling at their sides.

Lijena would have met a single Faceless One in combat. With the Sword of Kwerin and the magicks it possessed, she could defeat any one of the hell-riders. But only a fool seeking suicide would tempt the Sitala by standing against twenty of the demonic warriors.

Where are they bound? Even as she silently asked the question, she knew its answer. These and the four other squads of Faceless Ones she had encountered this day all rode northward toward the city-state of Yaryne that lay but a league away—Yaryne, her own destination!

Not for the first time, she wished that Count luBonfil had not been killed by the Faceless One. The journey to Yaryne had been long and dreary for her, and filled with the constant threat of discovery by Zarek Yannis' troops.

Lijena's hand tightened about the sword at her hip. Against magical beings it seemed invincible. Against human warriors the blade was nothing more than a finely wrought sword. When Edan had fashioned the sword for Kwerin, the mage had known the Bloodhawk's armies would be victorious over human troops and Raemllyn's first High King only needed a weapon to stand against the Faceless Ones.

The young swordswoman lifted her head again and strained to hear the faintest hiss or sound of the hell-riders. Nothing. Lijena rose and wiped off the mud the best she could. She looked worse than a beggar—a living beggar though, not one robbed of life by the Faceless!

Lijena climbed the muddy bank and stared about. Grasslands stretched lonely and deserted for as far as she could see. She released an overly held breath and drew in another. The tang of the salt carried on a breeze blowing off the Bay of Pilisi. Yaryne was close.

And at Yaryne, she thought, *then what?* Count luBonfil had spoken of a contact in the city, but had mentioned nothing more.

Lijena cursed the Sitala and the twisted fate they dealt her. The scores of Faceless Ones riding northward meant but one thing—Zarek Yannis would soon move against Prince Felrad and his stronghold in Rakell. Without the sword she carried, the prince and his armies stood no chance of defeating the unholy hordes of hell-riders.

Uncertain of her course, yet moved by a mounting urgency to find Felrad, Lijena Farleigh began to walk, her strides long and determined. In half an hour she topped a rise and looked down on Yaryne.

Being the daughter of a prosperous merchant did not blind Lijena to the ways of those with lesser means. Her own misadventures in the sewers of Bistonia had hardened her, made her more aware of how difficult it was to survive.

To show the gold coin she carried would be the same as signing her own death warrant. For someone in her present condition, golden bists would only draw the attention of the city guard. The soldiers would come and never believe that such a wretched specimen of Raemllyn citizenry had come by the money honestly.

So, Lijena stole!

The open shops and tents of Yaryne's bazaar provided a simple white blouse and a burgundy skirt. She would have preferred a pair of man's breeches, but decided they might draw unwanted attention.

A bucket of well water cleansed grime from face and hair, and a shadowy alley proved as practical as a perfumed boudoir for removing her old clothing and changing into the new. Carefully, she wrapped the sheathed Sword of Kwerin Bloodhawk in her old clothes, rather than strapping it about her waist. Again, a sword-armed woman would raise eyebrows and questions from citizens and soldiers alike.

She then strolled the streets of Yaryne, alert for any sign of Yannis' troops. Although armed guards patrolled the more heavily traveled boulevards, the rest of the city appeared relatively free of the usurper's soldiers, so far.

Lijena shivered, remembering the camp she had sighted to the southwest of the city-state. There, Yannis' forces gathered, and with them, the horde of Faceless Ones.

Lijena carefully double-checked the bundle she carried to make certain the sword hidden within remained concealed. Even with the sparseness of imperial troops, Lijena wanted to do nothing to draw any attention to herself. She had not come this far to be denied.

"There, you, boy," she said, calling to an urchin who crossed the street ahead of her.

The round-eyed waif looked around, then hesitantly approached her. "What is it, lady? An errand to run? A message to deliver?"

"Information," Lijena replied.

"Ah, lady, that I cannot give." The boy shook his head and backed away two steps.

"I haven't asked the question yet," she said. The direct approach failed, so she tried a more subtle route. "You live on the street. And I'm certain those keen eyes of yours miss nothing. There's precious little you don't know about that happens in Yaryne, I'd wager."

"Wager?" The boy's gleamed. "Information is a dangerous thing to sell, but perhaps we can wager."

Lijena didn't care how the boy rationalized the exchange. She needed to find Prince Felrad, or one of the prince's contacts, and had no way of doing so in a city alien to her.

"I need a name," Lijena said. "A gold bist says you cannot supply it."

"This must be an important name," the boy said. "It will be a difficult task for me."

She "wagered" two gold bists and asked, "Prince Felrad has an emissary in Yaryne. Who is it? How do I contact this person?"

"Felrad is a rebel," the boy said slowly. "High King Zarek promises to place anyone's head on a pike for trafficking with the rebel."

His large brown eyes stared up at her. Lijena debated adding a third coin to the pot, then decided against it. "Two gold bists is a large wager."

"Gold against my neck." The boy grabbed his throat as if he meant to strangle himself.

"I'll seek my information elsewhere, since you cannot help me." She turned away from the waif.

"Wait, lady, wait! I . . . I merely point out that there is great danger." The boy tugged at her sleeve.

"Not in Yaryne. There aren't many soldiers here." Lijena turned back to him.

"Show me the coins," he said. "I might be able to tell you about a certain brass merchant."

Lijena held out two coins and, as quick as she was, the urchin proved faster. He tapped the side of her hand hard enough to spill the coins from her upraised fingers. Before either bist struck the ground, the boy snared them in a tight fist and darted away.

Lijena's longer stride kept pace with the sneak thief until he dived into a hole in a wall too small for her to follow. She snatched at his disappearing feet, but the mud and dirt caking them provided little purchase. Like an eel, the boy wiggled free and vanished.

Lijena cursed and knew that her approach had been right, but garnering any useful information in this way would be almost impossible. If she persisted, she'd only attract unwanted attention. She returned to the market square and considered finding all the brass merchants within the city.

She discarded the idea. The urchin had probably lied about this, too. If she inquired at the dozen or more brass merchants she saw around the large market area, guards would alight on her like bees on honey.

She hurried through the bazaar toward the docks. It was to fortified Rakell she journeyed, not to contact one of Prince Felrad's sympathizers in Yaryne. Better to seek the prince in the city to which he summoned his armies than here.

Lijena attracted the stares, whistles, and catcalls of dock hands and sailors as she walked along. She ignored all, her gaze moving over the sails of the vessels in the harbor. The ships that came and went were all merchanters, none carrying the banner of Zarek Yannis.

"You," she called to a man supervising the loading of cargo onto a ship. "Where are you bound?"

"Evara," came the answer. "What's it to ye?"

"I need to book passage," she said. Evara lay on the eastern coast of Raemllyn, but the sea route had to pass Loieterland—and Rakell perched on the southernmost tip of that large isle.

"Can't be done. Against the new rules." The sailor spat. A green gobbet of phlegm struck the water and floated. "Qar-damned nuisance, they are, those rules. Cap'n decided it was easier to turn down all passengers rather than abide by them."

"What rules?" she asked.

"None sails without royal traveling papers, a pass o'port, they calls it." The sailor spat again. "If a warship stops us at sea and there's a passenger without proper *papers*"—the sailor made it sound like a curse—"they can seize ship and cargo and imprison the officers and crew. Rather be dead than a slave in the usurper's navy."

Lijena paled. She had found an honest man who denied her passage. A dishonest one would have taken her money and, at the first sign of a warship, thrown her overboard rather than face Zarek Yannis' wrath.

"How do I get away from Yaryne?" she asked.

"Not on any merchant ship," the sailor said. He turned and shouted, "You Nalren-cursed whoresons! Be careful with that crate! Damage it, and I'll have you chasing the ship all the way to Evara!"

Lijena drifted away and let the sailor supervise the loading. She considered stowing away, but this might prove doubly dangerous. If one of Yannis' war vessels discovered her, she died and lost the chance to get the sword to Prince Felrad. And if the captain of the ship discovered her, he'd toss her overboard without any qualms.

There had to be a way out of Yaryne and to Rakell! There had to be!

Lijena paced along the docks until foot-weary—then she saw it. The ship looked larger than most of the merchantmen in port, but this vessel carried no ordinary cargo. Gilt trappings dangled from the masts; the figurehead had eyes of diamond and teeth of ruby; the sailors were uniformed in the finest of gaudy silks.

And women moved languidly across the decks to disappear below!

Lijena had discovered a pleasure ship, one obviously belonging to a fabulously wealthy man. Who else might have so many provocatively clad women aboard a ship?

Lijena's gorge rose at the idea of those women being little more than slaves. Then her anger cooled when an idea formed.

"No," she said aloud. "This notion is too wild, yet . . ."

Lijena Farleigh had no friends in Yaryne. Count luBonfil's death stole any chance of finding allies needed to get her to Rakell. Nor would Lijena be satisfied in simply getting to the fortified city. She *must* place the magic-forged sword in Prince Felrad's hands. The movement of so many troops and the Faceless Ones indicated that lines were now being drawn for the largest battle since Bedrich the Fair was killed at Kressia.

Her aquamarine eyes narrowed as she studied the pleasure ship. *Naughty Goose* read the golden lettering on the prow. Shipping aboard as a crew member was out of the question. And passage? She doubted the integrity of any man who sailed such a ship. But as a concubine? Could she dare hope to hide among other women?

"Pardon, good sir," she said, grabbing a sailor's arm and stopping him as he passed. "This ship. Where's she bound?"

"The *Naughty Gooser?*" the man said, smiling lewdly. "She's off for Nawat, with the evening tide. From there, who can say? She sails at a whim. Heard rumors she'll be bound for Vatusia, but who can say?" The man winked suggestively. "Are ye as parched as I am? Let me buy you an ale."

"I thank you for the information. Such a gorgeous vessel," said Lijena, carefully keeping the loathing from creeping into her voice. "And she sails with the tide."

She disengaged from the sailor, turned and caught him directly behind the knee with the wrapped sword. The sailor teetered for a moment, then toppled headlong from the dock into the water.

"Sorry," Lijena said with all the insincerity she could muster.

Before the sailor could sputter and raise a shout, she pivoted and hurried toward the pleasure ship. Lijena stopped at the bottom of the gangplank, took a steadying breath, then boldly walked onto the deck of the *Naughty Goose*.

"What's it?" came a gruff question.

A man cloaked in orange and green silks pushed his head out of a hatchway that led below. For a heart-stopping instant Lijena thought she had run across Davin Anane's scurrilous companion, Goran One-Eye. She then saw that, despite the mate's penchant for garish clothing and a shaggy head of fire-red hair, he had both eyes.

"Good sir, where are my quarters?"

"Eh? How's this now? What quarters are ye askin' about?"

"Mine," Lijena said primly. "I have been . . . retained for the cruise to Nawat."

"Ye don't have the look of a concubine about ye."

"Indeed?" Lijena said, moving closer to the mate. Her hand stroked over his cheek and tangled in his thick, bushy beard. Again she was struck by this man's likeness to Goran One-Eye. "Allow me to demonstrate. After all, the master *did* retain me for this trip, and he said nothing about asking for my *exclusive* presence."

The mate heaved himself onto deck. One leg had been cut off just above the knee. He hobbled about on a peg leg carved from dark, richly polished *chiin* wood and inset with gold and silver bands.

"Rule of the ship. Never touch anything what belongs to the master." The mate frowned and peered at Lijena. "Ye have not the look of the rest about you."

"Should I keep the money, then, if you won't allow me aboard?" asked Lijena. She held out a few of the gold bists she still carried. "Or can I stow what little I have with me and go purchase more appropriate clothing?"

"Where do we sail?" the mate asked, still suspicious.

"What does it matter to me? But the master said we journeyed to Nawat, then to Vatusia, though he wasn't sure of that. I've never seen Nawat. I hear it's a fine city acrawl with lively diversions."

"It's a stinkin' piss-pit of a port," the mate growled. "Get your sweet arse below. And ye better have suitable clothing on before the master boards. If ye don't please him, I'll see ye tossed to the sharks."

"Thank you," Lijena bowed gracefully.

She didn't press her luck, but hastened down a ladder leading below the deck. No cargo was stowed here. The entire hold had been turned into an immense, floating pleasure palace. Rugs from Delu and Jyotis cushioned the floor, paintings beyond price were securely fastened to the walls, and plush pillows provided areas for—Lijena turned her thoughts from that. She desperately needed to leave Yaryne. If this was the only way, then she'd do it. Victory or defeat at Rakell might depend on her resolve.

Seeing no one about, she went to a small closet and opened the door. Inside stood various implements for preparing and smoking calokin buds. Her quick fingers pushed aside the narcotic-smoking equipment and tugged at a board in the back of the closet. Lijena had to use the tip of the Sword of Kwerin to pry loose the board. It took only seconds for her to wedge sword and sheath into the space formed. The board refused to slip back into place, but she doubted any would notice.

"You, what are you doing?" came a grating voice.

"Oh, nothing. Just looking to see if there was anything I needed to—"

"To steal, that's what you were doing?" A tall, shapely woman with rich, brown hair strode over and cast a quick glance into the closet. Lijena prepared to fight should this woman notice the board at the back of the closet. She didn't.

"What ugly clothing you wear. Are you making the journey to Nawat?" The woman arched a thinly shaped eyebrow, then her hazel eyes narrowed in obvious suspicion.

"Why, yes, I am—"

"Who cares what your name is? The master won't."

The woman tipped her head to one side and critically appraised Lijena. The daughter of Bistonia felt as if she were a cut of meat being evaluated by a master chef. The woman smiled and nodded. "I see why he selected you. There is a quality that will appeal to him, I am certain. A fire. He likes that."

"I am sure. But I must go ashore and—"

"No time. The master arrives at any moment. There is ample spare clothing. Go and change. Through those hangings. Do it, girl, do it *now!*"

Lijena offered no protest, but moved through a beaded curtain into a spacious dressing area. She hurriedly undressed and found lacy garments that seemed more air than material in one of four closets. She studied her reflection in a looking glass, turned, and decided to add another layer to hide what the first gown was obviously designed to expose. This time Lijena draped diaphonous silks around her. A third and final layer covered her body in a manner that would have been considered modest by the other women she had seen aboard this ship.

"The master arrives. Come and greet him," the woman outside called.

Lijena stepped back through the dangling beads and went cold inside. A tall, handsome man dressed in a *danne* work tunic and sporting thousands of bists' worth of jewelry stepped down the ladder and turned.

"Ah, Monni, you are as lovely as ever. And the others, the ones chosen for this trip? They are precious flowers to be savored, to be cherished one by one."

He went from one to another, lightly caressing, brushing quick fingertips across a cheek, smiling. When he came to Lijena she dropped to hands and knees, her forehead pressed against the floor.

"Master!" she said, her voice choked. "What is your wish?"

"To gaze upon your beauty. Rise and light my world with your beauty."

Lijena hesitated. She dared not show her face to this man. Not to Nelek Kahl, the slaver who had bought her and sold her to the mage Masur-Kell. She had vowed to kill him, and there was no way to keep the shock and hatred from her expression.

"Rise, my lovely," Nelek Kahl said.

Trembling with fear, Lijena Farleigh rose and stared into the steel gray eyes that met her gaze.

chapter 7

"IT WAS FOOLISH. It might have been our undoing!" Davin Anane's words contained a sharp reprimand.

The Jyotian thief glared at Awendala as she proudly displayed the bracelet draped from her fingers—a ruby bracelet she had stolen from Eznoh-Fadey's shop!

"Wasn't this the idea?" the young red-tressed woman questioned sweetly and batted long eyelashes innocently. "We had to find out how attentive the guards were. When Kulonna pretended to stumble and turn her ankle, they had eyes for naught else but her legs."

"Not just her legs, I'd wager," Goran One-Eye chuckled as he hooked an arm about Kulonna's waist and hugged her close. "This will be a fine theft, I feel it in my bones!"

"Your bones should to be ground to powder," Davin grumbled in disgust.

The risk Awendala had taken to steal a relatively cheap bracelet had endangered them all. Yet, he admitted a certain unvoiced pride in her achievement. If the opportunity had presented itself to him, could he have resisted?

Davin smiled, knowing the answer to the question. Had he been in Awendala's position, ignorant of this vast hoard of gold the gem merchant concealed, his quick fingers would have taken more than a single bracelet when Kulonna feigned the twist of her shapely ankle.

"Forget this bauble, Davin. What is done, is done. We have more important matters to attend—such as discovering where Eznoh-Fadey has stashed the gold." Goran winked at Awendala. "Once that is learned, all else is simple."

"Not even a muscle-bound oaf like you can tote away ten thousand bists on his back," Davin pointed out, leaning on the table and lowering his voice. "We'll need a sturdy wagon to carry the load."

"Aye, and steal a strong team of horses while you're at it. I have no desire to linger in Evara," Goran nodded, then drained the cup of wine he held. "Animals with strength to cross the Muu-Kou Mountains."

"We go eastward?" Awendala's head turned to Davin.

"To Yaryne. When we entered Evara, didn't Goran and I promise to assist Kulonna and you in reaching your final destinations?" the last son of Anane answered.

"Yaryne!" Joy filled Awendala's voice and beamed in her smile.

The young woman's unrestrained delight awoke a sharp, knotting pang of sadness within Davin's breast. Awendala sought the remaining members of her family in her homeland of Yaryne. When she found them, Davin knew their paths would part. The prospect of facing the inevitable sorely troubled him.

Awendala leaned close and planted a wet, sloppy kiss on the Jyotian's mouth. Davin weakly returned her smile. The Sitala had dealt her an evil fate for the past year until Davin and Goran had rescued her from the clutches of a power-hungry sorcerer. Parents dead—and worse—Awendala had endured much. Now she would return to her home with gold and such tales!

He looked at Goran, who sat with a silly grin running from ear to ear. The Challing had yet to realize that Yaryne meant that he would soon lose Kulonna, that the city was but a short journey across the water to Rakell—Kulonna's final destination. There she would serve as her father's emissary to Prince Felrad.

Or was Davin once more making the mistake of thinking of the changeling in human terms? Was a Challing even capable of love? Or did Goran merely see Kulonna as means to deeply sample the human pleasures he relished so? Davin didn't know.

"All right," the Jyotian said gruffly to cover his momentary lapse. "We know the guards can be diverted. I think it would be wise for Kulonna and Awendala to return just before the shop closes for business with a gift for the guards—drugged wine. At first the two men will protest, but our lovelies will persist."

"They *will* drink," Kulonna vowed with a wink and a smile.

"I'll find a wagon and team suitable for hauling such a weighty treasure. And you, Goran, will enter the shop and do nothing more than seek out ward spells. When I return with the wagon, we will both search for the gold."

"You think it is on the premises? Why would Eznoh-Fadey risk that?" The Challing frowned.

"What risk?" asked Davin. "Unless I misjudged the man, he isn't one to let such wealth stay beyond his grasp for long. No, my friend, he wants it where he can check it on a daily—hourly!—basis."

"Why did he tell Yannis' lackey that it would take a day to retrieve it?" This from Awendala.

"He hates to part with so much gold. Did you not hear the longing in Eznoh-Fadey's voice when he spoke of being elevated to Comptroller of the Realm? The man lives for gold."

Goran nodded his shaggy head. "There is truth in what you say." He then slapped his massive thighs and proclaimed, "Tonight we become rich beyond the dreams of our wildest avarice!"

"I'll fetch the wagon," Davin said, staring at his friend. "Remember, Goran, check only for spells until I return."

"Only the spells," the Challing assured him. "Though this part of your plan seems such a waste. I could have the shop clean of jewels while you bring the wagon."

"Only locate ward spells," Davin repeated firmly.

"Aye, just the magicks Eznoh-Fadey employs, nothing else," Goran nodded with resolve.

They looked down at the soundly snoring guards on the floor. Awendala and Kulonna had done their work well. Both women now waited at either end of the street, serving as lookouts.

Goran snorted. "The merchant isn't likely to place his full trust in such scurvy worms as these."

Davin glanced apprehensively at Goran. Golden specks of fire swirled in his good right eye. The witch-fire would blaze higher before the Challing had finished his examination of the store.

"I'll bring the wagon around back. Have the door open for me," Davin said as he slipped out the front and cast a knowing eye up and down the street. He saw neither Kulonna nor Awendala. A good sign: they hid well.

He hurried to the pilfered wagon a few streets distant. Wrinkling his nose at the noxious odor emanating from the tarpaulin-covered bed, he climbed into the wagon box and clucked the four draft horses forward. Gold and Goran would weigh heavily; he had stolen only the finest for this venture. Crossing even the low mountain passes in the Muu-Kous would test the four beasts' strength and endurance to their limits.

Davin found the alley behind Eznoh-Fadey's shop with no difficulty. Halting the team when the wagon's bed was even with the open rear door to the shop, he tied off the animals, dismounted, and slipped inside.

"Goran?" he called softly.

"What's that awful stench?" came his fellow thief's voice from the darkness. "You smell of offal!"

"I have a wagon half-filled with it." Davin shrugged.

"By Nyuria's poxied staff, do you intend to drive city guards away with the stench?" Goran moved like a shadow within the shadows, stepping to his friend's side. He pinched his nose with thumb and forefinger.

"Forget my offal odor! What spells does Eznoh-Fadey use to protect his jewels?" Davin demanded.

"That's a strange one," the Challing replied, and protested once more, "That smell is quite odious, Davin. Enough to make me reconsider our longtime partnership."

"The *spell!* What is protected?" insisted Davin, unable to contain his impatience.

"None of the jewel cases hint of even a trace of magic." Goran turned; his single eye blazed like a green beacon in the darkest of nights. "However, a wall in Eznoh-Fadey's office is heavily protected."

"Nothing else?" Davin crowded past Goran and went into the shop. Only the two guards' noisy snoring touched his ears. "No case is protected?"

"Not that I detect," said Goran. "And my powers feel . . . strong this night."

Davin could believe it. The witch-fire blazed so bright he could almost see by it in the darkened shop. With quick, economical movements, Davin went from one end of Eznoh-Fadey's shop to the other—fine jewels, bracelets, rings, and necklaces vanishing into a gunny sack. He tossed it over his shoulder and told Goran, "To this wall. Let's see what we really came after."

Davin marveled at the ease of the theft. Under ordinary circumstances, he would have been satisfied with such a magnificent take. Now he found himself considering this fine load of gems hardly more than an appetizer before a banquet, a feast of gold! All at the expense of Zarek Yannis!

"It cannot be too complex a spell," Goran said when they entered the office. "He had no mage come to apply it, so Eznoh-Fadey must mutter the chant himself."

"He paid heavily for that privilege," murmured Davin.

The Jyotian freebooter put down the sack of jewels and stood in front of the wall the Challing pointed to. It appeared no different from any other—except that Goran identified it as being ensorcelled.

"Aye, a princely sum," agreed Goran, "and I doubt the merchant is adept enough to remember the chant."

Carefully avoiding *the* wall, the changeling methodically examined every inch of the office's remaining three walls. Lifting a painting of a scraggly brown cow, the Challing yelped with delight. He pulled out a tattered slip of foolscap he'd found stuck behind the frame.

"As I thought! The merchant lacks the ability to memorize the guardian spell!" Goran held the parchment before him, letting the glow of witch-fire bathe it. "Let's see, invocation to the god Pliaton to restrain any of his thieving worshippers, then some minor imprecations, a portion here begging Yehseen for mercy, and a good finish demanding of Qar that he take the soul of any attempting to steal what lies beyond the wall."

"The spell places a *demand* on the Death God?" Davin felt gooseflesh prickle up and down his spine. He had little use of magicks or spells, even less when the names of Raemllyn's deities were invoked.

Goran shrugged. "It's not a very effective spell. I'm no mage, but I'm certain I can easily circumvent this, even with my powers so sorely held in check by this awkward human form."

"Do it then, and be done with it," urged Davin.

The Challing began to mumble the chant and wave his arms wildly in the air. The Jyotian watched in fascination as the green witch-fire flared more intensely. A tiny *pop!* sounded. Goran gasped and staggered back.

Davin's own gasp echoed that of his friend!

Not the ensorcelled wall but the Challing's left arm had been magically transformed into the foreleg of a goat.

"Fear not, Davin," Goran hastened before his fellow thief could speak. "'Tis not an effect of the incantation, but my own powers. I told you I felt the energies upon me this night!"

"Some wielder of magicks," Davin said with a disgusted grunt. It wasn't the force of Goran's ability at play, but the random effects of the on-again-off-again mystical power.

The Challing chuckled with obvious amusement as he concentrated, transforming goat leg back to human flesh that pulsated and writhed, eventually returning to the familiar form of Goran's left arm. "Now to try the invocation once again."

As before, the red-bearded giant read the chant from the parchment, while his arms waved and jerked in the air. When another "pop" sounded, he stepped toward the wall and squinted his good eye.

"That does it, I think. There shouldn't have been any noise as the spell collapsed, but then, as I said, I'm not a human mage, merely a Challing, which is a hundredfold superior." Goran looked over a shoulder at Davin. "Shall we examine Eznoh-Fadey's vault?"

"Where is it?" Davin puzzled.

The wall appeared unchanged, solid brick and mortar.

"Here," said Goran, walking forward.

Davin shouted, but the Challing ignored him and strode straight into the wall—and through it! His voice called anxiously:

"This is remarkable! Come, join me, Davin, and see for

yourself. Never have I beheld the likes of this before!"

Davin hesitantly advanced, hand outstretched. His fingers touched not unyielding stone, but cool mist—then his hand, all the way to the wrist, disappeared through the wall. Drawing a steadying breath to quell his dislike and mistrust of magicks, he stepped through the wall into Eznoh-Fadey's treasure trove.

For a few seconds, he stood speechless. Then, "Never have I seen such beauty!"

Stacked from floor to ceiling were chests brimming with gold bists. Yannis' emissary had asked for ten thousand, a king's ransom. Davin's quick estimate placed the wealth in this large vault at ten times that.

"Eznoh-Fadey must have been milking all upper Raemllyn to gather this much gold," Goran said in awe.

"Milking? He's been sucking it dry! He must receive all the booty collected by Yannis' pirate ships sailing the northern coasts."

"And more." Goran hefted one of the larger chests. His muscles stood out in thick cords along his arms and neck, silently testifying to the weight of gold coins inside. "That wagon had better have good axles, my friend."

"Let's not tarry," said Davin. "We have hours of work ahead if we are to empty this vault."

Goran and he made four trips from vault to dung wagon before he emerged with a fifth chest and heard the pounding of footsteps coming down the alley. He heaved the chest into a pile of dried offal and turned, hand on sword.

"Davin! Goran!" came a woman's warning cry.

"Awendala, what is it?"

"Demons!" she gasped when she reached his side. "T-the Faceless Ones!"

"What of them?" Goran deposited another large chest into the wagon. Wood groaned in protest beneath the weighty burden.

"One comes from the east. This way!" Awendala pointed to where she had kept watch.

Rapid footfalls from the opposite end of the alley drew the three's attention.

"Kulonna!" cried Goran.

"Faceless Ones!" the blonde duchess said between gulps of air. "There's one riding in from the west."

"Into the wagon, immediately," Davin ordered, ignoring the cold hand of terror that squeezed his heart.

"But the gold, Davin," pleaded Goran. "We've hardly begun to exhaust the wealth inside."

"If we find ourselves trapped in this alley, a Faceless One at either end, all the gold in Raemllyn will avail us naught. Get into the wagon and cover the gold with dung," the Jyotian commanded.

"What? Me? I am Challing!" Indignation rose in Goran's tone.

"Do it," Davin snapped as he raced back into Eznoh-Fadey's office.

He snatched up the discarded sack of jewelry and looked around for anything combustible. The desk and a few scraps of paper were all he could find. A tinderbox beside an oil lamp provide the needed spark to ignite a piece of paper. With flames licking toward his finger, he cast the burning paper atop Eznoh-Fadey's desk then spilled the lamp's oil on the flame. A tiny fire licked hungry tendrils across the desktop. He didn't remain to watch its voracious appetite spread to other parts of the shop.

"Hide these, too!" he called, swinging the sack to Goran in the back of the wagon. "Then get out of sight under the dung."

"You jest," said the Challing.

"Not unless you consider your life a jest!"

Kulonna silenced Goran's string of curses. "I'll join him. Three of us in the box will only draw unwanted interest."

The blonde duchess slipped over the back of the hardwood seat and crept under the tarp Goran held up for her.

"Even with such beauty joining me, it still smells like shit back here," complained Goran.

"Keep a close watch on our gold," said Davin.

Awendala smiled when she saw the Challing's response: he quieted at the thought of so much gold.

Davin snapped the reins atop the draft horses' backs, bringing them to life. Even though he and Goran had made only five trips to the vault, the load proved almost more than the massive animals could haul.

"Damn Jajhana for such bad luck!" Davin swore. "We could have had even more!"

"More? But this is so much. Davin!" Awendala's eyes widened when she looked back to the wagon's bed again. "The shop's on fire!"

"Fortune remains with us." Davin reined the team from the alley onto the street that ran before the gem merchant's shop. "That'll hold their attention for a few seconds."

Ice like a blizzard from the legendary land of Ianya suffused the young Jyotian's body, gripping muscle and sinew. Ahead in the street sat a Faceless One astride his fire-snorting horse. A sword of crystal fire dangled at its side. Unable to flee, Davin took the only course open to him—he continued straight down the street toward the hell-rider.

Beside him, Awendala's eyes had turned as round as saucers with fear. The Faceless One watched their every movement with burning-red eyes and a skeletal talon on the pommel of its sword. But it made no attempt to stop the creaking wagon. A nervous sigh escaped the young adventurer's lips as he drove the four-horse team past the demon.

"It's going on toward Eznoh-Fadey's shop," Kulonna's voice whispered from under the tarp. "We made it!"

"We got past one of them," said Davin, his heart still hammering wildly in his chest. He wiped sweat from his brow and left smelly dung streaks. He barely noticed. "What called them down like that?"

"Those minor imprecations?" Goran suggested. "Perhaps I misinterpreted them."

"When you countered the spell, you *summoned* them?" Davin's hands shook at the thought.

"It is possible the spell was more complex than I believed," the Challing replied as though it mattered naught. "Yes, that is probably what happened."

Davin's arms and legs went liquid, threatening to collapse and pool like jelly. Eznoh-Fadey had woven the ward spell more cunningly than they'd anticipated. They should have known that neither the gem merchant nor his master Zarek Yannis would ever be content with easily duped human guards or feeble spells that any mage could nullify. The spell that had been woven was intended to bring down the Faceless Ones on any who violated the trove of gold! Had it not been for Awendala and Kulonna, Goran and he would now be dead!

Davin clucked to the team, urging the draft animals to hasten their pace. "We ride straight for the Mountains of Muu-Kou. The more distance we put between the demons and ourselves, the better!"

"The fire you set illuminates the night." Goran's red head poked from beneath the tarp. "Such a lovely sight; but, the gold! We left far too much for that greedy bastard Zarek Yannis!"

"If the fire is hot enough, what remains will be melted into one giant nugget." For an instant, Davin's mind flashed with the vision of a small mountain of golden slag. "No great burden for a jeweler to cut off chunks, but it will make it more difficult to use. Few men commerce in raw gold. Bists are the coins of all realms. To have coins reminted will take months, even as much as a year. The usurper will not profit quickly from his ill-gotten treasure."

The clip-a-clop rhythm of hooves on cobblestone echoed through Evara's streets until the team pulled their heavy burden to the boundary of the city. On the road ahead, six mounted soldiers blocked their passage. Their heads lifted, and they stared at the approaching wagon, suspicion on their shadowy faces.

"Guards ahead, Goran. Prepare yourself," Davin whispered a warning from the side of his mouth.

The pile of dung shifted slightly as the Challing did as told without one muttered curse of complaint.

"What do we do, Davin?" asked Awendala.

"Reach over and slip the dagger from my belt. Use it if you get the chance, otherwise, just . . ." His voice trailed off as the officer of the guard approached the wagon.

"You, what's your business?"

"Ah, good sir, isn't it apparent? I sell night soil." Davin waved an arm toward the wagon's bed. "'Tis not the most profitable of businesses, but I manage to feed and clothe my family, as well as rid Evara of unwanted offal."

The officer wrinkled his nose. "I can smell your wares all too clearly. Where do you take it? There's naught along this road."

"Farms need my fine merchandise," Davin replied, eyeing

the five remaining soldiers who moved closer to surround the wagon.

"There are no farms from here to the Muu-Kous. Ground's too rocky," the officer said.

Another soldier added, "What weighs your wagon? The axles look as though they might snap at any instant. Dried turds weigh little."

"Here, good sir, look. Note the fine texture." Davin cupped his hands and scooped up a large portion of dung. In a quick motion, he threw it in the officer's face. At the same instant Goran exploded from under the pile, sword flashing death left and right.

Davin leaped from the wagon box, both feet striking the officer's chest and knocking him from the saddle. Before the slow-witted soldier recovered from the sudden attack, Davin freed his sword and skewered the downed man's unarmored chest.

Immediately, the Jyotian thief ducked, dropping under a vicious swing from another soldier on his left. He then twisted and lunged, catching the man in the solar plexus. Davin cursed as the man's dying body refused to yield back his blade. The soldier jerked to the side, sword still in his chest, disarming Davin.

Davin, now weaponless, faced another soldier. The look of pure hatred on this soldier's face told the freebooter that he'd just killed a valued friend. But before the soldier could advance for the kill, he stiffened and fell face forward from the saddle. The hilt of a dirk protruded between his shoulder blades. Awendala stood grimacing behind the man.

"Your hand is quick, my love." Davin dashed to the woman, gave her a quick kiss, retrieved his sword, and prepared to meet the rest of the soldiers.

There were no more guards to test his sword arm. They lay in growing pools of their own blood. Goran and Kulonna had finished them. Davin saluted the others with his sword, then said, "Pull the bodies off the road and hide them, then we travel to the mountains and freedom!"

"A rich freedom it will be, too," gloated Goran. The Challing turned and squinted at Davin. "We don't have to keep riding under that shit, do we?"

"No, friend Goran, fetch the soldiers' horses. This night, you ride in style! We all do!"

"In style we may ride," said Goran, wrinkling his nose, "but we still smell like shit."

Goran and Kulonna on stolen horses, Awendala and Davin atop the wagon box, they started eastward toward the Muu-Kou Mountains, away from Zarek Yannis' troops and the Faceless Ones.

chapter 8

LIJENA FARLEIGH ROSE from her position of obeisance and lifted her chin to face the slaver who she had vowed a thousand times to kill for selling her to the mage Masur-Kell. Now without sword or knife, she stood vulnerable in harem garb, certain that Nelek Kahl would recognize her and immediately cast her in chains, or worse.

As her eyes met Kahl's gray gaze, the woman Monni said, "Master Nelek, the captain requires you on deck. He said immediately."

"What is it this time?" Kahl pivoted from Lijena. "Must I attend to every detail?"

"Sire, it's the harbor police. Zarek Yannis' guard," Monni explained.

Lijena frowned. She couldn't see Kahl's features well, but the expression on that handsome face confused her. It appeared as though the notorious slaver did not fear Zarek Yannis' soldiers as much as he hated them.

But didn't the infamous Nelek Kahl operate throughout Raemllyn at the usurper's sufferance? The king often found it more agreeable that certain undesirable elements vanish rather than die; Kahl arranged for those non-permanent disappearances. If any of the slaver's victims were later required, they could be easily produced.

"All right, Monni, I'll see to it," Kahl answered, the irritation in his voice fading.

Only when the slaver hurried up the hatchway ladder and vanished, did Lijena allow herself the luxury of a silent sigh. That had been too close for comfort. Nor had her position improved that much! She would still have to face Kahl.

"Don't just stand around. We sail within the hour," Monni called to the women within the craft's opulent hold, bustling about as if she were the harem mistress.

Lijena bit back the words that formed on her tongue. Monni might *be* in charge of Kahl's concubines. Lijena dared not ask. To draw attention to herself might prove fatal.

Nelek Kahl and Amrik Tohon. Painful memories flooded Lijena's mind as she threw herself onto posh, fluffy feather cushions and tried to contain her anger. Amrik had been her lover, her betrothed in Bistonia. She had loved him above all others—and he had sold her into Nelek Kahl's hands.*

The slaver, in turn, had offered her to a mage for servitude that extended far beyond simple slavery. Masur-Kell's sexual tastes had been perverted and disgusting.

She had no glimmer of where Amrik Tohon had fled with his purse weighted from her sale into bondage. But Nelek Kahl would be hers before this pleasure ship reached Nawat. One dark night on deck and . . .

"Don't rip the cushions," Monni's sharp command sliced into Lijena's thoughts of venegence. "Sheath your claws and help with tidying up the hold." The taller woman stared curiously at Lijena, then asked, "Are you afraid of sea travel?"

Lijena caught herself and unballed her fists from the cushion, realized she had allowed her emotions to show. She covered by saying, "It is not sea travel that worries me. It's Yannis' patrols."

"The king allows our master free passage." Monni's upper lip curled in a sneer. "But the price of free passage is not obtained for free. Our master pays dearly for the privilege of wandering Raemllyn unhindered. That is why this . . . inspection is so odious."

Lijena nodded, not trusting herself to speak. How she wanted to rage aloud against Nelek Kahl. How she longed for his death after what he had done to her!

*Swords of Raemllyn, Book One, *To Demons Bound.*

Lijena's quick eyes did not miss the small dagger Monni carried tucked inside a broad, green-silk sash about her wasp-like waist. If she could only manage to slip the weapon free and hide it within the folds of her own clothing.

She felt the tides of revenge rise within her. A dagger, alone with Kahl on deck, a quick slash, and the slaver's worthless carcass would become fish food!

"What excites you so?" asked Monni, frowning. "The thought of our master having problems with the ignorant harbor guard?"

"The thought of the master," Lijena answered truthfully.

Monni shook her head and went to prod the other concubines into action. Lijena did what she could to tidy the already impeccably neat quarters. Then, when Monni was busy elsewhere, Lijena slipped on deck.

The peg-legged mate, Nelek Kahl, and a man dressed in a white linen uniform with ebony insignia stood in a tight group at the stern of the *Naughty Goose*. From the way the man in white—the captain?—gestured, his anger knew no bounds. Kahl spoke in a voice too low for Lijena to overhear, but the set of his body, the expression on his face, and the decisive hand motions bespoke an equal anger that was carefully held in check.

Lijena frowned, her eyes narrowing as she stared at the slaver. There was something else about Nelek Kahl, something so familiar, yet elusive. For several seconds she couldn't identify what it was about the man's appearance that troubled her so. Then a single name escaped her lips in a hissing curse of hate, "Davin Anane!"

Kahl the slaver could have been a twin of the Jyotian thief who had caused her so much woe and had ruined her life. Lijena blinked to clear the image of Davin and saw Kahl once again. The man did look like Davin—or how the thief might appear were he ten years older. A dash of gray salted Nelek Kahl's raven-black hair at the temples. His face showed a fullness that Davin lacked, and the slaver appeared heavier.

Lijena frowned. Although Kahl surely must live a life of indolent ease, something about him warned her against believing him decadent. To be certain, his physique was heavier than Davin's, but the man's body betrayed no hint of fat or flab.

Beneath the finery he wore, only muscle rippled. The Jyotian was whipcord thin and tough, while Kahl appeared stronger, but no less durable.

"... whoreson off the ship!" shouted the captain.

Kahl placed a reassuring hand on the officer's shoulder and turned. The wind caught his words and carried them clearly to Lijena. "He will be gone soon. Additional money will grease his palm to insure us a speedy passage to Nawat."

"And from there? Can we sail directly to Rakell?"

Lijena's aquarmarine eyes widened in surprise. Nelek Kahl sought passage to the heart of Prince Felrad's territory? Let him do just that! The prince would cut off the slaver's head and place it on a spike for all to see!

"Later, Captain Lattour. We will speak of this later. Be prepared for the worst after we leave harbor." Kahl slapped Lattour on the shoulder and left.

Lijena pressed close to the main mast as Kahl strode past without giving her heed. She released a pent-up breath and surveyed the ship around her.

A small skiff came along the *Naughty Goose*'s starboard side. She heard a ruckus from below and slipped back to listen without being seen. A man dressed in the uniform of an officer in Zarek Yannis' guard scaled a rope ladder that dangled down to the skiff. Nelek Kahl approached, an insincere smile on the slaver's handsome face.

"I am glad your inspection has gone well, Lieutenant. Give King Zarek my regards the next time you see him. It's been over six months since he honored me with an exclusive audience in his court at Kavindra."

The lieutenant tried to cover his confusion by blustering about harbor fees. He sought graft to allow the ship to depart, yet the slaver seemed on intimate terms with the High King. Lijena watched in fascination as greed and fear played against one another in a game of emotion.

Greed won.

A pouch of coins changed hands. She had no idea what the required fee was for the ship to leave Yaryne, but the lieutenant appeared more than satisfied with the weight of the leather bag he accepted from the slaver. And the look Kahl gave him when he turned to depart surely imitated the expression with which Black Qar greeted the newly arrived souls of the dead to Peyneeha.

Kahl turned and bellowed to Captain Lattour to get underway. The *Naughty Goose*'s crew rushed on deck like ants from a hill assaulted with boiling water. Lijena found herself caught up in the furor. Rather than draw unwanted eyes, she slipped back down into the hold in time for Monni to assign her new chores.

"It's been three days," said Lijena. "Where has he been?"

"What is it you don't understand?" asked Monni, lounging on a lace-covered cushion.

"Nelek Kahl. Not once has he left his cabin to . . . to come to us."

"The master is busy." Monni shrugged.

"But . . ." Lijena quieted, not wishing to make her concern obvious.

Kahl had kept his own company since leaving Yaryne. Why have a pleasure ship filled with lovely concubines and not once partake of the pleasures with which he surrounded himself? It made no sense.

Lijena had at first suspected that Kahl was less than a man, but none of the women even hinted at that—or that this trip to Nawat was different from any of the others they'd taken with Kahl.

Now and again the women's services were used to ease passage of the ship from harbor, she learned. The woman who had met briefly—very briefly from the brunette's description—with the port lieutenant of Yaryne had done so of her own accord. Kahl had not ordered her as a master might command a slave, yet the woman had done what was required.

Lijena Farleigh frowned at the notion that all the women aboard ship sailed willingly with Nelek Kahl. That made even less sense. Yet she discovered no other answer. These women chose the companionship of the most notorious slaver in all Raemllyn. Worse, they worshipped him like a god!

A sudden shift in course threw both her and Monni against a far bulkhead. From above came shouts and the rattle of steel, as swords were drawn from a normally locked box. Lijena peered up through an air grate and saw brightly dressed sailors testing the edges of swords and daggers.

"Monni," cried one of the other women. "What is wrong?"

The tall woman swallowed several times, her throat twitching nervously. "Pirates! Yannis' pirates!"

The phrase struck Lijena as odd, but in it she saw her opportunity. Weapons left nerveless hands in a battle. She might be able to recover a dagger in the heat of the fray and sheath the weapon in Nelek Kahl's treacherous heart before any were the wiser.

"Stay below!" shouted Monni, but Lijena had already climbed to the top of the ladder and was peering at the deck.

It was as the other woman thought. A small, fast warship, sporting Zarek Yannis' banner and royal insignia, cut across the *Naughty Goose*'s bow. Captain Lattour furled sails and let the pleasure ship drift dead in the water.

"We have bought safe passage!" the captain shouted to the warship. "What is the meaning of this? You disturb Nelek Kahl's peaceful journey to Nawat!"

The ship rocked hard, as grappling hooks caught the gilt-edged rails and pulled the two vessels together. An officer in Zarek Yannis' guard jumped from the warship to stand before Lattour.

"We know nothing of passage fees paid. Show me the receipt."

"Receipt!" bellowed Captain Lattour. "Thieves do not give receipts for what they steal!"

"Then you owe the crown a fee of . . . one thousand bists." The officer's eyes took in the expensive fittings and obvious wealth so blatantly flaunted.

"Not one copper!" Lattour retorted with a disgusted snort.

Kahl strode on deck from his cabin. Lijena frowned. It appeared that the slaver had hastily donned his expensive clothing. Beneath it she saw traces of a more serviceable tunic and breeches.

"Good sir, your master—and mine—has decreed safe and free passage for this ship," said Kahl.

"So you are the slaver Nelek Kahl," the guardsman sneered and spat on Kahl's boots. "I have no time for your kind, living off the flesh of your betters."

"As you live off the wealth of your betters?" asked Kahl in a voice that spoke of quick death.

Lijena blinked and her mouth fell agape. The pirate reached for a cutlass at his waist, but his fingers never closed about the weapon's hilt. He stood tottering a moment, then slowly sank to his knees to collapse face down on the deck. A jewel-studded knife protruded from the side of his neck. Kahl had struck quick and true. Lijena hadn't even seen the man's arm move!

No other signal to arms was needed. Sailors dropped from the cross beams like a flight of gaudy birds of prey. Steel flashed bright and clean in the afternoon sun. Death cries mingled with those of sorely wounded sailors.

Lijena had seen battles, but never one so efficiently organized. Kahl had known what lay ahead and had planned well to meet the challenge. In less than five minutes, the entire complement of Zarek Yannis' warship had been sent to the lowest levels of Peyneeha for Black Qar's celebration of death.

"Open the seacocks. Sink it," Kahl said, not even glancing in the direction of the warship. "I would make Nawat by the morning tide." With that, the slaver went below decks, as unconcerned as if nothing had happened.

Lijena saw her chance and took it. The instant Captain Lattour left the bridge to carry out Kahl's orders, she hurried on deck to the side of a fallen pirate captain and yanked the jewel-handled knife from his neck. A sluggish trickle of blood followed the slightly curved blade.

Lijena noted the flow coldly. How easily she now watched the draining of a man's life. Once, such a sight would have churned her stomach. Nelek Kahl was in part responsible for her horrible transformation from Bistonian lady to swordswoman. For that he would pay the dearest price of all.

Her earlier speculation about Kahl proved true; the man was no decadent dandy. To deal with the slaver would require caution. She wiped off the blade on the pirate's blouse, hid the weapon in the layers of her costume, and went below.

If they docked at Nawat on the dawn tide, then she had to strike during the night. And she would! Nelek Kahl would finally pay for the disgrace he had heaped upon her and the House of Farleigh!

chapter 9

BENEATH THE SLEEPING-SILKS, Lijena Farleigh caressed the sharp dagger she had drawn from the neck of the dead pirate. From above, the glow of the ship's watch lights filtered through the open hatch and grating to softly dance about the *Naughty Goose*'s pleasure-chamber-converted hold. Lijena's eyes moved over her surroundings. In the shadows, she saw and heard women curled in sleep atop plush pillows draped in the finest silks from the Isle of Pthedm.

The time for smoldering hate passed and the moment of action arrived. Tucking the weapon back into the flowing folds of her clothing, the daughter of Bistonia edged aside the silks, rose, and quietly crept to the ladder leading to the top deck.

"Where are you going?"

Monni's voice brought Lijena spinning around, her temples pounding. Monni sleepily leaned on an elbow atop her cushiony bed and lifted a low-burning candle. She blinked across the room at Lijena. "The master's requested us all to stay below decks until we leave Nawat."

"I . . . I feel sick. I need to go on deck for a few minutes of fresh air." Lijena's voice trembled, not from illness, but in fear of detection.

Monni peered at her more closely. "You don't look seasick. If some matter, a private matter, other than a queasy stomach, takes you above, beware. The master doesn't like us fraternizing with the crew."

"I'll be back in a few minutes," Lijena assured her.

Monni shrugged and returned the candle to the floor beside her bed as she nestled amid the pillows once again.

Lijena sucked in a breath to quell the racing of her heart. She had hoped to sneak on deck undetected. Now she feared that she had needlessly alerted the other woman. When Kahl vanished, his body sliding beneath the waves, Lijena's dagger firmly buried in his heart, Monni was certain to remember who had gone above this night.

Refusing to be denied the revenge for which she hungered, Lijena started up the ladder. Monni forced her to quickly alter her plans. She would kill the accursed slaver, return to the hold for the Sword of Kwerin Bloodhawk, then steal a skiff and escape in it.

Yes, she nodded to herself, *that will work.*

The *Naughty Goose* couldn't be far from port if they were to arrive at Nawat on the morning tide. Four or five hours at the most, she estimated. Besides, the pleasure craft sailed the Bay of Pilisi and was never too distant from land no matter what its location.

Lijena's head poked from the hatch. Nelek Kahl wasn't on deck. She hadn't expected the Sitala to be kind enough to deliver the slaver into her hands.

With a quick glance to assure she went unnoticed by the sailors on watch, she pushed from the hold and darted across the deck to the captain's quarters. Pressing an ear against the door, she silently cursed when faint stirring sounds came from within. Captain Lattour slept restlessly. The slightest sound might awaken the officer and alert him to the danger threatening his master.

Lijena hesitated. Nelek Kahl's life had to be severed with one quick, clean stroke of the stolen blade. Not only to avoid waking Lattour, but to save herself from the slaver.

Only a fool would give Kahl the opportunity to defend himself. The man was a merciless killer, highly skilled in the fighting arts. She repressed a cold shiver that sought to climb her spine, remembering the speed with which Kahl had struck yesterday. He had buried the knife she now carried hilt-deep into a pirate's neck without her seeing the motion of either hand or arm!

Like a shadow drifting across the silvery moonlit deck, she slipped to a companionway ten strides from the captain's cabin. The creak of brine-rusting hinges was lost in the rhythmic lapping of waves against the ship's hull. Lijena darted inside, her every sense alert and her slender body poised to meet attack.

None came. The passageway, bathed in the yellow glow of swaying oil lamps hung from the bulkheads, stood empty and silent. Like a she-cat, Lijena moved to the door before Nelek Kahl's quarters.

Her left hand gripped the latch and her right pulled the knife from the folds of her scanty attire. In a fluid, coordinated movement, she opened the door and ducked inside. A dark form lay on the bed. Heedless of the drumlike pounding of her head, Lijena struck without hesitation. In two silent strides, she crossed to the bed. The knife jerked high above her head, then fell.

She moaned in frustration as the blade plunged into the blanket and through, turning when the tip struck the bunk's hardwood supports beneath.

The gods frown on me! I've killed the slaver's blanket and nothing more! Lijena wrenched the knife from the rumbled blanket and sheets she had mistaken for a sleeping man. Fate still cheated her of revenge.

Pivoting, she surveyed the cabin. Empty. A curse died on her lips when voices came from outside. She stepped to the door, opened it a crack, and peered out. Limned in the moonlight, at the end of the companionway, stood Nelek Kahl and Captain Lattour.

So close, yet so far was her intended victim. She could rush forth and possibly kill Kahl, but not without forfeiting her own life.

The slaver shifted to face the ship's captain, giving her an unobstructed view of the man's face. Again she was struck by Kahl's resemblance to Davin Anane.

Davin Anane! The Jyotian kidnapper's name burned within her as brightly as her hatred for Nelek Kahl. The pair might have been born brothers. She could not sacrifice herself to slay Kahl when others also deserved her blade. She had let Davin

Anane live when last they met, not the next time! And Amrik Tohon would definitely feel the steel tongue of her blade lapping up his life.

Kahl and Lattour stepped around a junction at the end of the companionway. Lijena opened the door and stepped through the hatch, intent on returning to the hold, when the men's voices halted her.

". . . we arrive with the tide, sire," the captain spoke. "The watch has intercepted signals from shore."

"Favorable conditions, I trust," Kahl said.

"Aye, that they are. There's cargo to be picked up in Nawat. I myself saw the signal from Claw Point lighthouse. Three flashes and a long, slow blink."

"So, he still lives!" Nelek Kahl nodded. "I had not expected to see him again. The signal indicated someone travels with him. Who?"

"Can't say," admitted Lattour, "but he must be important. My guess is someone from Yannis' court in Kavindra."

"We can use a courier with good news." Kahl let out a sigh that sounded as weary as Lijena felt. "May Jajhana favor us. With what our noble lord can bring, we can defeat armies! Come to my cabin, we've much to discuss—and plan."

Lijena shivered and ducked into a small storage locker near the end of the companionway, waiting for the two men to enter Kahl's cabin.

Her mind railed against the treachery she discovered seething aboard this pleasure vessel. Zarek Yannis and Nelek Kahl were cast from the same mold. Prince Felrad gathered forces in Rakell, and the *Naughty Goose* sailed to Loieterland, obviously providing reconnaissance for the usurper. All the more reason to slay the slaver!

But now was not the time. There would be other opportunities to strike and, in the act, do Prince Felrad a double duty. Not only could she hand him the Sword of Kwerin, she would deliver the traitorous Nelek Kahl and Yannis' mysterious courier who would be joining the ship at Nawat.

Quickly, quietly, she returned to the hold unnoticed and slipped down the ladder. The candle beside Kahl's harem mistress had burned out, and Monni now lay deeply asleep. Only ship noises greeted Lijena as she curled up on her soft bed, closed her eyes, and drifted into dreams of vengeance fulfilled.

"No one on deck. For any reason," Monni said. Two burly sailors blocked the ladder leading topside. "It's the master's order."

"But..." Lijena's protest died on her lips. No other way on deck existed. Getting past the guards—and Monni—would be impossible without provoking a fight she couldn't win. Lijena subsided, fuming at her foul luck. The Sitala knotted her fate with bitter crochets each day. There was no way to spy on Nelek Kahl and Zarek Yannis' minions if she was trapped in the cargo hold of a pleasure ship.

Above, Kahl paced the deck as the *Naughty Goose* pulled into its harbor berth. Abruptly halting, he turned and shouted, "Captain, lower the gangplank. I go ashore immediately."

"But, sire, we've not yet moored properly. In a few minutes, we..."

Kahl silenced him with an impatient gesture. The slaver then climbed atop the railing and grabbed a trailing line. Giving it three stout yanks to test its strength, he jumped and swung out, lightly dropping to the dock.

By the time the *Naughty Goose* lay securely moored, Nelek Kahl had disappeared amid a throng of workers at the far end of the dock. Captain Lattour barked orders for several of the sailors to accompany their master. Without question, they hurried from the ship, frantic bodyguards left far behind the man they were to protect.

Kahl's long strides brought him outside a harbor tavern with a gaudily painted sign that proclaimed the establishment to be the Full Sail Inn. The slaver heeded not the rowdy noise that came from within. His attention focused on the man and woman dressed in black who emerged through double swinging doors to greet him. A slow smile split the slaver's handsome face.

"Berenicis! The gods favor us. I feared we would never meet again!"

The Lord of Jyotis, Berenicis the Blackheart, stepped forward—Yannis' former master mage, Valora, a few paces behind. Berenicis' knees bent, as though to lower himself in obeisance. Kahl's firm hand gripped the dethroned lord's shoulders, halting him.

"You forget our surroundings, Berenicis," Kahl said. "To kneel before me here would bring an army down about our heads."

"My Prince, forgive me. The joy of seeing that you still live robbed me of my senses for a moment," Berenicis stood, his eyes lifting to Kahl's face, then lowering.

"Forgiven," Kahl nodded. "Now tell me of your quest."

"Again, my liege, I must ask for forgiveness." Berenicis' shoulders sagged. "I have failed you. The Sword of Kwerin Bloodhawk is lost to us."

chapter 10

DAVIN ANANE WIPED the sweat from his eyes and squinted as he studied the narrow pass. The wagon burdened with the Eznoh-Fadey's—and Zarek Yannis'—stolen gold would barely scrape through the rocky notch in the hillside.

"Aye, it'll work," Davin said more to himself than to the women or Goran One-Eye.

The Challing lounged in the back of the wagon, long emptied of its original cargo of dried dung and spread with a soft bed of straw purchased from a caravansary in the foothills.

"As long as you're the one doing the work, 'tis fine with me." Goran sprawled on the hay, his seeking hands underneath the surface.

Davin shook his head, realizing that his friend ran covetous fingers through the vast, golden treasure trove hidden there. He turned his attention back to the narrow pass.

"I'll need help—help only a Challing can give." Davin said with an amused smile on his lips.

He phrased the request in a manner that Goran couldn't refuse. The changeling-trapped-in-the-body-of-a-man constantly boasted of Challing superiority over humans. Davin wasn't above playing on this and the way that Goran took a juvenile delight in showing off his prowess for Kulonna.

"What is it?" Goran said, resigned to moving his huge bulk

from its soft bed. He patted Kulonna on the flare of a hip as he jumped to the road.

"See those rocks?" Davin pointed to the formations that precariously teetered above. "If we bring them down onto the road, that should block pursuit."

"What pursuit? No one follows us!" Goran rolled his single eye in exasperation. "Davin, my dim-witted friend, we've committed the perfect crime! Why trouble yourself so with phantom pursuers?"

The Challing's words echoed through the hills, rebounded off mountainsides, and folded back on the wagon.

Davin answered in a soft voice, "It is not wise to advertise our deed so blatantly."

"Who's to hear? We are alone." Goran turned and grinned lewdly at Kulonna. "Alone in the most delightful way possible, that is."

"The rocks, Goran! Zarek Yannis won't permit thieves who plunder his war chest to escape without giving chase. He requires every copper for the battle with Prince Felrad." The Jyotian stared at his friend, hands on hips as though scolding a child.

"So he'll send Faceless Ones?"

Even as he spoke, Goran realized the gravity of that prospect. Hell-riders and their mounts never tired, fought with inhuman strength and skill, and followed spoor like a well-trained hound.

"I'll see what can be done," Goran conceded. "Move the wagon up the road." He dusted off his hands and started scaling a steep rock incline like a fly on a wall. "Whoever maintains the road will have naught good to say of this day, I assure you."

"As long as we're alive to listen to his complaints, that's fine with me," Davin answered while he climbed back onto the wagon box beside red-haired Awendala.

A snatch of the reins brought the four-horse team to life. The beasts strained against the gold-weighted wagon; wooden wheels creaked as they laboriously rolled forward through the narrow pass. A safe distance beyond, the heir to the House of Anane turned and waved to the Challing. Goran perched high atop the boulders—back against the side of the mountain, feet against the pile of rock that Davin had spotted.

Goran groaned a grunt that echoed up and down the canyon as he shoved with calf and thigh. The Challing's face turned crimson, rivaling the redness of his beard and mane, before the grinding of rock drowned out his grunts. When the pillar of stone came free, the sound exploded like a clap of thunder and dust filled the narrow notch. Goran stood and bellowed out a cry of delight at the destruction he had caused.

Rock and debris now entirely filled the narrow pass. If the Faceless Ones did trail, the hell-spawn would have to abandon their mounts and climb over the rubble, or find another route on which to follow. Either way, Davin felt safe that the wagon could outdistance the hell-creatures.

"Such strength," cooed Kulonna when Goran climbed back into the wagon.

Awendala and Davin exchanged amused looks when Goran avidly slipped into the blonde's open arms to receive his reward for the display of brute force.

"We're making good time," Davin said to his own lovely companion, attempting to ignore the delighted squeals and giggles rising from the wagon bed behind him. "The mountains should be behind us in another two days."

"At least by then we'll be across and moving downhill," Awendala replied with a wide-eyed glance over a shoulder. "That will aid the horses."

"Might be more difficult. I'll have to set the brake, or risk the wagon running over the team."

They fell silent, Davin aware of the warmth along his right side as Awendala pressed close. He felt at peace with himself for the first time in almost a year. The Muu-Kou Mountains stretched to the azure sky and isolated Davin in a way that he found curiously satisfying.

At peace. The Jyotian sighed and admired Awendala from the corner of an eye. Her fiery tresses stirred in the slight breeze that slid down the mountain slope. Ethereal, Davin decided, as he bathed in her beauty. Her milky skin shone like alabaster in the warm, spring sunlight, adding an animation to a woman already wondrously alive.

It was not the mountains, or the solitude they provided, that was responsible for the deep peace he sensed, but rather this woman who rode at his side. He smiled, once again marveling at how quietly she had entered his life, until he now found it difficult to imagine life without her.

With Awendala beside him, Lijena Farleigh, a year's race across Upper Raemllyn, the horror of the Narain and Lorennion's Blood Fountain, even the deadly potential of the Sword of Kwerin, seemed worlds apart from the moment he now lived.

"Why are you smiling?" Awendala nudged him lightly with an elbow. "A private joke?"

"Nothing of the sort." Davin's grin broadened. "Maybe I'll tell you when we stop for the night."

Awendala craned her neck and peered at the cloud-dotted blue above. "It gets dark early in the mountains."

"So much the better!"

"Davin, look! We're almost out of the mountains!" Awendala stood and peered to the east. "I've gotten so tired of seeing nothing but rocks all around."

"Tired?" A frown creased the young thief's brow. "I thought you were happy here?"

"But look! The plains. And take a deep breath. You can taste salt water in the air. We're not more than a day's travel from the Bay of Zaid."

Davin nodded. He looked back over his shoulder. Goran sat with his back against one side of the wagon while Kulonna napped.

"We'll have to find some way of getting over to Rakell," said Davin.

"I thought you were familiar with this area." The Challing lifted a bushy red eyebrow.

"It's been many years since I journeyed this way. Getting to the Isle of Loieter isn't difficult—usually. But remember our cargo. It'll take a large ship to port this much gold to Rakell and Felrad."

"Come, come, friend Davin. You're not seriously thinking that all this truly belongs to your throneless prince, are you?" Goran stared at his companion in arms. "We stole the gold, so it belongs to us! You can't simply squander it by giving it away to some pauper-pretender whom we've never met."

"Would you spend your declining years fleeing the Faceless Ones?" Davin's tone was harsh. "Unless Prince Felrad regains the throne, Yannis' influence will spread like a plague. I doubt Zarek Yannis has any love for thieves like us."

"Does any ruler?" Goran One-Eye brushed off his fox-fur eyepatch, then ran slow fingers through his tangled, fire-red beard. "Still, it might be worthwhile if your Prince Felrad realized he had two such stalwart supporters. If Yannis offers Comptroller of the Realm to that toad of a jeweler in Evara, what might Felrad offer two such as we?"

Davin offered no answer. This gold was not to buy appointments for Goran and himself, but to aid Felrad in the struggle to regain a throne rightfully his.

"For once I believe you might be correct, Davin son of Anane. These purloined coins are an investment in the future," Goran mused. "They may be the key to opening even the most secure of vaults to us, eh?"

Still, Davin did not reply. The Challing's view of honor and his own were divergent, at the least. Davin, who had tried to avoid Raemllyn's political entanglements for so many years, now served Felrad, a man whom he had never seen, for one reason—the prince opposed Zarek Yannis. Only through Felrad could Anane's last son hope to avenge the death of Raemllyn's High King Bedrich the Fair. Aye, and even savor the possibility of driving his own steel into the usurper's heart.

"But," Goran continued, "we don't have to give *all* the gold to Prince Felrad. We deserve some of it for our trouble and—"

"Davin!" Awendala cried out. She grasped the Jyotian's right arm and tugged. Then she reached across his midriff to pull forth a dagger from his belt.

Davin blinked in confusion. Then he saw what the sharp-eyed Awendala had already sighted. Tiny puffs of dust rose from horses' hooves on the plain that stretched before them.

"Goran, we have company. To the left. At least four riders, maybe more."

Davin urged the team of draft horses to hasten their speed, but the rocky road and the wagon's weighty burden impeded a pace quicker than steady plodding. The young freebooter cursed the Sitala as he watched the riders cross the plain and pull up a bowshot's distance from the wagon. Six there were, not four. None spoke or gestured, merely stared at the approaching wagon.

"What do they want?" asked Awendala.

"Brigands," Goran muttered. "They want our blood!"

"They'll find more than they bargained for," vowed Davin. "There are only six of them."

"Ten," came Kulonna's choked voice. "To the right. Look!"

Davin jerked about. The blonde was right. While he had watched the dusty approach of the six riders, four others had crept close. He turned and looked back along the rocky trail. His heart sank when he saw a full dozen riders following them.

"This must be a profitable route," Davin said. "How else could a band so large make a living from robbing travelers?"

"Davin, what are we going to do? We can't fight off more than twenty armed warriors." Awendala's knuckles burned white from the intensity of her grip about the knife's hilt.

False hope sprang neither to Davin's tongue nor heart. He saw little chance for escape. Even if they abandoned the gold, the brigands wouldn't be content with simple robbery. Rape might be only the beginning for women as lovely as Awendala and Kulonna—and for Goran and himself, Davin saw only death. Highwaymen left no victims alive as witnesses.

"Goran, where do we make a stand?"

The Challing shrugged his massive shoulders. "Never have I seen so many in a band."

"They must plunder the entire region," Kulonna, now fully awake, stared about in horror. "Between the mountains and the Bay of Zaid might be a rich road."

"Rich, pah!" exploded Goran. "All there is in the entire area is Salim, and that's a poor town. Poor. Why, they even outlaw gambling within its city limits!"

Davin drew the wagon to a halt in the shadow of a low boulder. He would've preferred a larger stone—a mountain!—to guard their back, but the riders took them in an open area just as they left the foothills of the Muu-Kous.

The fight will end quickly, Davin thought when he dropped to the ground and freed tempered steel from leather sheath. Nor did he deceive himself about who would be the victors.

Over fast it might be, but the cutthroats would well-know how the last of the House of Anane fought and died!

"Awendala, Kulonna, protect our backs," Davin ordered. "Any that try to get to us over the boulder, stop them."

Both the women were armed with daggers. Pitiful weapons that would wilt quickly under the shadow of the forest of swords sprouting all around.

Davin planted his feet squarely and waited for the attack. Goran leaped from the wagon and stood in a wide-legged defiant stance beside him. The Challing hefted a heavy war ax to his shoulder, leaving no doubt that this band of brigands would pay dearly in pain and death before they sent human and Challing souls into Black Qar's embrace.

"Good day," Davin called out. He held no hope that these men were more than they appeared, but he held his attack until certain. "Do you collect road fees for the local lord?"

Two of the riders laughed harshly. The apparent leader leaned forward in the saddle and said, "Surrender your arms and you'll not be harmed."

Davin snorted. "Surely you don't expect even the fool of fools to believe such a lie."

"As you will." The band's leader shrugged then waved his followers forward. "Take them!"

From all sides, swords leaped clear of scabbards, and spurred heels dug into equine flesh.

A battlecry roaring from chest and throat, Goran took two hasty strides forward and swung the double-bladed ax in a level arc that caught the nearest rider's horse in mid-chest. The animal screamed as a crimson spray fountained from its open body. The poor creature died of shock before its spasmodically twitching body toppled. Its rider somersaulted forward over the animal's neck, hitting the ground flat on his back.

One step brought the Jyotian beside the gasping man. Davin's right foot lashed out, connecting squarely with the man's temple. The brigand groaned, then collapsed, unconscious.

Davin had no time to make the condition permanent. Four riders circled him and charged. Davin parried one slicing sword meant to sever head from torso and received a painful but shallow cut across his back from another. He spun and thrust, but his sword tip skewered empty air that had contained his retreating assailant only a heartbeat before.

Beside him the Challing grunted with every mighty swing of his chosen weapon. However, only one in five of the battle-ax's blows sank home.

Nor could Davin aid his friend; he was too busy fending off those seeking his own life. He fought like a berserker lost in the rage of bloodlust. Again and again, his longsword raked out, striving to cut the horses' legs out from under them and bring their riders tumbling to the ground. To no avail! The brigands, like men born to the saddle, eluded his best efforts.

Worse, he sensed the men merely toyed with Goran and him, waiting until their arms grew too weary to lift sword or ax before they moved in for the kill. A time that grew closer and closer.

The young thief held no hope for his own life, yet Awendala and Kulonna might be spared. While the band was occupied with Goran and himself, the women might—just might—escape in the wagon!

"Awendala," he cried out.

No answer came.

A quick glance to the wagon revealed the two women had fallen to four brigands who held them pinned down in the hay. Awendala still struggled. Kulonna either had ceased to fight or had been knocked unconscious—or worse!

Ducking beneath two blades, Davin moved beside the wagon and lashed out with his sword. The razor-sharp tip opened a gash on one of Awendala's captor's cheeks. The brigand shouted angrily, but Davin's ploy failed. The man clung tightly to his redheaded captive.

"Davin, there are too many of them. Who'd have thought we'd end our lives in the wilds? Still," panted Goran, "it's been a good week since Evara. Kulonna makes this almost worth the end!"

Davin attempted to block a war club that plummeted toward Goran's unprotected head. The length of gnarled wood brushed aside the Jyotian's tempered steel. The Challing fell face forward into the dust and lay there unmoving.

A second blow from the heavy war club took Davin's sword from his hand. He ducked, grabbed for the fallen weapon and felt the air rush from his lungs as a heavy body smashed into his back, pinning him to the ground.

Davin Anane flailed about weakly. Through blurred eyes, he saw a glove studded with links of chain mail rise, flash in the warm spring sun, then descend.

Daylight fled and darkness swallowed him.

chapter 11

"THOUSANDS WILL PERISH." Undisguised relish rang in the voice of Raemllyn's usurper, High King Zarek Yannis. The leanly built ruler lounged in the Velvet Throne, grinning. "This battle will rival Kressia, where I destroyed Bedrich's army. My Faceless Ones will grind Rakell into the dust!"

"There are problems, my liege," said Hamor-Lorn, the High King's most recent master mage.

The white-haired, white-bearded sorcerer refused to be intimidated by Zarek Yannis, and this made him less desirable in the king's eyes, he realized.

But Hamor-Lorn had spent two score—and more—years advising minor lords and petty dukes and even low kings. Sheer power did not awe him; that Zarek Yannis controlled a power thought lost for ten thousand generations puzzled the aging mage, but did not prevent his tongue from speaking when there was need.

"Of course there are problems," Zarek Yannis snapped, irritated that this impudent, weathered wizard attempted to undermine his elation. "Look, Hamor-Lorn. Look! Tell me what you see!"

Hamor-Lorn closed his eyes. A living tableau formed in his mind, a scene of bustling activity that Yannis saw from the window of the throne room. Kavindra buzzed with the movement of troops, but it was not on this that the High King wished the mage to turn his mystical eye.

Hamor-Lorn centered his thoughts on his inner vision and focused attention farther afield. There, in Yaryne and other ports on the Bays of Pilisi and Zaid, he saw Zarek Yannis' warships moving in and out of harbors. Over a hundred of the vessels, which acted more as pirates than official warships, docked and prepared to carry troops to Loieterland. Supplies to support a siege were loaded into waiting holds. Immense engines of war were dismantled and stored in cargo bays to await the order to sail forth and invade the Isle of Loieter.

Most of all, Hamor-Lorn sensed the movement of the Faceless Ones. Massive numbers of the demon-riders converged on Yaryne. From all Raemllyn's realms they rode, their mounts snorting flame and dancing on fiery hooves. Those hell-spawned monsters chilled Hamor-Lorn, as did their uncountable number; he had not realized Yannis had summoned so many of the demonic warriors from beyond the void. But he feared them naught. He had lived too long to fear man or demon.

Hamor-Lorn smiled slightly. Did he fear even the gods? Until he confronted one directly, he would not know. Yet the mage thought his courage would be adequate to stare in the dark gaze of Black Qar, whether the Death God be male, female, or *thing!*

"None of your ships' captains will carry the Faceless Ones," Hamor-Lorn said. "All refuse."

"No major problem that," Yannis answered, flicking a mote of lint from his robes of woven silver and gold. "If they continue their refusal, they will be replaced—after being turned over to the Faceless for the hell-riders' amusement!"

"Such is not the proper course, my liege," Hamor-Lorn warned, a sharp edge in his tone, though his eyes remained closed to maintain the mystical vision. "Sea captains are fearless men when confronted with physical danger, but they are a superstitious lot. Execute one and all will openly oppose you. Without your vast fleet, you have no chance of ever reaching Rakell and Felrad."

"The Battle of Rakell will etch my name in history!" cried Yannis, refusing to accept the sorcerer's words.

Without his mind's open eye, Hamor-Lorn stared at his king and saw madness. Zarek Yannis had defeated Bedrich at Kressia through treachery—and the Faceless Ones. One trusted commander had betrayed Bedrich, allowing a hundred of the Faceless to break through the now-dead ruler's ranks and destroy the center of Bedrich's powerful and popular army. Unless Zarek Yannis withheld information, Hamor-Lorn knew of no traitor in Felrad's rank, nor did his vision reveal any.

And without the Faceless Ones on Loieter, Hamor-Lorn saw no way to sure victory.

"They will obey me or die!" raged Zarek Yannis. "I will not be opposed in this. We will assemble the army at the gates of Rakell and batter them down. Only when I have Felrad's head on a spike in my capital will there be peace in Raemllyn."

Peace? Hamor-Lorn shuddered. Even a bell-capped fool would not be deceived by Zarek Yannis' utterance. Only one glance at the monarch's flushed face was needed to confirm that Zarek Yannis was greedy for power, not a quiet countryside.

Hamor-Lorn nodded, not in agreement with his liege, but in acceptance. Avarice he understood. The mage had no idea what drove those who were truly altruistic—like Felrad.

"We need to be careful in choosing the ships that will convoy the Faceless Ones to Loieterland," said Hamor-Lorn. "I have chosen several whose captains are less likely to protest, if certain bonuses are guaranteed."

"Do it," said Yannis, obviously tiring of the counsel.

"Not all these, uh, bonuses, will be in the form of gold."

"Give them what they want. The Faceless Ones must be assembled before Rakell's gates if I am to triumph."

Hamor-Lorn inclined his head. At least Zarek Yannis realized the source of his power. Without the Faceless Ones to secure a beachhead, the main force could never land. And once supported by the human army, the hell-riders were again needed to breach the walls of Rakell and hold back the defenders long enough for the army to enter the city.

"Not a man, woman or child shall survive," Zarek Yannis continued. "They are all to be slaughtered. No quarter will be given. The carnage will make even Kressia look pallid in comparison."

"There is no indication that Felrad's true strength lies within the fortress," Hamor-Lorn warned. "My best scrying spells are turned away by the pretender's mages."

Zarek Yannis sat erect. Thin eyebrows arched high. "What of his mages? What magicks do they conjure to protect Rakell?"

Hamor-Lorn shook his white head. "I have been unable to compile a roster of those sorcerers most likely to be within the city. Whoever Felrad has recruited, they are powerful enough to deflect my magical spyings. But I do not fear their spells."

"How well do you cover our plans with magic?" Zarek Yannis leaned to the edge of the Velvet Throne. "There is no way Felrad can scry the staging area?"

Hamor-Lorn hesitated. Although he had no personal fear of the High King, the magician knew he had to phrase his response carefully.

"Any mage will find only normal activity, if magicks are used. But there are spies in Yaryne and Nawat and other parts of Upper Raemllyn who will not be deceived."

"What?" cried Yannis.

"Spies who see with eyes and not magical spells," explained Hamor-Lorn.

"My troops have ferreted out all such traitors to the Velvet Throne!"

"As you say, my liege. But there exists a possibility that some might be . . . coerced into revealing much to Felrad's agents. The buildup of your army and the travels of the Faceless Ones cannot be concealed for long. Felrad must know by now that you intend to confront him in Rakell."

Hamor-Lorn found it impossible to think that a wily tactician of Felrad's ability could remain ignorant of Yannis' invasion force. Magicks were not all the forces that moved in this world; human eyes and wagging tongues provided much information not available even to the most adept mage.

"We leave for Yaryne—and Rakell!" cried Zarek Yannis.

The ruler shoved away from the throne and stalked out of the room. Wearily, Hamor-Lorn's eyes opened. Heaving a heavy sigh, he slowly followed, his mind planning the spells he would need to guide the invasion force to the Isle of Loieter. Even with a successful landing at the gates of Rakell, Hamor-Lorn knew that it would not be the simple battle Zarek Yannis thought.

Felrad had been hard at work fortifying Rakell for months, maybe all the years since his father's defeat.

Hamor-Lorn smiled wanly. In one thing, Zarek Yannis was right. The Battle of Rakell would rank with that at Kressia, where Bedrich the Fair had died. There would be those hell-spawned Faceless Ones and thousands upon thousands of human troops—and magicks.

Oh, yes, Hamor-Lorn thought, *there will be magicks. I shall see to that!* Zarek Yannis' mage walked faster, almost eager for the coming battle. If Yannis' name became permanently etched in history, then that of Hamor-Lorn would also be remembered.

chapter 12

LIJENA FARLEIGH DRIFTED casually through the hold of the *Naughty Goose,* deftly disguising the anxiety that tortured each passing second. Above, two sailors, under Nelek Kahl's command, stood guard, blocking the exit to the deck.

The daughter of Bistonia glanced about. Monni's watchful eye remained on her as it had all morning. The woman studied her every movement like a veteran prison warden.

Lijena smiled honey-sweet, while silently cursing. Her trip topside last night had captured Monni's attention. Since awakening, Lijena had sidestepped the woman's barrage of subtle, probing questions, especially those concerning lovers, husbands and children, and family.

Again, Lijena's brain whirled with myriad unspoken curses. She had been careless last night. Her desire for revenge had muddled common sense. She should have made certain Monni and all the other women were soundly lost in their dreams before attempting to climb to the deck. Now Monni's suspicion was aroused.

Feigning weariness, Lijena walked slowly across the lushly appointed cargo hold, listening intently as she went. When muffled sounds of conversation came from directly overhead, she slumped down next to a bulkhead and pressed her ear against the highly polished wood.

It didn't help. The sounds of the crew moving on deck

muffled the voices. The natural creaking of the ship's hull and the lapping of water drowned out much, and the occasional sharp cracks as the hull crashed repeatedly into the Nawat dock assured anonymity for those above.

Still she persisted, catching snatches of conversation from those above.

". . . Valora will gain us entry into Rakell," came a voice tantalizingly familiar to Lijena.

Valora! Lijena's eyes went wild. That was the name of the sorceress who had led the Faceless Ones against Davin Anane after their escape from Lorennion's keep in the Forest of Agda. She strained, trying to identify the man's voice that came from above.

"She was recently the usurper's master mage."

Lijena's heart hammered wildly. It was the same Valora! Nelek Kahl had brought aboard one of Yannis' mages! The only purpose had to be circumventing the ward spells that Prince Felrad had ordered cast to protect Rakell. The battle for the Velvet Throne drew near and Lijena listened—or tried—to the plans!

". . . need it. Very dangerous without it . . . Sword of Kwerin must be recovered."

Lijena's wildly pounding heart almost stopped when she heard Nelek Kahl's clipped tones speak of the very sword she had hidden in the small locker not ten paces away. The slaver knew of the ensorcelled blade's existence and sought to return it to Kavindra and Zarek Yannis!

Lijena's mind raced. By accident, she had stumbled into a conspiracy of traitors to Raemllyn's true ruler. She had to act—and quickly. Killing Nelek Kahl still ranked high in her mind. For all he had done to her—and for his opposition to Prince Felrad—he must die. But to attempt it now, with one of the usurper's mages aboard, would be suicidal. When she moved, it must be done swiftly, without hesitation. And the Sword of Kwerin Bloodhawk must be saved!

Rakell. The Isle of Loieter. She had no doubt that the *Naughty Goose* was destined to sail for Prince Felrad's walled fortress, rather than Vatusia as Monni and the other women had mentioned. What vile mission did Zarek Yannis send Nelek Kahl on? Whatever it was, the mage and the other who had boarded ship played an important role.

Lijena fingered the dagger tucked away in a silk sash around her trim waist. This knife would find its way into Kahl's heart; she vowed that much. If necessary, she'd stand and fight the mage. Perhaps Valora would fall prey to the Sword of Kwerin. The sword's power worked only against magicks. And it was quite capable of draining the life of a wizard; she had proven that when she had killed Aerisan in Bistonia.

"Welcome, master, lord, lady," greeted Monni. The woman's words pulled Lijena around to see the trio who descended the ladder from the deck.

The other concubines huddled close. Again, Lijena sensed something amiss with them. They whispered among themselves but did not show the type of obeisance she expected of concubines in the presence of their master. And Nelek Kahl did not seem to demand or even expect it.

What slaver ignored discipline among his possessions?

Kahl dropped to the deck of the cargo hold, then helped down a woman robed entirely in black. Lijena shyly tucked chin to chest to avoid Valora's cold, ebony eyes. The sorceress' recognition would destroy any hope she had of either vengeance or delivering the Bloodhawk's sword into Felrad's hands.

Valora's dark gaze darted about the hold, finally coming to rest on the locker containing the Sword of Kwerin. Lijena tensed. Valora's face went totally impassive, and she took a step forward, only to be halted by the sandy-haired man who dropped lightly to the deck beside her.

"Valora, we need your expert advice," said the man.

Lijena Farleigh's wrath almost erupted in a fiery fury that sent her across the room, dagger held high, ready for the kill.

Berenicis the Blackheart!

How the Sitala, all Five Fates of Raemllyn, served her! And now Jajhana, Goddess of Chance and Fortune, turned a sunny face her way. Not only could she kill Nelek Kahl, but her blade would also drain Berenicis' lifeblood.

Like another man might employ a hound, the dethroned ruler of Jyotis had used the demon that once possessed Lijena to lead him to the wizard Lorennion's forest keep and the long lost sheath of the Sword of Kwerin Bloodhawk. He had professed that he sought the magic-empowering sheath for Felrad. All the time he had conspired with Raemllyn's foulest slaver—and Zarek Yannis!

Berenicis' gray eyes slowly took in the assembled loveliness of the concubines. Again Lijena imitated shyness and dipped her chin to avoid the man's attention.

How she hated this noble-born Jyotian! Berenicis had repeatedly betrayed her. It had been from the Blackheart that Davin Anane had stolen the Sword of Kwerin. In this, at least, Lijena saw that Davin had been correct. Berenicis Blackheart was a traitor and not to be trusted.

Even as the thought of the magical sword crossed her mind, Lijena saw the sorceress Valora turning like a compass needle toward the locker where the sword lay hidden.

"Valora, come; *Kahl* needs our advice." The mocking tone and the unusual emphasis that Berenicis placed on the slaver's name puzzled Lijena. It was as if lord and sorceress shared a joke untold to the others.

"Lord Berenicis will certainly be eager to finish any such meeting satisfactorily," said the dark mage. "A man of his tastes will be unable to resist such beauty."

Lijena sensed warring undercurrents rage between the two. Valora taunted Berenicis. Why shouldn't a lord and former ruler of Jyotis be allowed to sample the earthly delights available in a slaver's seraglio? Yet Valora implied that such would never occur. Nelek Kahl did not avail himself of his concubines. Why shouldn't Berenicis the Blackheart? Lijena had no doubt about the lord's sexual tastes. He had made them abundantly clear to her as they journeyed to Lorennion's Blood Fountain.

The trio climbed back to the deck. Lijena listened as their tread crossed the deck and went to Kahl's cabin, but try as she did, no sounds echoed down to betray the topic of their urgent meeting.

Lijena Farleigh sank deeper into the pillows cushioning her. For the moment, she would have to be content with her sudden turn in luck. The gracious Goddess Jajhana had delivered two of her enemies into her hands. The time would come for the death strike—and then there would be two fewer scoundrels to blacken Raemllyn with their presence.

chapter 13

PAIN—SHARP, SHOOTING pain that transformed the world into angry streaks of blazing red and devouring black lanced through Davin Anane's skull and sliced into his brain. The young adventurer groaned and received a mouthful of dirt for his trouble.

For a second he was certain that the sizzling jolts of twisting agony knifing through his head were some insidious torture provided by Black Qar's principal demon, Nyuria, in the lowest of hells. An eternity of damnation to pay for a short lifetime as a roguish scoundrel!

In life, not death, lay the source of the Jyotian's pain. And he remembered how he had come to this sorry condition. He stiffened.

The slight movement betrayed him.

"This one's awake," a man's voice boomed above.

The hard toe of a boot dug into Davin's ribs, forcing him to his back. The heir to the House of Anane moaned, caring not that he displayed weakness before the brigands. There was nothing more they could do to him that could increase the agony.

The band of cutthroats proved him wrong. Awendala screamed!

Davin's eyes shot open, and he struggled to get his feet beneath him. A boulder-knuckled fist to the side of his jaw sent him tumbling to his backside.

"She's in no danger." It was the band's leader who spoke. "Unless . . . your answers fail to please me."

Davin blinked and frowned up at the man, instantly regretting the slight facial movement. Demonic fingers of pain worked their way behind his eyes and gouged in his brain. Still, Davin sat rock-steady, with only a tilt of his head in acceptance of the brigand's demand.

Why should common thieves plying their trade along a poorly traveled road care to interrogate prisoners? Why even take prisoners?

"He'll tell you whatever he thinks will please you, Lieutenant," said another man holding a sword tip against Goran's throat, even though the red-haired giant lay unconscious.

The man's odd comment increased Davin's puzzlement. Why address the leader as "lieutenant?" Captain, perhaps, or by name. But as "lieutenant?" It made no sense.

"We were on our way to the seacoast," Davin said.

Even these few words rattled about painfully, echoing deep within his skull. He took several calming breaths to quell the nausea that churned his stomach. Gingerly touching his throbbing head, he found a large, blood-dampened lump. Other than this, he seemed no worse for the encounter.

Davin's gray eyes shifted about. But was there hope for escape? Goran One-Eye lay flat on his back in the dust, and the two women were tied securely in the bed of the wagon. For the gold, Davin had no hope. It would be lost—but the exchange of gold for life was one he'd make every time, especially when the life was his own.

"You traveled full across the Muu-Kou Mountains?" the leader asked.

"Aye. We come from Evara. What's wrong in that? We're simple farmers seeking a market for our hay."

"Simple farmers selling hay?" The leader laughed harshly. "Dressed as you are, I'd sooner think you common thieves."

"What's wrong with our dress?" asked Davin, looking down and regretting the clothes all had purchased the moment they entered Evara. His finely woven, colorful garments bore a few stains from the long, hard journey through the mountains, but other than this, they were of obvious quality. "Not all farmers seek to look like bumpkins."

The leader grabbed Davin's hand and, with thick thumb gouging the underside of the Jyotian's wrist, forced fingers to splay widely. "The calluses are wrong for a farmer. See? This spot on your index finger. A sword balances there. You're more likely to wield a sword than a plow."

"I've gold to offer. Take it in exchange for our lives," Davin said, pulling free from the man's grip.

"Who do you support?" demanded the one with sword tip at Goran's throat.

"In what?" Davin asked. For his trouble, he received a light cuff to the side of the head.

"All Raemllyn boils with rebellion," said the one named lieutenant by his men. "Where do you stand?"

"Davin," came Kulonna's voice. "There is nothing more to tell these swine." She groaned as an unseen captor silenced her words.

Davin spat. "The Faceless Ones chased us from Evara." He spat again. "Zarek Yannis will never defeat Prince Felrad!" He spat a third time.

"Lieutenant, this one fits the description of the one we've been alerted to look for."

"Bring her down."

Two men lifted Kulonna from the wagon's bed and roughly shoved her in front of the leader.

The head of the brigand band rubbed at a darkly stubbled chin. "She has the look of nobility about her. But if it is true, what's a lady doing consorting with scum like those?" He pointed at Davin and Goran.

"She's been kidnapped," Davin said hastily. "We kidnapped her. Her father's Duke Tun. He'll pay a fabulous ransom for her return."

"Kulonna, daughter of Tun?" asked the brigand leader and received a sharp affirmative tilt of the blonde's head in reply. "Your Grace, forgive us. We did not recognize you. Shall we put these kidnappers to death?"

Davin reeled. This made no sense unless. . . .

"Prince Felrad's men!" Davin gasped the answer.

"Who else?" The leader glared at him, then turned back to Kulonna. "Your Grace, we'd been told you journeyed by sea, but were lost. How did these two come to kidnap you?"

Without answer Kulonna's right hand shot out and tore open the man's tunic. Beneath lay the forest green uniform of Prince Felrad's army. Her eyes widened.

"Davin Anane and Goran One-Eye, the big one, are our protectors, not kidnappers," the beautiful young duchess explained. "He lied. He . . . he thought you were Yannis' sympathizers and sought only to save my life."

"Prince Felrad is desperately in need of the message you bring to Rakell," said the lieutenant. "Is it favorable?"

"Yes! My father will unite with the prince against Zarek Yannis!"

The lieutenant bowed again. "We will escort you directly to the coast and arrange for transport to the Isle of Loieter. Rakell prepares for the coming battle. The way is more dangerous than ever. Not only Yannis' troops but his Faceless Ones patrol the coastline."

The lieutenant looked down at Davin and asked, "You spoke truthfully when you said you fled the Faceless Ones?"

"We did. We stole something very dear to Zarek Yannis in Evara, and the hell-riders were set on our trail. We eluded them in the mountains." Davin nodded and winced as new lances of agony ripped into his skull.

"They are tenacious trackers. Jajhana smiled on you."

"And on Prince Felrad," Davin added.

"Wait," came Goran One-Eye's weak voice.

The barrel-chested giant opened his one good eye and peered up at Davin. The Challing had obviously been feigning unconsciousness while he had listened to every word that had passed. Davin saw no dancing, green witch-fire—only the red of a bloodshot eye.

"Consider your words carefully, Davin. Hastily spoken sentences could cost us a fortune. Consider first. Please!"

His friend's voice was so plaintive that Davin felt a twinge of guilt for what he had to do. But, without the transportation this lieutenant could provide, they might never reach Rakell.

"We traveled to Yaryne in search of a ship to carry us to Loieterland," said Davin.

"Then Jajhana smiled when she brought us across your path," the lieutenant said. "Reconnaissance reports indicate Yannis' troops mass for an invasion in Yaryne. Hundreds of warships have put into the port. Thousands of troops make their repulsive presence known to the good citizens of the port."

"And the Faceless Ones," chimed in another soldier. "Hundreds of them converge on the city awaiting ships to carry them to Rakell."

"You would have been captured easily," the lieutenant added.

"My home!" A choked gasp came from Awendala, who pushed from the wagon. "Is all lost to me?"

"If family and friends support our prince, I fear it is so." The lieutenant's gaze rolled to the ground. "Yannis' spies have ferreted out hundreds of those loyal to Felrad in Yaryne. Daily they are executed as an example—to strike fear into the hearts of the remaining populace."

Tears streamed from Awendala's eyes as she groaned and shuddered. Davin stood on shaking legs and went to her. The lieutenant nodded to a soldier; Awendala was untied. Davin put his arms around the red-haired woman who had lost so much. Her parents ensorcelled and killed, now her home turned into a military camp by the usurper of the Velvet Throne. Davin held her close. His soothing palms and gentle whispers seemed so inadequate. Awendala clung to him, her body quaking as she sobbed.

"But you *do* have a way of getting us to Rakell?" Kulonna asked. Her tone was that of a woman born of royal blood, not the wench of a common thief.

"For you, your Grace, yes."

"For my friends, also," Kulonna demanded.

"It will be difficult to justify it. You can appreciate the problem of traversing the Bay of Zaid with so many of Zarek Yannis' warships on patrol. We lack the vessels commanded by the usurper."

"It is necessary that we reach Rakell and Prince Felrad," Davin said. "We have something of great value to him."

"This thing you stole from Yannis in Evara?" The lieutenant's eyebrows lifted.

"Look in the wagon. Under the hay."

"No, Davin, please," moaned Goran.

The Challing slumped into a red-haired pile of dejection when the lieutenant brushed away the hay to reveal the chests of gold.

"So much!" the officer cried. "And you give it all to Prince Felrad?"

"What good is gold when a tyrant such as Zarek Yannis sits on the throne?" asked Davin.

"Do you really want me to answer that, friend Davin?" Goran asked. "We can buy . . ."

Davin cut the Challing off with a wave of his hand. "We've discussed this, Goran. Consider it an investment in a future free of Zarek Yannis."

"Prince Felrad sorely needs financing," admitted the lieutenant. "My own troops have not been paid in over three months."

"Take your pay, then," said Davin, "and we'll carry the rest to Prince Felrad."

Davin watched as emotions played across the lieutenant's face. But his head shook in denial of the offer. "No, we've lived off the land. We can do so as long as necessary. The prince needs this more than we do. Take all of it to him."

Goran gaped at such generosity, and Davin knew that they had done the right thing. With men such as this answering Prince Felrad's call to arms, perhaps the chance to defeat Zarek Yannis did exist.

"This is the boat?" Davin Anane asked skeptically. "It looks as if it'll sink the instant it's launched."

"Aye, it has that look," said the weathered fisherman to whom the boat belonged. He chewed a bit of *mylo* weed, spat through the gap left by two missing teeth, then pointed to sea. "See that? Storm movin' in on the bay. Sooner we get afloat, the sooner we can get into it."

"You're crazy!" Goran snorted. "This leaking monstrosity would sink in calm weather. Take us into that storm, and we'll all end up tangled in Nalren's seaweed beard!"

"Watch that ye don't profane the God of the Sea!" the old fisherman warned. "The boat's stronger'n she looks. Zarek Yannis' ships will heave to when the teeth of the storm bites deep enough. That's our only chance to reach the Isle of Loieter and Rakell."

"What do you see, Goran?" Davin stood beside his friend.

The Challing's one good eye of gold-flecked jade burned green with witch-fire.

"'Tis no ordinary storm," Goran answered. "Magicks weave across the water. But their source eludes me."

"Perhaps,"Awendala suggested, "Felrad's wizards cast spells to guard the isle."

"Or the usurper uses sorcery to hide his invasion force," Davin added darkly.

"No matter," said Goran. "It's magic-born and doubly dangerous for us. Mayhaps we should bury the gold and return for it later."

"Goran," Davin reprimanded. "We've agreed that the gold belongs to Prince Felrad."

"Belongs is such a *strong* word," the red-bearded giant replied. "After all, Zarek Yannis stole it from the citizens of Raemllyn, and aren't we citizens of this fine realm? Therefore, in reality the gold is ours. We merely reclaimed what had been stolen from us."

"Your logic is askew," said Kulonna. "But I love you, in spite of that greedy streak. Give freely of the gold, and I'll see that it is made worth your while."

"And when did you start claiming Raemllyn as your homeland?" Davin asked. "I thought this world was but a ball of mud compared to the glories of your Challing realm of Goh-wohn?"

"It is," the changeling grumbled, then lovingly patted Kulonna on her backside and pulled her against his massive frame.

Davin and Awendala slowly walked to where the soldiers loaded the chests of gold onto the fishing boat. The ponderous weight of each new chest caused the boat to creak and groan in protest, but the craft's hull sank no more than a finger's joint deeper into the water beneath the incredible bulk. As heavy as the gold was, it proved a minor burden for the boat.

"Can bring in bigger catch than any other two boats," the fisherman bragged. "She's a fine old boat, she is. And never has she been put to better use than running Zarek Yannis' blockade of Loieterland."

"You do realize that the storm's of magical origin?" Davin asked, uncertain that the old man's mental faculties were still intact.

"Won't be the first I've weathered." The fisherman gripped a thick hawser with strong hands. "One storm's just like another, no matter where it comes from." He pulled on the line and brought the boat's stern around so that the boat headed out into the bay. "Lieutenant's got the gold loaded. We tarry here too long. The sooner we leave, the sooner I can return. The wife's got a good pot of fish-head stew aboiling. Hate to miss a meal like that."

Davin couldn't tell if the man joked or not. He certainly didn't jest about getting underway. Casting off the lines, he readied the boat for sailing.

"May Yehseen favor you," the lieutenant bid them farewell. "And your service for the prince will not go unrewarded."

He clasped Davin's shoulders, started to grab Goran, and decided against it when the Challing growled at him. But the lieutenant wasn't to be stopped from lightly kissing Awendala on the cheek and bowing to Kulonna and kissing her hand.

"May we all be successful against the tyrant," Kulonna said.

"The boat!" cried Goran. "It's leaving!"

With that, the Challing scooped Kulonna into his arms and jumped, barely reaching the deck before the boat drifted too far from the dock.

While the fisherman and two others worked the short, triangular sails, Davin and his friends moved to the prow and stood studying the storm ahead.

"The clouds churn constantly," said Goran. "Yet, see how they remain fixed in one spot over the water? That's a storm bound by magicks."

"Yannis might be launching his attack," Davin repeated his earlier thought. "If so, we've come just in time."

"To die?" grumbled Goran. "We should have let the lieutenant deliver the gold you so generously gave away."

"I must speak with Prince Felrad and let him know of my father's support for the cause," said Kulonna. "Whether you went or not, *I* have to go to Rakell."

"You'd've gotten lost without me," Goran mumbled and looked back at the boiling clouds of gray and black. "Yon storm reminds me of how I lost my eye. It was . . ."

Before the Challing could spin yet another farfetched tale

of his missing eye, gale-force winds howled down on the small craft, driving the four backward. Goran protectively huddled above Kulonna, his bulk forming a windbreak for the young blonde. With Awendala caught in the hook of an arm to lend her support, Davin fumbled the latch to the boat's cabin door, opening it. All four tumbled inside away from the chilling force of the storm winds.

"Never hit winds so strong this far away from the isle before," the fisherman called to his four passengers above the raging gale. "It's going to take fancy sailing to get us in. The wind's trying to push us back to the mainland."

Cunningly using the sails to tack into the powerful storm, the old sailor maneuvered his vessel on a zig-zagging course. Four hours he fought the gale before announcing, "We're less than a league from Loieterland, though you'd never know it."

Davin peered out of the cabin into the towering black clouds. It looked as if some berserk god had drawn a line through the water. On this side the air, though turbulent, was clear. Through the dark veil ahead, Davin saw nothing. And they sailed into that unknown water realm in a leaky fishing boat laden with enough gold to sink a craft twice its size!

"Here it comes!" cried the fisherman.

The warning came a heartbeat before the winds doubled their howl and heavy rain lashed the boat. Even inside the cabin, the four were drenched with salt water driven through cracks in the walls. The small craft pitched from side to side, tossed about by the battering waves.

The gold served, rather than worked against them, Davin realized. It's weight was the ballast that kept the boat from capsizing in the churning seas. As it was, the fisherman kept the boat's prow into the waves and let the powerful waters crash over the decks.

"A league of this?" asked Awendala, moving closer to Davin. "We won't make it."

"We will," Davin insisted.

He felt oddly confident that they would, in spite of the magic-spawned storm. Hadn't they stolen this gold from under the nose of Zarek Yannis' regional comptroller? Hadn't they evaded the Faceless Ones? Who could stop them?

Davin actually laughed. He felt more alive and ready for battle than he had in months. Nothing could stop him—not usurper, not mage, not god!

Even as his confidence soared, the boat shuddered as though a titan's fist struck the side of the craft.

"What's happening?" Kulonna's head jerked up in horror.

"Magicks," Goran said so softly that Davin barely heard his words. "I feel a force directed against us. Not just the storm, but something more."

Another battering-ram-hard blow shuddered through the boat. Timbers creaked; the vessel listed.

The fisherman ducked inside from his post on the sails. Dripping water, he shook all over. He stared at his four passengers, his expression telling more than the words that followed:

"Something's caving in the side of my boat. Can't see what's causing it."

"Magic!" Goran's good eye flamed with green. "I feel it. I feel it!"

Again the battering force struck the ship, almost turning the boat on its side. The splinters from the broken hull floated about the craft in the foaming sea. Again the unseen fist of magic slammed home. The boat heaved and listed heavily.

"We sink!" the fisherman cried out in terror as though the danger to his craft had just penetrated his mind. "Prepare to abandon ship!"

chapter 14

"Three war ships," Captain Lattour said from behind the wheel of the *Naughty Goose*. "They sail toward Yaryne. What should I do, liege?"

Prince Felrad, who was known throughout the realms of Upper and Lower Raemllyn in his guise as Nelek Kahl, leaned on the railing and peered into the misty distance. He relied on the captain for information, but the burden of decision always rested upon his shoulders. The handsome man ground his teeth together.

Should they run, should they stand and fight, should they hope that Zarek Yannis' ships failed to spot them? What? So much depended on his every decision.

If he made a small error now, all Raemllyn might be ground under the tyrant's heel. Rakell would fall. Thousands of stalwart supporters would die in a vain battle—or worse! Prince Felrad shuddered at the thought of any loyal to his cause being turned over to the Faceless demons Zarek Yannis had somehow summoned after so many years of banishment.

So much rested upon his every decision, and Felrad, son of King Bedrich the Fair, felt the weight.

"They pass by. None has noticed us—or will," said Valora. The dark-tressed sorceress stepped beside the prince.

"How is this?" Felrad turned to the woman who had so

recently been allied with his bloody enemy.

"A simple spell. They look in our direction, but see nothing save a surfacing narwhal." Valora smiled, and Prince Felrad saw no humor in the expression. "Or perhaps they find a sea monster of unbearable aspect. I cannot say. I merely cast the spell and allow their lookouts to interpret as their feeble minds and confused eyes see fit."

"You provide me with sorely needed support. For this I thank you."

The prince turned his gaze once more to the distance and the coming battle. Truly it would surpass Kressia, where his father had fallen, in the bloodletting. Aye, even in importance! Should he die by Zarek Yannis' hand, there would be none left to oppose the usurper. If he failed to regain the Velvet Throne, the people of Raemllyn would suffer Yannis' rule for untold years to come.

"You are right to worry," said Valora.

"Oh?" The prince glanced at Valora. "Is it not your place to reassure me rather than cast doubt on the outcome?" He did not question how this cold, dark-eyed mage had so accurately read his thoughts.

"We both have much to lose if you fail," Valora replied. "Zarek Yannis has no love for any mage. For me especially, after I have turned against him. . . ." She shrugged shapely shoulders.

Prince Felrad found himself considering Valora as a woman in that moment. He shook himself free of her sexual allure, wondering if it came from natural attraction or magicks cunningly woven to bind him to her.

"We both live or die at Rakell," he said. "I openly welcome your choice to support me—or at least war against Yannis."

Valora smiled.

The smile awoke a feeling that Felrad stared on an incredibly beautiful and totally alien creature. Valor might be a human female in form, but something inside her had died—or changed. Still, Prince Felrad needed any ally against the usurper at this juncture.

"Why do you maintain this charade?" asked the sorceress.

"Why do I pose as Nelek Kahl, the slaver?" Prince Felrad laughed, feeling hollow inside. "What other guise allows me free passage around Raemllyn? I need to contact my supporters, no matter how scattered."

"You could send lieutenants."

"No," disagreed Prince Felrad. "I require personal contact to insure their loyalty. The people need to see that I am no figment of some overactive imagination. In this fashion I have raised an army, funds, and the chance to truly oppose Zarek Yannis."

"In Nelek Kahl's clothing you went to Kavindra and issued the challenge?"

"The greatest risk I have ever taken, but one which has given me the greatest support." Felrad smiled.

As Kahl, he had entered Raemllyn's capitol of Kavindra on a slave-buying expedition. And as Prince Felrad he boldly climbed the four hundred and four steps to the top of the Tower of Lost Mornings. From the Forum of Truth he had shouted his challenge to Zarek Yannis. Then, again as Nelek Kahl, accursed slaver, he had taken his caravan of slaves and begun the long journey overland for Yaryne.

"Nelek Kahl does not suit you?"

"No, he is not to my liking. Commercing in the flesh of others ill suits me. Yet it is necessary to maintain the fiction of Kahl's existence. I take lovely women and trade them with ancient, despicable mages for the information they can provide. A part of me dies even as hope for my final victory against Yannis grows."

"This vessel is filled with much guilt for you, then," observed Valora, taking a malicious glee in mouthing each word.

To her surprise, Prince Felrad laughed joyously. "Yes. Although this time I take great pleasure in the *Naughty Goose*'s journey, perilous though it is. These are no slaves, no concubines, no souls being bartered."

"There are many women in the hold," began Valora, confused.

"All wives and lovers of men who await them in Rakell. From Kavindra to Yaryne I gathered them. Tongues wagged about the infamous Kahl's slave caravan. Only a few knew the purpose."

"These are not concubines?" Valora's confusion grew. "You do not make use of them as such?"

"They are loyal subjects—wives and lovers of soldiers who have proven their loyalty to me through great sacrifice. Of course I don't 'use' them, as you suggest."

His indignation brought a deep bow of apology from the sorceress. "Prince Felrad, I fear that I have offended you."

"Continue to call me Nelek Kahl. Although most aboard ship know my true identity or have guessed it by now, some may not. If anything happens, it is best that they not know."

"In this you are wise. Caution is its own reward, my Prince," Valora said.

"And what will be yours, Valora? What reward will you expect after Zarek Yannis is defeated?"

"I am sure Prince Felrad is as generous as Nelek Kahl. However, there will be time for such discussion after the battle is joined and won."

Prince Felrad's attention returned to the Bay of Zaid stretching before the ship. Sharp gray eyes fastened on the storms ahead.

"Yes," said Valora. "Those are produced by Yannis' mages. Simple spells, of no consequence. I can counter them long enough for the ship to sail into Rakell."

"And then?" asked the prince.

Valora's pale face lightened a shade. "Then," she said slowly, "the true battle commences."

chapter 15

"THE STORMS, HAMOR-LORN," Zarek Yannis demanded of his master mage. "Are the storms' winds intense enough? Their fury must be of such might to batter down Rakell's gates. They must open wide the way to my invasion force. Felrad's portals must be shattered before my armies even land. Do you understand that? They *must!*"

Hamor-Lorn nodded slowly, hands secreted within the folds of his robe to keep the High King from noticing the patterns his fingertips traced. The mage found little to fear, even in Kavindra when Zarek Yannis' rages often flared like the soul-consuming flames of Peyneeha's lowest level, but now his fingers wove spells to ward off the Faceless Ones.

Not a mere dozen or two of the hell-spawns patrolled the streets of Yaryne, but fully a hundred. The white-haired wizard closed his eyes and allowed his mystical senses to rove. He dared not scry the city; he took in only fleeting impressions of the magicks aswirl about Yaryne—impressions that told of the arrival of even a greater horde of the Faceless.

How had a mortal such as Zarek Yannis called back a legion of the demons? No mage, sorceress, warlock, or witch since Nnamdi in the days of Kwerin Bloodhawk had held the power to call forth the hell-riders from their realm of existence. What secret did Zarek Yannis, no master of the black arts, possess to allow him to command those fearless, invulnerable fighters? To gain such knowledge Hamor-Lorn would give much, much indeed.

"The storms grow in intensity, Majesty," Hamor-Lorn answered his master. "No fewer than six mages control the gales. The entire Isle of Loieter has been cut off from the rest of the Bay of Zaid. Felrad cannot get supplies in—or escape."

"We sail now, then!" Zarek Yannis exclaimed with unrestrained relish.

Hamor-Lorn cringed. The High King had been unbearable during the arduous journey from Kavindra to Yaryne. He ranted like a madman, again and again briefing any and all in his retinue about the impending battle to crush Rakell, making certain all knew his plan, that nothing was going amiss. Loieterland would be his final victory, he screeched time and time again, leaving Hamor-Lorn to ponder whether the prospect of direct, face-to-face combat with Felrad had not driven Zarek Yannis mad. The High King had never been the same, or so Hamor-Lorn reflected, since Felrad publicly called his challenge from the Tower of Lost Mornings in Kavindra.

Hamor-Lorn's eyes opened and he glanced at the six mages standing in a line on the opposite side of the chamber. One of his apprentice mages signaled him. The master sorcerer frowned; from the pinched expression on the woman's face, he knew she bore ill news.

"A moment, Majesty." Hamor-Lorn contained his anxiety in slow, restrained steps while he moved across the room to garner whatever bad tidings his apprentice carried.

"Well?" The old wizard arched a reprimanding eyebrow before the woman even spoke. "Out with it."

"A ship has breached the wall of storms, Master." Wide brown eyes blinked in an attempt to conceal their fear.

"What? How?" Hamor-Lorn reeled under the pronouncement. It couldn't be! "I cast the spells myself. All you do is maintain them. How could anyone . . ."

The mage abruptly cut off his tirade. A single answer blazed in his mind. Like a curse the name tore from his lips, "Valora!"

"I fear you are correct, Master," the apprentice said. "I worked with Valora. There is a certain . . . tenor to the spells she casts. This countering spell carried her familiar signature."

"What information did you gather from this breaching?" demanded Hamor-Lorn.

"Information? I do not understand." The sorceress blinked again.

"Fool! Every spell leaves a residue, a hint to the sorcerer casting it, a trace of those affected by it. You always examine what another has done to learn, to assure that your own work is without flaw. Did only Valora enter Rakell, or did she take an army with her?"

"I . . . not many, Master. A . . . a few. A shipload. No more," the woman answered.

Hamor-Lorn's lips drew into a thin line. "This might be to our advantage."

"What is it, Hamor-Lorn? What hampers our attack? I would be done with this." Zarek Yannis gestured impatiently for his mage to return to his side.

Hamor-Lorn dismissed the apprentice and rejoined the high king. "Good news, Majesty. Felrad has been detected on the Isle of Loieter. When you attack, the pretender will be at your mercy."

The wizard only guessed. But who else would the traitor Valora serve?

"He must not escape. No, Hamor-Lorn, he must not. The storms ring the isle?" Yannis asked for the thousandth time that day.

"Entirely," Hamor-Lorn assured his anxious king. "My apprentices assure me of hurricane-force winds at every point around Loieterland. Only when our fleet approaches will the storms lift to allow us through. We will land at the gates of Rakell!"

"And crush Felrad!" cried Zarek Yannis. The High King spun and ran to a parapet that overlooked Yaryne's main avenue. "There! There is the weapon that will destroy Felrad and all who pay allegiance to Bedrich's whelp!"

Hamor-Lorn's fingers worked faster, forming the ward spells. In the street below rode the Faceless Ones, four abreast and extending for as far as the mage could see. Those hell-spawns rode with cowled heads turned upward, so that their burning eyes rose to greet their lord and master.

Yannis saluted them as they passed. Each of the demonic warriors, in turn, clutched the hilt of crystal-fire sword in skeletal hand. The echoes along the cobblestone streets grew deafening as each fiery horse's hoof struck the paving stones at precisely the same instant. The impact sent steam sizzling into the air, carrying the nose-burning scent of sulfur even to the heights of the Yaryne palace tower from where Yannis gazed at the horrible parade.

"My loyal troops," Zarek Yannis said.

Hamor-Lorn watched his king's physical change. Yannis' expression transformed from one of nervous anticipation to transcendence. He straightened, chest expanding. This was a commander, a ruler of men—and demons. It was as though Yannis drew strength from the hell-riders who passed in review.

"There are many others loyal to you, Majesty," said the master mage. "A full twenty thousand await transport to the Isle of Loieter."

"Half my entire army," mused the king. He looked up, as if considering this point for the first time, although it had been discussed until the mage had tired of hearing it. "The ships? Are there enough ships?"

"Over two hundred, Majesty, each capable of carrying five hundred men. The first wave will land on Rakell's beach and begin the siege. Within four days the ships will return to Yaryne, take on the other half of your invasion army, and return to reinforce those who went before."

"There will be no need of reinforcements," Zarek Yannis said with certainty. "The Faceless Ones will be enough. They will drive forward, destroy the gates of Rakell and move inward, herding Felrad's pitiful defenders before them. My troops will march in their wake, and slay everyone who lives. Everyone!"

Hamor-Lorn pondered. King Yannis made it sound simple. The wizard did not mention that Valora now cast her lot with Felrad.

And what of the Sword of Kwerin Bloodhawk? What had become of it? Hamor-Lorn's agents throughout Raemllyn had been unable to find it. For a time, Felrad's agent Berenicis Blackheart had it while he sought to reunite it with its magically empowering sheath.

Hamor-Lorn frowned. Something had happened in the forests of Agda. Lorennion, the foremost sorcerer of Raemllyn, had been dealt a severe blow.

And sheath and sword? What of them? Hamor-Lorn had his suspicions. Strange occurrences that had led to his predecessor's death in Bistonia might be explained by the presence of the Sword of Kwerin. But who wielded it? Not Berenicis. Felrad himself?

If so, the battle for Loieterland would be even more vicious than Zarek Yannis anticipated.

"We sail, Hamor-Lorn. The sooner we arrive at Rakell, the sooner Felrad dies!"

"We sail, Majesty. On the tide." Hamor-Lorn cast a final glance out the window at the last column of Faceless Ones riding to the docks to embark. His fingers worked on a final ward spell, and it required all Hamor-Lorn's willpower not to fervently hope that the ship bearing those hundred demons to Rakell would sink.

But he knew that, without the Faceless Ones, Zarek Yannis had no chance of defeating Felrad.

What *had* become of the Sword of Kwerin Bloodhawk? The old sorcerer had no answer. And if the usurper knew, he said nothing. What had become of Kwerin's legendary blade? The battle's outcome could depend on Hamor-Lorn discovering the answer.

chapter 16

LIGHTNING, JAGGED BOLTS of actinic power that walked the underbelly of clouds like twisted spider legs of living light, sliced the dark sky above the *Naughty Goose* with eye-searing violence. Thunder crashed, rolling between black, mountainous storm clouds, dissipating only when drowned in another deafening clash of energies.

Hidden beneath a swaying skiff that hung from its riggings, Lijena Farleigh defied Nelek Kahl's orders and Monni's watchful eye by being on the pleasure ship's deck. In truth, she had crept from the hold to appraise the storm's force, wishing to be prepared to salvage the Sword of Kwerin Bloodhawk should the vessel be unable to weather the raging elements.

She stayed, enduring the cold deluge that soaked her to the bone, because of Valora!

A sizzling bolt arced from the boiling blackness overhead and seared into the *Naughty Goose*'s top spar. The air exploded with a crackling hiss. Wood parted and burst into flame. Fiery splinters plunged downward, hailing to a sputtering death across the drenched wooden deck. The pleasure craft, now unbalanced in the howling gale, heaved, listed, and fought the mounting wave crests.

Through it all, Lijena saw a lone figure on the bow of the ship. Standing as if nothing untoward happened was the dark mage Berenicis had brought on board.

Valora lifted her hands high. In the lightning Lijena almost mistook the sorceress for the ship's figurehead. Valora's hands reached upward, to touch the mist churning in front of the ship, to deflect the raging storm clouds, to draw the lightning from the sky.

Lijena gasped when a massive bolt of purple-green lightning struck the mage. Her horrified cry vanished in the roar of the sea and the groaning protests of the ship's timbers. When the dazzling afterimage of the lightning passed, Lijena stared in bewilderment. Valora still stood at the prow, her hands and arms upraised as though beckoning the deadly bolts into her willing embrace.

Again, again, and again, the lightning answered the sorceress. Spitting and sizzling, the ragged bolts lanced from the thunderheads to dance across the mage's hands and down her arms. An unearthly glow radiated from Valora's palms. It spread clinging to Valora's arms and outlining her body. Winds whipped back the robe the sorceress wore to reveal a body trimmer and more youthful than Lijena had thought.

Hardly more than a child, Lijena realized, mesmerized by the sight of the sorceress battling the magic-evoked gale winds.

Child or not, Valora fought and drew down the powerful thrusts of Yannis' mages, her own spells somehow transforming the raw energy into a countering force that opened smoother seas for the *Naughty Goose*. The heaving and tossing of the deck beneath Lijena didn't slacken, but neither did it grow worse.

On both sides of the ship rose hundred-foot walls of gray-green water, struggling to crush the craft and all aboard.

Valora held back the massive mountains of water! Still the lightning bolts seared into her outstretched arms, drawn to the woman as though she were a statue of iron. And from the mage's fingertips hurled magic bolts of her own. The potent blasts tore through wind and rain to rip into the churning, black thunderclouds above, rending them.

"Hurry!" Valora's head twisted, and she cried to Captain Lattour who manned the *Naughty Goose*'s wheel. "You must hurry! More than one mage opposes me. I cannot hold back their combined strength! Hurry, damn you, man! Hurry!"

Another barrage of blasting bolts leapt from Valora's hands

as a tidal wave rose before the tossing ship. Rather than breaking atop the vessel, the wave opened—a narrow tunnel cut through the water's heart. Lattour spun the wheel, sailing his ship through that watery mouth.

"Rakell!" came the cry from the bridge. "She's gotten us through to Rakell!"

Half obscured in mist still, Lijena saw Nelek Kahl, Berenicis and Captain Lattour on the deck. The captain and Kahl now struggled together on the wheel to keep the ship on course, while Berenicis stood to one side, looking smug. Lijena turned her attention back to Valora—and beyond.

Truly, it was Rakell! The storms had prevented sight of the port city with its massive docks and extensive warehouse district, but it was to the fortress that Lijena's eye naturally gravitated.

The fortress of Rakell stood on a low hill past the center of the city. Walls of fitted stone blocks capped with *chiin* wood towered one hundred feet into the air. Lijena's knowing eye evaluated the fortress' success in repelling attack. Although a considerable plain stretched around the fortress where Zarek Yannis might bivouac and build his war engines during a long siege, the walls looked impregnable. Prince Felrad had taken the time to build well.

But Lijena despaired. To fight a defensive battle implied a lack of troops to carry the war directly to Yannis. She sighed. The prince fought in the only fashion possible for an underdog. He lured the usurper to him. Prince Felrad chose the site and kept the high ground, but the disadvantages were equally telling.

Should Zarek Yannis triumph, all would know Prince Felrad had fought his last battle. Rakell provided the core of his power. Crush it and the rebellion died forever.

Lijena closed her eyes and pictured the Faceless Ones riding across the stripped-bare plain to the *chiin* wood gates of the fortress. What magicks did Prince Felrad have to repulse such an attack?

She knew of none—save the weapon she carried. The Sword of Kwerin Bloodhawk had to be placed in Prince Felrad's hands soon.

First, she had a mission to accomplish. With Rakell within

swimming distance, the water inside the magically induced storm glassy smooth and calm, she had a dagger to deliver to Berenicis the Blackheart and Nelek Kahl.

Lijena touched her hidden dagger, scurried from beneath the skiff, and started for the bridge—when a hand froze her in mid-stride. She stumbled and went to her knees, unable to move.

"Why aren't you below with the others?" came Valora's voice. "You were ordered to stay in the hold so you would not interfere with my carefully conjured magicks."

"I . . . I . . . didn't . . . know," stammered Lijena.

Terror rattled through her brain. Valora stared directly into her face. Surely the woman would recognize her from that night in the mage Lorennion's keep. She had to get away. Lijena's legs refused to move. She fought to stand, but couldn't. Her legs felt as though they had been stripped of muscle.

"Go below now, you silly bitch! We dock soon." With that, Valora stalked off toward Kahl and the others.

Lijena found, as soon as the mage released her grip, that she could stand. The magicks from the sorceress's fingers faded instantly. On shaky legs, Lijena obeyed and scurried below.

Why hadn't the woman recognized her? Lijena could only guess. Maybe the drenching rain that plastered her hair against her skull like a wet cap had disguised her.

Or perhaps on that night when she had stood with Davin Anane as he battled Valora and her guard of Faceless Ones, the sorceress's attention had focused on Davin and the Sword of Kwerin Bloodhawk, rather than one of Lorennion's demon-enslaved serving wenches. Whatever the reason, Lijena thanked Raemllyn's gods for her fortune.

By the time she was able to walk without trembling, the *Naughty Goose* had docked.

"All ashore, all ashore," cried Monni, smiling and crying. "Oh, it's so wonderful to have finally arrived. So wonderful!"

Lijena frowned, bewildered by the woman's high spirits. She knew they had come through the hurricane and into the eye of the storm. Soon, Zarek Yannis' might would be unleashed against Rakell and the fortress.

"Are you overcome with joy at finally arriving?" Monni asked Lijena. No sarcasm tinged the words. Monni truly meant what she said. "You look strange. Pale."

"I am weak from the storm. Seasickness," Lijena explained lamely.

"I remember. You did not weather the journey well, even in calm seas. Let me help you. Who awaits you?"

Lijena almost said Nelek Kahl and Berenicis, then bit back the words. Lijena only smiled and allowed Monni to interpret the grin in whatever way she wanted.

"Can you make it up the ladder?" asked Monni, obviously anxious to get ashore.

"Go on. I can make it by myself. Don't tarry because of me." Lijena watched Monni's grateful nod.

In a flash, the woman scampered up the ladder, ducked through the hatchway, and ran across the deck.

When she and the other women aboard disappeared down the gangplank, Lijena pivoted and dashed to the locker where she'd hidden the Sword of Kwerin. Seawater had soaked into the wood and caused the loose board to swell; still, Lijena's fingers were enough to pry loose one board. With a sigh of relief, Lijena pulled free the magical blade and its empowering sheath.

"For Prince Felrad," she said softly. "But first, Kahl and Berenicis will taste this steel."

To her dismay, however, the slaver and Berenicis had already gone ashore. On deck, Lijena stood and stared in confusion.

A crowd of men and women pressed close to the gangplank. Lijena couldn't understand the scene unfolding before her. The concubines, Monni with them, had rushed into the arms of men on the dock. It struck Lijena more as a homecoming than as a docking of a slave ship filled with concubines. However, the boisterous joy faded quickly and the crowd dissipated, returning the dock area to frantic activity.

Everywhere she looked, she saw the preparations being made for Zarek Yannis' invasion. Stunned and unsure of herself, Lijena Farleigh went down the gangway and stood. She looked around and saw no one she recognized from the ship. Even Captain Lattour had vanished.

Kahl and Berenicis will not elude me as long as they remain in the city! Lijena refused to be denied.

Taking time to go back onto the *Naughty Goose* and change

into blouse, breeches, and boots, Lijena left the ship and walked into Rakell to locate the two she had slated for death. Only when revenge sated her could she locate Prince Felrad and deliver the Sword of Kwerin. She prayed her search would be short and the killing quick and clean. Invasion seemed imminent.

chapter 17

"THE WORST PART of imprisonment," Goran One-Eye groaned, "is the separation from Kulonna. By Nyuria's arse, why is it taking them so damnable long to verify her story? I'm well on my way to rotting!"

Davin Anane glanced at his friend. For the Challing, the bars around them served as a second prison. Not only was he confined by the rock and steel of their cell, but the protective spells woven around the city of Rakell robbed him of his shape-changing ability. Were it not so, Goran might have altered his form and wiggled through the bars, securing both their freedoms.

"A week! A whole damned week in this stinking hole!" Davin vented his own misery.

In truth, the Rakell prison wasn't as bad as some that had held the Jyotian freebooter. The cell's stench had long ago numbed his nose to its constant odor. New straw to cover the floor was brought every second day. And two meals a day, the evening's with meat, were shoved through the bars. But the idea—the insult—of incarceration when they'd meant only to *bring* gold to Felrad rankled the heir to the House of Anane.

"They think we're spies for Zarek Yannis." Goran slumped on a cot that was dwarfed by his massive bulk. He held his shaggy-maned head in his thick hands. "We'll be executed when the usurper begins his attack, wait and see. Easier to be done with prisoners, even if they are innocent."

"If Kulonna cannot convince them, what about Awendala?" asked Davin, not expecting an answer from his friend. "She is an honest woman. How can any doubt her word?"

"Would an honest woman travel with the likes of us?" Goran groaned without glancing up. "If we are to walk as free men once again, Kulonna is our only chance."

Davin dropped to his own cot, his mind replaying the events that had led to their accommodations in Rakell's prison. The fishing boat that had brought them through the storm had been crushed by Yannis' magicks. Yet the old fisherman had somehow managed to steer his shattered craft to shore before the boat came apart at its seams.

Davin swallowed a twinge of guilt. The old man had given his life for his passengers, remaining at the sails of his boat until waves washed him overboard. Yet the Jyotian had never learned his name. On the mainland, a bowl of fish-head stew had long gone cold waiting for a husband to return for his dinner.

After the fisherman had been swept away by the waves, Davin remembered little of it. The cries of the two crewmen had rung in his ears as the water sucked them under. Then the battering waves had swept him from the sinking deck.

Awendala? Kulonna?

He didn't know. He vaguely recalled Goran altering his form to become seaborne. Davin remembered water in his mouth and burning into his lungs—and a long tentacle wrapping about his waist to hold him above the crashing surf. Goran had rescued him.

But what of the others? Davin didn't know.

Goran thought the women had reached the safety of the beach, that he might have also saved them. However, the storm and the magicks driving it had confused the Challing, erasing those moments in the crashing waves from his memory. Goran didn't even remember when and how he had shape-changed.

They still live, Davin told himself. *Awendala and Kulonna have to be still alive. Have to be!*

A cold shudder quaked through the Jyotian's muscular body. Surely the gods could not be so cruel—to rob him of the woman he loved when their time together had been so short. Not when their whole lives lay before them.

"I view this as an example of human stupidity." Goran flopped to his back atop the cot. "We should have remained on the mainland and spent the gold on ourselves. Yet, *you* insisted on 'returning' it to Felrad. How can man or Challing return something that never belonged to that person? We stole the gold fairly, and at great personal risk, may I remind you? It was ours!"

Ignoring his friend's ranting, Davin pushed from his own cot and paced. His gray eyes examined the cell's every detail for the thousandth time in his week of imprisonment. With every stride he prayed Prince Felrad's guards would appear to announce that all was well—or Kulonna would convince the petty bureaucrats that she was, indeed, Duke Tun's emissary and had come to embrace the Prince.

Neither happened. Davin raged against the iron bars in the cell's window.

Beyond the barrier to freedom, in the city, he saw preparations for invasion. Civilians stripped their homes and fled for the interior of Loieterland. Merchants gave what they could to the forest-green-clad soldiers, then torched the rest to prevent it from being used by Yannis' troops. Everywhere were soldiers, all laboriously readying themselves and city for the impending assault.

Stretching on tiptoe, he gazed at the uppermost spires of the fortress that jutted above the city's rooftops. So near, yet so far from him. He ached to be within that fort, to be standing at Felrad's side.

An ironic smile twisted the Jyotian's lips. The Sitala relished such twists in the fates they dealt to common mortals. During the years since King Bedrich's death, he had professed to care little whose hindquarters warmed the Velvet Throne of Raemllyn. He had even begun to believe that lie himself.

Now that he realized how important it was for the House of Anane's last son to pledge his sword arm to the true heir, he found himself locked away in prison, accused of being one of the usurper's spies.

"We should have followed her and reclaimed the sword!" Davin hissed between clenched teeth. "Black Qar take her!"

"The skinny wench still gnaws at you, eh?" Goran crossed his arms under his shaggy red head and stared up at the rock ceiling, his one good eye unblinking. "I'd thought Awendala had worn you out, and that the wench Lijena no longer crossed your mind. You humans. I'll never understand. We Challings know how to enjoy life, at least while in human form."

"Lijena is not what I. . . . Never mind!"

Davin could never explain to the Challing it was the Sword of Kwerin Bloodhawk he yearned to hold and not Lijena Farleigh. He grasped the iron bars in an attempt to rattle them—an action that only increased his frustration. They were too securely set in the hard rock wall to budge.

"On your feet, you two," a clipped command sounded from behind Davin.

The young adventurer pivoted and stared at an officer sporting field-grade rank, standing at the door to their cell. Did Felrad send such high-ranking officers to carry out executions?

"Hurry, you louts! I've orders that you are to be taken before the Prince," the officer shouted impatiently. He then turned to a half-dozen armed troops standing to his right. "Clean them, then bring them to me outside."

"Outside?" asked Davin.

He staggered and stumbled, clumsily brushing against one of the guards when they entered the cell. As he tried to regain his balance, Goran rose, slipped on the straw covering the floor, and crashed into the Jyotian's side. Together the pair fell heavily.

The officer stood glaring at them. "Return the cell key you just took. And be quick about washing up. Prince Felrad is a busy man. Why he wants to see the likes of you, only Yehseen can say."

With a shrug, Davin handed back the cell keys he had stolen in his seemingly clumsy fall. If they'd found out nothing else, they weren't being taken outside for execution. Not unless Felrad participated in such exercises personally.

Almost cheerful for the first time in a week, Davin Anane and Goran One-Eye marched from the cell to bathe and make themselves presentable for Prince Felrad.

Davin Anane stiffened as he walked into Prince Felrad's audience hall. Seated on a low throne, the man with the thin moustache, dark hair slightly silvered at the temples, and piercing gray eyes had to be Prince Felrad.

Two steps down from the throne's dais stood Berenicis the Blackheart.

"Ah, Davin, my brother!" Berenicis called his false greeting of joy and waved a welcome arm.

"Brother!" Goran's head jerked around, his good eye going round. "The snake called you *brother!*"

"Aye, that I am," Davin managed to spit with contempt before his body went rigid once again.

A woman dressed entirely in black mage's robes stepped from behind the throne.

Valora! Davin's mind balked against the travesty that filled his eyes.

"My brother, you appear shocked to see us." An amused smile played across Berenicis' lips.

Davin's attention focused on the dethroned ruler of his homeland, the man who had destroyed the House of Anane. "I'd thought—hoped—you and the usurper's traitorous bitch had died in Agda's wood."

"Davin, such sentiment ill becomes you. I thought we had agreed to place such pettiness behind us, to let bygones be bygones." Berenicis' smile widened to a smirking grin. "Have you met Prince Felrad?"

To the seated man, Berenicis turned and bowed. "Highness, may I present my brother from Jyotis, Davin Anane, heir to the House of Anane?"

Prince Felrad nodded, lifted a hand, and motioned Davin forward.

Davin's eyes narrowed as he drew closer to the prince. He had seen this man before! But where? Elusively, a half-forgotten memory flitted about within his mind like a shadow. Then it surfaced, dark and ugly.

"Kahl! Nelek Kahl!" Davin blurted. "You're the slaver Kahl!" He *had* seen this man before—selling Lijena Farleigh to the magician Masur-Kell in the city of Leticia.

"Some know me by that blighted name." The prince's chest heaved as though weighted by unseen sorrow. "That guise provides freedom to travel Raemllyn otherwise denied me by Zarek Yannis. It is my understanding that you have come to aid us."

"My friends and I . . ." Davin stammered in bewilderment

and tilted his head toward Goran One-Eye to cover his dazed mind. This was Nelek Kahl, the most notorious slaver in all the realms of Raemllyn! And he allied himself with Berenicis and the sorceress Valora! ". . . arrived a week ago with a shipment of gold stolen from Yannis' comptroller in Evara."

"Highness, Davin is a most expert thief," Berenicis interrupted, still smirking. "I'm sure my brother's few coins will prove useful."

"He brought twelve hundredweight of gold," Prince Felrad said. "More than merely useful, I would say."

Berenicis' mouth closed, and the Blackheart swallowed whatever words might have been on his tongue. His eyes, the same gray as Davin's, although glinting a steel-edged coldness, shifted to his fellow Jyotian.

However, Davin's attention was caught by Valora's dark gaze. Zarek Yannis' former master mage studied him as if he were a specimen trapped for experimentation.

Davin repressed a shudder. The witch was not to be trusted; she was capable of anything. Surely Felrad must see that! Or was it that he didn't mind. The prince *was* Nelek Kahl.

"Your generous contribution to my dwindling coffers is gratefully accepted and appreciated." Prince Felrad's gray eyes moved from Berenicis to Davin.

"The theft doubly harms the usurper, Highness," Davin bowed awkwardly.

He found himself hard-pressed to pay homage to this man. Although Davin's journeys and hardships for the past year had been completed and overcome in the name of Raemllyn's rightful ruler, was Prince Felrad a better choice than Zarek Yannis? Davin Anane could not deny the doubts that assailed him.

"Kulonna has spoken well of you," Prince Felrad said. "Simply escorting the lovely daughter of Duke Tun to Rakell is an incomparable service to me and the rebellion."

"Kulonna lives then?" Davin's eyes widened, aspark with hope. "And the other maid, Awendala, who traveled with the duchess, what of her?"

"She also survived the storm that Zarek Yannis sent against this isle." Felrad nodded.

"Why's it taken us a week of rotting in your jail if you took the gold and knew of Kulonna's parentage?" Goran, who had stood silent until Kulonna was mentioned, abruptly stepped toward the dais. Green witch-fire blazed in his good eye.

"Your friend's tongue needs training." Prince Felrad shot a glance at Davin, but no anger tinged his words. Nor did he attempt to hide his smile of amusement when he looked at the Challing. "To answer this, Goran One-Eye, I have only just arrived in Rakell. My officers were overly cautious due to the possibility of infiltration by Yannis' spies."

"Would spies buy their way in with such a trove of gold?" Davin posed.

"Perhaps. Yannis is capable of anything. Yet, in all likelihood it was doubtful that his spies would attempt such a ruse. That is why you were not executed on the spot."

"What of the fisherman whose boat brought us?" Davin asked. "Was he washed ashore?"

Felrad glanced to an officer standing at the side of the room. The man shook his head and lowered his eyes.

"Apparently no trace of the man or his crew was found. We can only assume that Yannis' magicks overcame our loyal subjects." The prince settled back, then looked from Valora to Davin and Goran. "You know one another?"

"We do," Davin said, cutting off any possible response from Valora.

Davin found it difficult to believe the renegade mage held any true loyalty to Prince Felrad, yet he didn't dare so advise the pretender to the Velvet Throne. Nelek Kahl or not, Prince Felrad appeared no one's fool; he had to know a pit of vipers surrounded his temporary throne.

"The Blackheart was an ally in time of need," Goran spat with unrestrained contempt.

Again, an amused smile lifted the prince's lips when he turned to the former Jyotian ruler and the sorceress. "Berenicis, Valora, please attend the matters we discussed."

Felrad then watched as the Blackheart and the dark mage bowed and exited the room. When they were gone, Felrad motioned for Davin and Goran to approach closer.

"I am greatly in your debt. Your gift of gold has provided needed ships to augment a lamentably small fleet. Since Zarek Yannis launches from Yaryne, every ship we sink on its way to Rakell saves lives here," Felrad said.

"We have seen some of his privateers along the northern coast," Goran commented. "The usurper can muster a fleet of several hundred war vessels."

"Well over two hundred, within the Bay of Zaid and the Bay of Pilisi." Prince Felrad nodded grimly. "And they already sail for Rakell. But along the way they will find ships purchased with your captured gold. Those ships have been ensorcelled to explode and burn should one of Yannis' vessels sail too close. If Jajhana favors our endeavor, we might sink several dozen of the usurper's troop-laden ships."

"The ones with the Faceless aboard would be enough," Davin added.

"Agreed." Prince Felrad's hands opened and closed, as if around the hilt of a sword.

"What of the Sword of Kwerin Bloodhawk?" asked Davin.

"What?" Felrad's gray eyes widened. "You know of the blade?"

"Berenicis has not mentioned our mutual encounter with the wizard Lorennion?" This from Goran One-Eye.

Prince Felrad frowned, but said nothing. And for Davin, the dark expression spoke more than words. "Berenicis has reasons for all he does. This I know well from the days he drove me from Jyotis branded a murderer."

"The sword," prompted Prince Felrad. "What became of it? All Berenicis said was that he'd lost it. Do you have it? That would be a greater gift than all the gold in Raemllyn."

Davin quickly explained how Lijena Farleigh had gained possession of the blade—and how she had put it to use against three of the Faceless Ones.

"Three less of the demon-spawns to fight at the gates to my stronghold," said Felrad. "I am more indebted to you than I realized."

Prince Felrad settled deeply into the throne's cushions. "I know of your personal differences with Lord Berenicis. Aye, and even how my father Bedrich the Fair wronged your mother. . . ."

A jolt of reawakened pain shot through the young Jyotian. A humorless smile touched the corners of his mouth. How artfully Felrad avoided calling him brother, though Bedrich had sired them both.

"Judge not Bedrich harshly," Felrad continued. "He was not called the Fair for naught. Remember that in your time of troubles and need, Bedrich found himself faced with Zarek Yannis and his horde riding out of Lower Raemllyn."

Davin said nothing. He had often held the same thought. It did nothing to restore the House of Anane or breathe life back into his mother.

"As to Berenicis and yourself, it must be as Berenicis said. The time has come to place the past behind us. We must rally as one to assure that Raemllyn as we love it has a future."

Felrad paused as though expecting an answer from the adventurer. Davin remained silent. "If you seek to overthrow Berenicis through me, then you have journeyed to Rakell on a fool's mission. I have promised to reinstate Berenicis on his throne should we prove victorious against Yannis and his armies. Considering the antagonism of the other rulers toward my attempts to regain the throne, Berenicis may well be seated as lower king of the coast along the Sea of Bua from Yow to Cahri. One as predictable as Lord Berenicis has his uses."

"My quarrel with the Blackheart has nothing to do with his service to the throne, Highness. Nor did we journey here to seek boons from you. We only ask how we may serve in the battle against Zarek Yannis," Davin finally spoke with an outward coolness. Inside he seethed. Berenicis ruling almost all of western Raemllyn's coast? Unthinkable!

"Your sorely needed sword arms will be enough for now," Felrad replied. "My apologies again for not rescuing you from my prisons earlier. I trust you can understand and forgive my officers. My presence was required at Nawat and Yaryne before Yannis moved in his troops."

"We thank you for your consideration," Davin bowed.

He nudged the Challing in the ribs. Goran grunted and performed an awkward half-bow.

"To show my gratitude, please accept the use of a suite of rooms within the fortress. I am sure you will find the accommodations far superior to those you've enjoyed the past week." Prince Felrad's tone of voice indicated that the audience had come to an end.

Bowing again, Davin and Goran quickly left, and one of

Prince Felrad's field officers stepped to the spot they had vacated, a sea chart in hand.

Outside, Goran asked, "How do we find these rooms? If there is anything worth stealing, let's take it and be off. We can make our way to Vatusia before the assault begins."

"We stay," said Davin. "We owe it to the Prince."

"To a man who surrounds himself with snakes like Berenicis and Valora? Ha!"

"Exactly for that reason. He might not know their true color."

"Some ruler! The man's idea of gratitude is sorely lacking. We deliver him wealth, and he offers us the opportunity to be killed in return," Goran complained.

But the Challing was soon singing a bawdy song off-key as they wandered the bare stone corridors of the Rakell fortress in search of the promised suite. A serving maid beckoned them down an arched corridor and pointed toward a door at its end.

The instant Davin opened that highly polished cherrywood door, he knew they had found the right rooms.

"Awendala!" he cried as the red-haired woman rushed to his arms. They kissed until Goran roughly shouldered them aside to pick up Kulonna and spin her about.

"Have they kept you here since you washed ashore?" asked Davin, looking around the sumptuously appointed rooms. "Some prison!"

"Without you, dearest Davin, it has seemed bleak." Awendala's passionate kiss left no doubt that she meant every word.

Arms circling one another's waists, they moved to the center of a large room where cushions had been scattered. Davin gratefully sank to one, with Awendala beside him.

"Where's Goran?" he asked. The Challing and Kulonna had vanished into another room.

"Do not think of them, Davin. Think of this." Awendala kissed him again.

This time, Davin took time and care in returning her gesture.

When Awendala broke off, gasping for air, she said, "Oh, how I've missed you!"

"And I have missed you. If only Zarek Yannis' attack wasn't already launched."

"He comes?"

"Yes, Nyuria burn him forever!"

Awendala looked at Davin carefully before saying, "There's more. What is it?"

Davin heaved a deep breath. He didn't want to speak of it, yet it gnawed within his breast. "Berenicis the Blackheart."

Awendala edged away slightly, shocked by the bitterness of Davin's voice. "What has this Berenicis done? You have mentioned some to me, but nothing to make you so angry."

"What's he done? What's my *brother* done?" Davin laughed harshly.

He poured himself a flagon of wine and downed it without tasting the fine vintage. He drank half of another before he spoke. "Yes, Awendala, he truly *is* my brother. Or half-brother."

"But he was ruler of Jyotis!"

"And we are both bastards of Bedrich the Fair."

"You have claim to the Velvet Throne? But Felrad . . ."

"Prince Felrad is direct and blood-legal heir. Who knows how many illegitimate sons and daughters were left by Bedrich? Our former High King believed in using his right to share the beds of noble-born ladies in his realm while he traveled throughout Raemllyn."

"As you said, such is the High King's right," Awendala replied. "But what of Berenicis?"

"A jealousy born of two brothers sired by the same father but by different mothers," Davin said. He explained that after Lord Anane, his legal father, had been killed in a hunting accident, Bedrich made Jyotis his home away from the capital Kavindra. "Months he spent in our halls. Openly he loved my mother, and openly he declared me his son. And that was what fueled Berenicis' hate."

Davin detailed how Berenicis plotted and killed his own legal father to rise to Jyotis' throne. "He then turned against our house. Taxes, legal battles won in courts where Berenicis' judges ruled, slowly reduced us to peasants living on a small plot of land. Yet, we survived. The land was rich and game abounds in Jyotis. For nothing else was needed, at least for my mother and me. For Berenicis, it wasn't enough. He arranged to have his own chamberlain murdered. There were those in his court who willingly accused me of the crime. I was arrested and thrown into prison."

Davin paused and downed the rest of his wine to wash the bile from his mouth. The alcohol did nothing to lessen the pain. "Helpless against the Blackheart, my mother could do naught but worry—worries that developed into a sickness that robbed her of life. And I escaped Berenicis' dungeon and fled Jyotis vowing to one day repay my brother for all he had done!"

"What of Bedrich? Why did he not intercede?" Awendala's arms pulled Davin to her.

"My own thoughts, then. I was certain the High King had betrayed the woman he loved and the youth he called son," Davin said. "Only after the Battle of Kressia's Plain, and Bedrich's death, did I realize that while Berenicis methodically destroyed the House of Anane, my father fought for his very life—and failed."

"The prince sets great store by Berenicis' talents," said Awendala, a frown of doubt marring her delicate beauty. "I've overheard much in the past week. Without him and the traitorous mage who dresses only in black, Felrad believes there is little hope for success against Yannis and the Faceless Ones."

"Fear naught, my precious," said Davin. "I know how Prince Felrad values them. And I will not settle my grievance with either Valora or Berenicis until the battle has ended."

Nor was he prepared to place unquestioning trust in a prince who would assume the guise of one as despicable as Nelek Kahl.

As if Awendala read the worries troubling his mind, she drew closer, pressing warmly against his body. Her lips sought his and soon all thought of death and vengeance fled, replaced by love.

chapter 18

LIJENA FARLEIGH STROLLED the main street of Rakell, her gaze lifting to the stone battlements of Prince Felrad's fortress. Although no expert on military design, she admired the massiveness of the structure, the strong, powerful lines of its gray walls.

A feeling of invulnerability and security radiated from the stronghold. Lijena nodded her silent approval. Zarek Yannis could well spend many years laying siege to Rakell's stronghold—years the usurper didn't have.

If word carried through Raemllyn that Prince Felrad made a staunch stand here, the populace would rally to the Prince's banner. Lijena estimated that Zarek Yannis dared bring no more than half his troops to the Isle of Loieter in answer to Felrad's challenge. The remainder were needed to put down petty uprisings and civil disorders in the rest of the realm. Though feared, the usurper was not loved or even liked by a majority of his subjects; the first hint of military weakness would bring about immediate civil war throughout his kingdom.

Lijena sighed. Only Prince Felrad provided the focus for all that power, though. Petty warlords might strive for supremacy in isolated areas, but Yannis' grip was unshakeable. Felrad, dead King Bedrich's only legitimate son, stood as the sole noble-born whom all could agree was the true heir to the Velvet

Throne. The fate of the kingdom rested on the Prince's ability to stage successfully the forthcoming battle.

Years—Lijena estimated the structure's strength to stand against the usurper's armies when she glanced back at the fortress—*if Yannis' armies were merely mortal!*

She could only pray to the pantheon of Raemllyn's deities that stone and mortar might repel the hordes of Faceless Ones that the usurper commanded.

Around the daughter of Bistonia, the people of Rakell bent their backs to the task of preparing for the invasion. Work that did not contribute to that end was ignored, left unattended to gather dust from the bustle of passing carts and wagons that hauled heaping loads of food into the fortress in preparation for a lengthy siege.

It seemed to matter little to most of the citizenry that soon they'd be burned out of house and home, that their city would be in ruins. For a people who faced possible extinction, their spirits seemed to soar. Lewd jokes about Zarek Yannis and his mating habits with various small animals were shouted back and forth between groups of workers who busily stripped two blacksmith shops and loaded equipment into carts. Laughter rolled along the avenue.

Others proclaimed proudly that they would take all their vital possessions into the fortress, then put the torch to their own city to prevent Yannis from using it to quarter his troops. Lijena didn't doubt the sincerity of those claims. The usurper's human forces would be greeted by charcoaled timbers and ashes when they landed on Rakell's beaches.

But Lijena knew that the human contingent of the invasion force would be the lesser part. Zarek Yannis depended heavily on the demonic Faceless Ones. Her hand rested on the hilt of the magical sword once wielded by Kwerin Bloodhawk. At the dawn of Raemllyn's history, the blade had returned the Faceless Ones to their own Qar-damned world of dimension. In Prince Felrad's hand, it could do the chore again.

Lijena turned toward the fortress, winding through city streets until her strides brought her to a denuded plane surrounding the towering structure. As her booted feet carried her across the barren land, her lips uplifted in another smile of approval.

Zarek Yannis would find no cover here. The ground had been scorched—whether by natural flame or blasting magicks, she didn't know.

The crunch of her soles atop the burnt plain evoked images of the near future. In Lijena's mind's eye blazed a tableau of the dead and dying that would soon be stacked shoulder high on the ground. She shuddered, remembering the battlefield she had crossed in the journey from Agda to Bistonia. There had been no victors that day—except for Black Qar.

Reaching the lofty gates of the fortress, the frosty-haired swordswoman readied lies to persuade the guards to allow her entry. She passed beneath the portal without incident. Scores of green-clad soldiers hurried about her, and none paid her the slightest mind except to cast an appreciative eye in her direction.

Was security this lax? Lijena wondered. What if Yannis sent a saboteur into Rakell? Poisons in the water, food supplies destroyed, a postern gate left open at the wrong time; any of a dozen fatal tactics might be pursued by a spy within the walls.

The hilt of her sword warmed to her touch. Lijena stopped and stared at the top of the fortress' high walls. Seated cross-legged, quietly chanting, burning incenses, and appearing oblivious to the bustle below were several men and women in dark robes.

Prince Felrad protects his refuge by magic, she realized. Lijena had no idea what reaction a spy's entry into Rakell's fortress would produce. She could only guess that any with malicious intent would be noticed and quickly dealt with.

Unchallenged, she walked into the center of Prince Felrad's powerful stronghold. The intense activity around her had momentarily driven from her thoughts the primary purpose in coming here. She would hand over the Sword of Kwerin to its true owner after she finished her personal business with Nelek Kahl and Berenicis the Blackheart. Her fist closed so tightly around the sword hilt that her knuckles glowed white.

Shouts drew her attention to the left. She glanced down a narrow alleyway that ran off the main avenue she walked. Her heart quickened.

Kahl! Lijena hastened into the alley, stumbling over scattered debris and dodging crates carelessly discarded. Before she reached the far end of the alley, she knew her revenge would be complete. *Berenicis!*

Both turned and moved northward along another street; still they were within her grasp!

Lijena exploded from the mouth of the alleyway and spun after the pair. What she saw froze her from toes to the pit of her stomach.

"Davin!" The name almost choked her. How could it be?

The Jyotian adventurer stood next to Nelek Kahl, engaged in an animated discussion. Kahl nodded often, then smiled and slapped Davin on the back. Lijena watched through narrowed, unblinking eyes of aquamarine.

Memories of avowed love flittered through her mind—the love Davin Anane had proclaimed for her. Lies! All of it had been lies. And she had almost believed those lies—almost.

Now she knew the horrible truth: Davin Anane and the slaver were in league. That Berenicis stood a short distance away while they talked implicated the three in her misery. No matter that the animosity between Davin and Berenicis seemed real—they had all wronged her.

Nelek Kahl had bought her from her betrothed, Amrik Tohon, and sold her to a cruel mage. Berenicis Blackheart had betrayed her and attempted to trade her to Lorennion for the sheath to the Sword of Kwerin.

And Davin Anane? His crimes were the worst of all. She had been possessed with a demon at his behest. He had lied to her, made promises to love only to gain advantage, had humiliated and degraded her at every turn.

All three would now die!

Lijena's hand closed on the sword's hilt. Against mortals the blade functioned as any other devoid of even a hint of magicks. No matter! The edge was sharp, and Lijena was skilled. She sucked in a steadying breath and strode forward.

Her plan for vengeance raced through her mind. A quick draw and hard downcut would neatly sever Berenicis' head from his shoulders. She would step back, widen her stance, slash backhanded, and open Nelek Kahl's gut. By this time Davin Anane would have recovered from his shock of seeing his soul allies dying in pools of their own blood. She would have to lunge forward and take his sword arm. Thus disabled,

Davin Anane would fall quickly to her sword.

Berenicis, Kahl, then Davin Anane last, and her quest for revenge would be sated!

Lijena tried not to break into a run that would attract their attention. But Jajhana did not favor Lijena Farleigh that hour. From the walls of the fortress came the cry, "Zarek Yannis! His ships land! *The Faceless Ones!*"

All three of her intended victims pivoted as one and ran toward the central keep of the fortress. Lijena attempted to follow, but the sudden rush of people in the streets blocked her. The trio of villains vanished from her sight.

Personal vengeance would have to wait. The cries that rang out about her told her the time to find Prince Felrad was at hand!

chapter 19

SOUL-SHATTERING THUNDER rolled over the stone walls of Rakell's fortress. Beyond those massive walls came the screams of men and women who ran from the abandoned city to seek sanctuary with their chosen prince.

The ground trembled beneath Lijena's feet, and deafening thunder crashed overhead again. The storms that had stayed offshore now pounded relentlessly against the fortress. A wall of gale-whipped rain raked across Rakell, drowning flames that had been set to destroy the city and rob Zarek Yannis and his troops of shelter.

Yet no rain fell inside the fortress' staunch walls. No wind gusted. Even the damp smell of a storm failed to reach Lijena's flared nostrils.

Dumbfounded, Bistonia's fairest daughter stood in the middle of the street, along with hundreds of others, confused and bewildered. She looked toward the fortress' entrance. Green-clad soldiers slammed the massive gates and barred them as the last of Rakell's citizens stormed through. Although their movements were crisp and smart, the soldiers' expressions said that they were as confused and frightened as everyone else.

Her gaze rose slowly, past the gate's giant locking bars to the walkway circling the walls. There the mages she had seen when first entering the fortress still sat and chanted. A red nimbus bathed their huddled bodies. They shimmered, fading in and out of focus. Closer they leaned, so that each touched another. Like the links of a steel chain, the physical contact augmented their power. The red light surrounding the clustered magicians flared outward in a glowing sphere.

"They hold back Yannis' mages!" a woman shouted behind Lijena. A man answered in a breathless voice. "They're doing it! By the gods, they're doing it!"

Lijena stared with mouth agape. The power directed against that small knot of sorcerers mounted. Even though she was no mage, Lijena felt it. The Sword of Kwerin's tingling magical sense burned beneath her grip, fueled by spells and magical forces now assaulting the fortress.

The man who had cried out so joyously a few seconds earlier gasped in terror.

A *thing* rose above the wall!

A serpent it was! But like no serpent Lijena had ever seen before.

Fully as thick as a horse, the coiled horror lofted through the air on dragonlike wings attached midway between tail and head. And that head! A viper's head, flat and triangular. Unblinking yellow-green eyes, slitted by the blackest of blacks, glared down on the fortress.

Writhing with the sinuous grace of a reptile, the black-scaled creature battered and lashed at the walls. Jagged chunks of stone and mortar the size of boulders tore from the ramparts.

Screams rose from those trapped at the base of the fortress' wall, terror-filled cries that abruptly died beneath the hail of shattered masonry. Twenty men, women, and children lay crushed and mangled beneath the fallen stone.

The shrill screams rose the instant the winged giant fluttered from the boiling black cloud that had borne it over the battlements. The flying serpent dipped. Strong jaws gaped, then snapped closed. Three died, bodies severed in twain. Lijena could no longer distinguish whether the victims were men or women.

Again and again those gargantuan jaws opened to expose a mouth filled with serrated teeth. And when they closed, Felrad's minions lessened by one, two, five.

The mages struggling on the walkways atop the fortress

walls held back only the imponderable force of the magical storms Zarek Yannis sent to blast the Prince's stronghold. They were powerless to stop this ravaging magical beast whose ilk had never before been seen in Raemllyn.

Lijena stood and stared, knowing what she must do—and fearing it. The creature alighted on stubby, taloned legs that protruded from its scaled belly beneath its wide wings.

Lijena swallowed and drew a deep breath.

And gagged! The stench of death surrounding the serpent was like a foul wind blowing directly across an open graveyard. The monster's neck arched high, and it glared at the crowds that fled below it.

Lijena stared up into yellow eyes fully the size of a warrior's round shield. Hatred reflected from those giant orbs—the hatred Zarek Yannis harbored for Prince Felrad.

Steeled by the resolve that she held the only weapon that might stand against the winged gargantuan, Lijena unsheathed the Sword of Kwerin Bloodhawk and advanced. Against ordinary mortals, the sword proved of no more use than any other weapon, but against the magical. . . .

Lijena Farleigh hoped it worked as well against this gigantic beast as it did against the Faceless.

A wing swept along the street at knee-level. Ten soldiers who rushed toward the monstrous serpent died—arms, legs, and torsos sheared off in a bloody welter.

Lijena judged distance, saw the wing sweeping toward her—and swung.

The spell-forged blade bit deeply without a trace of resistance. Like steel through water it cut, clearly severing the leathery appendage. Green ichor spewed into the air from the creature's wounded side. The serpent *thing* screeched . . . in anger?

In pain?

Had she truly wounded it? Lijena didn't know. Nor did she have time to consider the clash of magicks her hand, wrist, and arm worked. Regaining her balance, she spun, lashing out with the Bloodhawk's sword once again. For the second time, the ensorcelled blade found magic-spawned flesh.

An open, questing talon flew through the air and vanished into nothingness. A shower of ichorous blood fumed and boiled around the weaponswoman. Vapors hissed into the air wherever the creature's blood struck the ground—fumes that she was certain were deadly if inhaled.

Holding her breath, Lijena rushed forward with the Sword of Kwerin held high.

Whether she slipped on the bloody street or was nudged by the unseen hand of some magnanimous god or goddess, she didn't know, but she fell. Face down she tumbled atop cobblestone, her magic-forged sword clutched before her in both hands.

Lijena felt an instant of slight resistance when the blade's honed tip sliced into the giant serpent's exposed underbelly. In the next heartbeat, fetid air exploded around her. A searing gale-force wind lashed above her head. Flames licked over her back, burning away her clothing as if she'd brushed into a fiery furnace.

The *thing* vented a scream that held nothing in common with any living creature. It writhed, and it vanished as quickly as it had appeared.

Lijena lay on the ground, gasping, sucking cool air into her lungs. Then she rose, hands clutching to her the scorched remnants of her clothing. She glanced around, gaze alighting on a soldier who had died in the fray. Repugnant as it was, she rose, stripped away the man's hand-tooled leather tunic and green uniform. With shaking hands, she donned them, then cleaned the blade. Her eyes rose to the sky.

The storm clouds boiled and threatened around the fortress' heights, but no new demons leaped to attack the walls. Unspoken praise for the mages' ability died on Lijena's lips.

Those valiant few sorcerers had perished, their lifeless bodies dangling limply over the edge of the walkway. In their place stood a lone figure dressed entirely in black. A woman who wildly waved her arms, while her hands traced arcane signs in the air to fight back the storm Yannis' wizards hurled against the stronghold.

"Valora!" Lijena gasped aloud.

She blinked, once again lost in confusion. Did the treacherous bitch now cast her lot with Prince Felrad? It must be!

Valora singlehandedly held back Zarek Yannis' entire magical attack. In the lightning flashes, Lijena saw the sorceress' pale fingers working in complex patterns. From her fingertips danced a series of fat blue sparks that leapt up into the engulfing, roiling cloud. Every spot in the cloud that the sparks touched hissed and exploded and normalcy returned.

Like wildfire, the spot in the thundercloud spread until only fluffy, small white clouds drifted away from Rakell. The clear, clean blue sky appeared, and a bright spring sun beat down on the fortress. Valora relaxed, hands lowered to rest on the edge of the wall.

Valora serves Felrad? Lijena shook her head, unable to accept what she had witnessed. *And Berenicis? What of Kahl and Davin?* It couldn't be. The knaves disguised themselves as Felrad's allies while they plotted to destroy Raemllyn's true ruler. That had to be it!

More than personal revenge fired the heart of the daughter of Bistonia. Valora had provided a brief respite for Yannis' attack. Lijena knew that she had to work quickly if she wanted to find Davin, Kahl and Berenicis. When Yannis struck again it might be too late. She *had* to find the three and kill them! Not for herself, but to save the world!

Hand on sword hilt, Lijena started in the direction in which the trio had disappeared when the attack had begun. The central keep rose stolidly in the center of the fortress. Lijena found herself caught up in the flow of men and materiel entering a side door. She didn't mind. The anonymity of the crowd allowed her to keep a sharp eye out for the men she sought.

She left the workers and slipped to a side corridor that ran to the prince's deserted audience chamber. A voice called out, stopping her before she entered:

"You, there! What are you doing here?"

Lijena looked up. An officer in Felrad's guard approached, ready to draw his blade.

"I . . ." Lijena stumbled, gathered her thoughts, and began again. "I have a message for Lord Berenicis. Where can I find him?"

"Berenicis?" The officer frowned and shook his head. "Haven't seen either him or Prince Felrad since the attack began."

"Berenicis is with Prince Felrad?" Lijena cursed under her breath. Why did the pretender to the Velvet Throne choose to ally himself with such scum? Didn't Felrad realize the de-throned Jyotian ruler's true colors?

"Aye, that he is. But the other ones. I forget their names. They are upstairs."

"The others? Davin Anane and Goran One-eye?" she asked.

"Those are the ones." The officer brightened. This intruder obviously knew those who so disturbed the normal workings of the fortress. "They and their women have the suite at the far end of the upper living-quarters corridor."

"It is Berenicis I seek." Lijena started to ask after Nelek Kahl, but the guard had already moved on in response to a small altercation outside.

If Berenicis and Prince Felrad were on the walls overseeing the battle, and Nelek Kahl was someplace she didn't know, then Davin Anane was the one she'd first deal with, even though Lijena's pleasure would have been greatest saving that black-guard for last.

She found the stairs and mounted them, spiraling upward until she came to the living quarters. The corridor was emptied. Lijena hastened to a door at the end of the hall, edged it open, and peered inside.

Two women paced relentlessly. Lijena strained to overhear them as they talked.

". . . the first attack failed. What will that Qar-damned fiend do next?"

A redheaded woman answered the blonde, "Zarek Yannis only toys with the prince. Those weren't the true attacks. When he unleashes the Faceless Ones, *that* will be the beginning of the battle."

"Prince Felrad's archers find it impossible to reach Yannis' human troops. They've camped too far away," the blonde said. "That means Zarek Yannis is constructing siege machines—catapults."

"You are more familiar with such tactics," said the redhead. "But for my part, I do not intend to idle away the hours while Davin is fighting for Rakell. I intend to join him."

"Agreed," the blonde answered with sudden resolve. "What do they take us for? Flowers to be hidden away for only a moment's viewing? All that we endured to reach this point must show our worth!"

"This against a Faceless might not be much, but it is better than no dagger at all!" The redhead lifted a knife high and let it glint in the sunlight that entered from a window.

At the same instant that she hefted the blade, she saw Lijena peering in the door. The red-haired woman jerked upright and asked, "Who are you?"

"I am a messenger," Lijena answered hastily to cover the discovery. "I am supposed to give a message to . . . Davin Anane."

"He and Goran are patroling the walls, awaiting the Faceless Ones' attack," the blonde replied.

"I must find Davin." Lijena found herself staring curiously at the two women.

They were not what she'd expected when the guard had revealed Davin and his one-eyed friend were with women. The blonde had about her an air of nobility, dignity, and strength.

With the other, the one with whom Davin Anane obviously traveled, Lijena wanted to find fault. Although there was a wild look in those emerald eyes, she read more, too: intelligence, worry, suffering and strength, even love. Love for Davin Anane? Was this possible? Lijena's hand relaxed on the hilt of her sword.

"Is something wrong?" the redhead asked.

"No, nothing. Nothing is wrong. You are to stay here," Lijena ordered.

The blonde stiffened, her blue eyes narrowed. "We will accompany you. I am Duchess Kulonna and demand to be taken to Prince Felrad. My friend Awendala will accompany us."

Lijena had been correct in assuming this was a woman of noble birth and unaccustomed to taking orders. How was it she came to be with the uncouth red-bearded giant Goran, Lijena wondered.

For an instant, Lijena's resolve wavered, then it returned steely strong. She guessed that the Prince conferred with others; among them might be Nelek Kahl, Berenicis and Davin Anane. If this duchess could take her to her enemies, all the better. "We will go together, then."

With the Duchess Kulonna and the red-haired Awendala to get her through to Davin, her mission would be accomplished that much sooner. The only question was whether she could also kill Nelek Kahl and Berenicis before turning the Sword of Kwerin over to Prince Felrad. Lijena decided to take the chance that she could. The confusion of the attack masked much. Why not three more deaths?

"We tarry too long," said Awendala. "The waiting is gnawing at me."

Lijena found her heart going out to the woman. Lijena tried to shake the feeling. Perhaps the woman did love Davin Anane, unaware of how treacherous the Jyotian thief truly was. And Lijena was no stranger to love. Chal, her dead Chal, had taught what it was to love and be loved.

The three left the central keep and walked briskly down the streets toward the fortress wall. The citizens recovered from the first attack wave and worked with quiet determination to prepare for the inevitable. Without incident, Lijena reached the base of the stairway leading up to the ramparts.

"We must see Davin Anane immediately," she announced to a guard who blocked the way.

The green-clad man turned and looked up. Lijena's heart almost stopped. Above, Davin spoke with Nelek Kahl!

"He's not to be disturbed. No one goes up unless it is commanded by the prince," the guard finally replied.

"We have information . . ." Lijena started.

Kulonna pushed her aside. "I am the Duchess Kulonna, daughter of Duke Tun. I demand to see Davin Anane. It is a matter of vital importance."

The guard refused to be swayed. But while Kulonna occupied him, Lijena slipped behind the man and started up the broad, stone steps. The Sword of Kwerin Bloodhawk whispered softly as she unsheathed the blade that had slain demons. It would now kill both Nelek Kahl and Davin Anane.

She reached the top of the stairs and stopped, looking over the charred plain around Rakell. Lijena gasped when she saw the size of Yannis' army. She had imagined it to be large, but reality outstripped her mental picture of the scene. Thousands of soldiers, at least twenty thousand, stood ready for the signal to attack.

And standing amid bright, orange flames that danced from the hooves of their mounts were the Faceless Ones. Her mind reeled at their number—more than she'd thought existed in this or any dimensional reality.

Lijena jerked around, sword ready. Yannis prepared for the spearhead thrust of the gates of the fortress with the Faceless demons. She had to kill those she sought and turn the sword over to Prince Felrad before the attack.

Her heart sank when she found the Jyotian thief again. Nelek Kahl had vanished and Berenicis the Blackheart was nowhere to be seen. Only Davin Anane leaned against the stone coping. So be it! He alone would perish before Lijena gave the Sword of Kwerin back to its rightful owner.

She ran forward, blade high. Lijena Farleigh's entire concentration focused on the spot at the back of Davin's neck where the sword would sever his spinal column. Her muscles tensed as she jerked the magical sword high and brought it plummeting down to meet its target.

chapter 20

THE SWORD OF Kwerin Bloodhawk fell like the razor-honed blade of an executioner. And with the cold eye of an executioner come to deliver justice, Lijena Farleigh aimed the weapon's edge to sever Davin Anane's neck in a single blow and send his head leaping from his body.

Although the last son of the House of Anane neither flinched nor ducked, that deadly blade never reached its target.

Lijena gasped and groaned in frustration and alarm when the sword froze in mid-air a fraction of an inch from Davin's vulnerable exposed neck. A massive hand, thick fingers clamping about her wrist like steel bands, held the sword immobile, cancelled the power of her blow as though her arm's strength were that of a newborn babe.

She twisted, turned, and struggled to free herself, but the viselike hand around her slender wrist proved too strong. *"No!* By the gods, no! I will not be cheated. Not now! No!"

"Bah! It's always the skinny ones!" Goran One-Eye glared at Lijena and shook his red-maned head in disgust. "As I've told you again and again and again, Davin my reckless friend, it's always the skinny ones who give you trouble."

The Jyotian thief pivoted at the sound of the Challing's reprimanding voice. His gray eyes went wider when he recognized the sword's wielder. "Lijena!"

"You should guard your back more carefully, Davin," Goran

continued, obviously enjoying his friend's awful position. "If it weren't for my singularly keen eye, quick hand, and superior Challing strength, you would now be fully enwrapped in Qar's embrace. Davin, this streak of trust you carry will surely result in your death one of these days when I'm not there to protect you."

"Lijena!" Davin repeated, dumbfounded.

With a ripple of muscle along his brawny arm, the grinning Challing lifted Lijena until only her toes brushed the stone of Rakell's battlements. Bistonia's fairest daughter twisted, attempting to transfer Kwerin's Sword from right hand to left and finish the task she had started.

"None of that," the Challing chided with a waggle of his head.

He grabbed Lijena's other wrist and held her suspended by both wrists. She kicked, boots slamming into the changeling's shins. If Goran noticed, his gloating grin did not droop to reveal it.

"Nothing has changed." Davin's numbing daze passed, and sorrow filled in his voice as he stared at his would-be assassin. "I find myself with mixed regrets in this. I hoped that one day we would again meet, but I feared it would be like this."

"Beast! Swine! Traitor!" Lijena shrieked out her rage and frustration.

Others along the ramparts glanced around, located the source of the cries, then turned back to Zarek Yannis' army standing outside the fortress' gate. What were one woman's curses when the Faceless Ones rode forth for an assault against the stronghold?

"Beast? Perhaps. Swine, that I won't deny. But traitor? Never!" Davin marveled at the woman's wild beauty.

Even in such a murderous rage, he found her attractive. Yet, gone were the aching pangs of love that had once suffused his breast when he stared at this frosty-haired beauty. If he had worried about the strength of his feelings for Awendala, he now knew. The fiery-tressed woman from Yaryne had completely won his heart.

"Not a traitor? What of you and the slaver Kahl? You and Berenicis? You and Valora?" Lijena struggled, still unable to break free of the powerful hands binding her wrists.

Davin frowned. "My love for Berenicis has not grown since we traveled with the Huata. We have an uneasy truce for Prince Felrad's sake. Valora has aided the prince, and for her I have no feeling one way or the other. But what is this about Nelek Kahl?"

"The slaver. You and that soul-selling fiend are in league!"

"She must be the only one in Rakell who doesn't know!" Goran snorted.

The barrel-chested Challing moved with blinding speed, grabbing the magical sword from her right hand and transferring both of Lijena's wrists to his left fist. Even though her struggles continued unabated, the Challing held her easily at arm's length.

"Know *what?*" demanded Lijena. "That you are a shape-changing, hell-spawned whoreson? That I spit on you both?"

Goran spun her about so that her spittle missed and sailed through the air toward the gathering Faceless Ones. Several soldiers alongside mistook her gesture as one of defiance against Zarek Yannis and cheered.

"The slaver you so condemn is none other than Felrad," Davin answered.

"Liar!"

"She *is* the only one in Rakell who doesn't know," Goran said with obvious amazement. "Not only is she skinny, she's also stupid!"

"I came here from Nawat on Kahl's pleasure ship. I know that he and Prince Felrad are *not* the same!" Lijena attempted to plant a booted toe in Goran's groin and found herself snatched rudely from the ground.

"She even travels with him and fails to see the truth." Goran shook the helpless woman. "Let me drop her over the side, Davin. Please."

Without so much as a grunt of strain, Goran hoisted Lijena up and over the battlements to dangle her there like a living marionette. The hundred-foot drop beneath the swordswoman did not slow her kicking feet nor her curses. If anything, she fought the harder!

"Goran! Bring her back behind the wall," Davin shouted at his friend. "I have no desire to see Yannis' archers use her as a target."

With obvious reluctance, Goran One-Eye heaved Lijena

back and cast her down to the stone flagging. She glowered at the pair of rogues from her hands and knees.

"Careful that she doesn't bite your leg," warned Goran. "Her teeth are small, but they look sharp enough to take off a kneecap. The way her spittle foams, she well may be rabid."

"It's true," Davin said, ignoring the Challing and pleading with Lijena. "Kahl and Prince Felrad are the same man. The prince used the slaver's guise to enable free movement about Raemllyn. Yannis never questioned a slaver who paid all the proper bribes. How else do you think Felrad succeeded in entering Kavindra and issuing the challenge that brought Yannis here?"

"Prince Felrad is a good man. He'd not trade in human flesh, even to fight the usurper." Lijena spat again.

Davin's chest heaved, and he sighed in exasperation. "You came here on the ship from Nawat with him. Think, woman, think! Did nothing during the trip strike you as unusual?"

"Kahl kept company with Berenicis Blackheart!"

"Berenicis is Felrad's agent. We both knew that when we encountered him in the Huata caravan, although I doubted his claim. Was there nothing else?" Davin demanded.

"Kahl did not make use of the concubines," Lijena admitted reluctantly. "That seemed unusual for a slaver with such a black reputation."

"Those weren't concubines aboard the ship, you bitch wench!" This from Goran One-Eye. "Those were wives and lovers of men already in Rakell. Felrad traveled about gathering them to him, 'purchasing' them as necessary to reunite families. An odd practice, but one he performed."

"Although they knew the danger was greater in Rakell than in other parts of Raemllyn, the women wanted to be with their husbands. Prince Felrad, in his disguise as Nelek Kahl, helped them come here." Davin added while he motioned impatiently for Lijena to get to her feet.

"I've never heard such a crack-brained story in all my life," Lijena's anger flared anew as she pushed to her feet. For a moment, she had almost believed the two thieves.

"I have." Goran snorted in unrestrained disgust. "You should hear *his* campfire tales of how he loves you."

"Goran!" Davin arched an eyebrow to silence his friend. To

Lijena, he said, "This is the truth. I know of no other way to prove it than to give you back the Sword of Kwerin. Do with it as you see fit."

Davin nodded to Goran One-eye. "Give her back the sword. Let her do her worst."

The Challing started to protest, then shrugged his massive shoulders. Humans were too emotional and did things that led them to suicidal action, yet that uncertainty thrilled him. Goran silently admitted to himself that returning the sword would prove an interesting experiment.

Lijena yanked the blade from Goran's hand and stared at Davin. "You know what I will do with this?"

"Go on, kill Berenicis. It's nothing more than I desire. I suppose you'll try to kill me, too. Do so, if you doubt my story."

"That Kahl is Prince Felrad?"

"There's an easy way to prove it," Goran offered, "though I'd hate to interfere in such a touching scene. I also doubt she desires proof of the truth. Find Felrad and introduce the two, Davin. If that doesn't convince her, she's skinny, stupid, and *blind*. Besides, her sword rightfully belongs to the prince anyway."

Lijena's grip tightened about the hilt of the magic-forged sword, but the blade did not rise. "Take me to Kahl. If his explanation ill-suits me, then I shall have both your hearts. Then I take the head of this fat one for good measure." She glanced at Goran to leave no doubt of whom she spoke.

"*Fat!* You called me fat!" Goran bellowed his indignation. "By Nyuria's pitchfork, the skinny wench *is* blind! Davin, let me toss her over the wall and be done with her for once and for all. She's been a painful thorn in our sides far too . . ."

A howl like that of hounds unleashed from the bowels of lowest Peyneeha rent the air. Thoughts of betrayal and personal vengence died before that unholy yowl. Beyond the fortress' walls, the Faceless Ones charged!

Across the barren, charred plain, thundered a full hundred hell-riders. Their demonic horses' hooves kicked embers into the air rather than sod and dust—a fiery shower that sparkled and flared in the afternoon like bits of the sun itself. Now those hooves provided the only sound of attack. After that one, blood-chilling battle cry, the Faceless Ones rode silently, bony hands clutching their swords of crystalline fire.

The stronghold's defenders did not still their voices. Shouting defiant curses down onto the demon warriors, Felrad's archers unleashed their first flight of arrows. Like a black cloud, the whistling missiles arched into the air and fell short of the front of the Faceless Ones' rank. A second flight hailed from the ramparts but heartbeats later—steel heads and wooden shafts finding their targets.

The Faceless Ones rode on, their mounts' long strides unfaltering.

"They do not fall!" Lijena gasped in horror. "See? That one has a dozen or more arrows embedded in its body and still it comes. And there, that demon carries at least six shafts. Still they charge!"

"Not for long," said Goran. The Challing stood as if frozen. The flames of witch-fire burned within the depths of the changeling's single, gold-flecked jade orb. "They ride—for now."

Even as Goran spoke, a hush settled over the Rakell defenders. Through the silence came a strong, high voice; Valora worked her magicks!

Yannis' one-time master mage chanted, invoking the spells that might save Felrad's troops from the demon-born riders. The air about the stone fortress crackled as though alive with an unseen force that radiated outward from the black-robed sorceress.

"The Faceless! They fall!" a soldier two strides from Lijena shouted.

Every hell-rider that had been struck by an arrow writhed in the saddle as Valora's spell took effect. The arrows' protruding shafts glowed a brilliant red.

With a prayer of hope on his lips, Davin watched the Faceless Ones struggling to yank the offending barbs from their bodies—and fail! One after another, the arrow-skewered Faceless lost control of their demonic mounts. The fire-hooved animals veered wildly, colliding with other horses that ran at their sides. Though no hell-horse toppled, here and there the Faceless Ones fell from their saddles. It was as if the demons had drunk too much summer wine and now suffered the heady effects.

"They collide with each other, aye, and they fall," Goran said. "I see much out there, but this only slows them. The Faceless do not die."

Davin saw that the Challing spoke the truth. For every Faceless One with a magical arrow disorienting it, two more rode through the ragged rank to attack Rakell's gates.

"More arrows!" Lijena urged the archers on the ramparts beside her. "Give them more arrows!"

A third flight launched, as if at her command. But these shafts seemed to move through treacle. Slowly, inch by agonizing inch, they crept away from bowstring, into air, toward the top of their arc, then downward. The charging Faceless Ones were already well past when the arrows struck.

"Zarek Yannis' mage casts his spells," said Goran. "Valora cannot cope with her counterpart and his assistants. Valora is alone. Oh, why cannot I summon more!"

The Challing's head jerked back, and he glared at the heavens. A roar more bestial than human rolled from Goran's chest and tore from his twisted lips. The heart of frustration, anger, and rage dwelled in that anguished cry.

Davin's right arm snaked out and wrenched Lijena from the Challing's side as the Jyotian backstepped. Whether by intent or sparked by Goran's helplessness, Davin didn't know, but the changeling's entire body was abruptly enveloped by the glowing green of witch-fire.

Again the Challing threw back his head and roared at the heavens. Like a comet, the flaring witch-fire leapt from Goran's flesh to coalesce above his head and fountain into the sky. Outward it raced, arcing above the Faceless Ones.

It exploded; huge gouts of green fire showered down on the hell-riders. Every demon touched by that emerald witch-fire trembled and quaked. Arms, legs, and heads vanished beneath the fountain of Challing-born magicks.

Even this failed to stop the Faceless as they smashed fiercely against the gates!

Weakened by the burst of magicks that had torn from his body, mind, and soul, Goran One-Eye staggered, stumbling back against the battlements for support. Even with solid rock behind him, his legs refused to support his massive weight.

The Challing collapsed, his single eye rolling dizzily in his head.

Along the ramparts, Felrad's soldiers struggled with pots of boiling oil, moving the caldrons to davits, tipping them, and spilling the fuming contents onto the demons.

Such a searing rain would have sent human soldiers scurrying back in screaming retreat. Not so with the Faceless Ones. They seemed no more troubled than if they'd stepped out into a gentle spring shower.

"They're through the gates!" a cry of horror rose from within the fortress.

Davin's head jerked around as he helped Goran to his feet. A spike of ice jabbed at the base of his spine. *"Awendala!"*

The Jyotian's flaming-tressed lover stood at the foot of the stairs leading from the wall to the staging area immediately behind the gates. She stood only a few yards away from the invading Faceless Ones!

"Kulonna!" This from Goran who now saw his blonde duchess at Awendala's side. "What is she doing here?"

Davin didn't answer, but spun about and grabbed for the Sword of Kwerin in Lijena's hand. The daughter of Bistonia jerked it away from his fingers, defiantly staring at him, daring him to try for the blade again.

Davin made no attempt. He wasted time with the madwoman when Awendala's life was in danger. Twisting about, the heir to the House of Anane raced down the steps, steel sword in hand. He leaped from a landing, alighting before the oncoming horde of hell-horse mounted demons.

Like a madman who saw his death and no longer feared, Davin hefted his blade in a two-handed grasp and met the attack. He slashed and hacked with a berserker's fury upon him. Nor did he care that his sword did little more than cause the Faceless to rein around him.

"He can't fight two of them!" cried Lijena to Goran when she saw a pair of the demons swing from their fire-snorting horses and move toward Davin.

The Challing didn't answer. Goran followed his companion-in-arms down the stairs to take a wide-legged, defiant stance at Kulonna's side. His heavy, double-edged battle-ax swung in wide arcs, not killing as it would have with human foes, but keeping the demons at bay.

Bastard-born whoreson or not, Lijena could not let Davin die thusly. *She*, not Yannis' demon warriors would be responsible for sending his soul to Black Qar, and in her own time!

The Sword of Kwerin Bloodhawk hefted high, she took the steps leading below three at a time. Reaching the landing, she leaped to where Davin battled so futilely against the two Faceless Ones.

"Don't let them touch you. It is death!" she shouted a warning to the Jyotian swordsman.

Davin staggered back beneath the force of an overhead blow delivered by a Faceless One directly in front of him. Steel sword met weapon of demonic fire—and the steel lost. The blade nicked, chipped, melted at every point of contact with that potent crystalline weapon.

Victory burned in the coal-red eyes flaring within the Faceless' cowl as though they saw Davin as a dead man. Again the blade of crystalline fire rose for the killing stroke.

Lijena interposed herself between Davin and the demon. The Sword of Kwerin leaped up to shatter the creature's sword, then plunged downward. The tip of the magical blade touched the Faceless One's chest and skewered it from breast bone to spine.

The monstrous creature gave a curious sigh, as though relieved that death claimed it, then crumpled to the ground to evaporate in a steaming cloud of greasy black smoke.

Davin dived and tackled Lijena, throwing her out of range as the other Faceless One attacked. Its blade missed—then its hand was crushed into powder by the side of Goran's heavy ax.

Davin looked up to see the Challing deftly flick the ax sideways and catch the Faceless One at eye level. The demon staggered back and fell flat on its back. Dead? Davin didn't know. All that mattered was that it no longer moved.

"The demon's own blade!" Lijena shouted as she shoved to her feet. "Take up the Faceless One's sword!"

Davin cast aside his melted blade and hesitantly reached for the Faceless One's fallen weapon. His fingers closed about the hilt. Like a vapor it moved in his grip, responding to the slightest flick of his wrist with ease. A grin spread across his face. Although not the Bloodhawk's blade, the sword would serve his purpose. Without further pause, he stood and faced a demon warrior who charged down on him.

Ducking beneath a sword stroke meant for his head, Davin swung the blade of crystal flame with both arms, aiming not at the rider, but its mount. Like a blade of steel cutting into mortal flesh, the demon sword he wielded slashed into the animal's left hindleg.

Horse and rider fell. The latter never rose again. Lijena was on the Faceless before it could scramble to its feet. The Sword of Kwerin Bloodhawk rose and fell, and one less demon threatened Felrad's stronghold.

There was no time for words of praise or even appreciative glances. The Faceless still reined their hellish horses through the fortress' open gates. A fighting team born of desperation—Davin Anane, armed with his demon-forged blade, and Lijena Farleigh, wielding a sword once held by Raemllyn's first High King—met the attack.

Davin cast but one glance over his shoulder. His eyes found Awendala and Kulonna as Goran hastened them up the stairs to where Berenicis the Blackheart waited at the edge of the battlement walkway. When Goran turned and raced back down the stairs, Davin's attention once more returned to the fray, with the knowledge that the woman he loved was beyond danger, at least for the moment.

chapter 21

BERENICIS THE BLACKHEART watched as the Faceless Ones drove forward through the cascades of Valora's ensorcelled arrows and breached the massive gates of Rakell as if those ponderous wooden slabs meant nothing. A pang of fear rose and died within the man as new possibilities came to him. Berenicis appreciated the stark power inherent in those hell-riders as much as he feared them.

The Jyotian lord walked to the edge of the walkway and peered down into the area immediately behind the gates. To his surprise, Prince Felrad's troops had allowed the Faceless Ones in by unbarring the gates.

He frowned. That could only mean that they attempted to allow a portion within, then bar the gates and hoped to eliminate the demon-spawns inside the fortress. By the time the remaining Faceless battered down the gates, Felrad's protectors would be recovered and ready for a second assault.

Or so he viewed the tactic of desperation. It was a madman's plan. But then Felrad was a madman to even think of opposing the usurper's army of mounted demons. In the end, all within the fortress would perish, and he along with them. Unless he could . . .

By the gods! What is this?

Below, a frosty-haired amazon met the hell-riders without fear. The blade she wielded exploded with a shower of blue-white sparks when it met the Faceless' swords. And should her steel nick or merely touch one of the demons, the creature dissolved in writhing black smoke.

Lijena! Berenicis' mind raced. The weaponswoman below was Lijena Farleigh! And in her hands was the Sword of Kwerin Bloodhawk!

How had she and the ancient blade come here? Had Felrad known of her presence and kept it from him? The dethroned ruler of Jyotis didn't know, but the spell-bound sword explained the gates that closed below. Protect the sword wielder at all costs!

Hell creature after creature fell before that singing, blazing sword. This was not Prince Felrad's only weapon, Berenicis saw. The prince had withheld much from him, and against this perfidy Berenicis seethed.

Davin Anane picked up one of the Faceless Ones' crystalline swords and used it against the demons. Goran One-Eye proved less effective with his battle-ax, but still the trio presented a frightful weapon against Yannis' demons.

Berenicis' agile mind worked through the possibilities. If he had been the one to return with the Sword of Kwerin, he would have been a hero in Prince Felrad's eyes. No longer. Those three turned the tide of battle against the Faceless Ones, and for that they would be held in Felrad's favor. And Berenicis knew none of the three would be inclined to aid Berenicis the Blackheart in his dream of total domination of Raemllyn. Worse, either Lijena or Davin might request Berenicis' head as a boon from their prince!

"Felrad might actually carry this day if he can destroy all of Yannis' hell-riders. The gods be damned," Berenicis cursed aloud.

"What?"

A feminine voice drew Berenicis' attention. Kulonna and Awendala came running up the stairs, panting heavily as they reached his side. The Jyotian lord's gray eyes sparked at recognized opportunity.

"Come with me," Berenicis ordered. "We must hurry if we are to carry out the prince's wishes."

"What? Prince Felrad is there." Kulonna pointed to where Felrad and Valora stood, working out new magical tactics to employ against the Faceless Ones outside the closed fortress gates.

"There isn't time for a discussion. Our prince commands!" Berenicis grabbed Kulonna and tugged her toward a distant staircase.

Without the duchess, Berenicis had nothing. With her, he held a valuable bargaining point with Zarek Yannis—and more. The usurper's power would be diminished this day, win or lose. With Duke Tun swearing allegiance to Zarek Yannis—on pain of his daughter's torture and death—northwest Raemllyn would come under the usurper's tight rein.

"No, damn you. Release me and explain yourself." Kulonna tried to jerk free, but couldn't break the lord's grip.

Awendala rushed to her aid. "Release her!" She brandished the dagger she'd taken from Davin.

"Come with me. Felrad has ordered me to take you to safety," Berenicis said.

"You seek to flee like a craven!" accused Awendala.

Berenicis moved like a striking snake. Releasing Kulonna, his right hand freed a dirk at his waist while his left hand grasped Awendala's wrist. He stepped forward, turned, and drove the dagger into Awendala's heart.

She gasped, straightened, then fell from the walkway to crash into the paving below, no more than a dozen paces from where Davin Anane and Lijena fought the Faceless Ones.

"You. . . ." Kulonna's eyes widened. "You're no coward. You're a traitor!"

"Traitor?" mocked Berenicis. "Hardly. Always, I have been true to my own best interests. With others now preeminent in the prince's pantheon of heroes, I stand little chance of gaining even the throne of Jyotis, as he'd promised. To obtain the Sword of Kwerin Bloodhawk, Prince Felrad would do anything—anything!"

Kulonna fought, struggling to pick up a weapon, to wrench free, to stop Berenicis. The Blackheart laughed and drove a short jab to the point of the blonde's chin. Kulonna sagged into unconsciousness.

Berenicis threw her over his shoulder like a sack of meal and descended the small, spiraling stairs to a dirt path that led along the fortress' inner walls to the stables. There Berenicis tossed Kulonna over the back of a waiting saddle and horse, then mounted.

A small trap-maze, a swift sword to dispatch the guardsman, a hidden door in the wall, and Berenicis rode out toward Zarek Yannis' distant skirmish lines.

Only his bearing, and the promise that Yannis would skin alive any who failed to deliver a refugee from Rakell, bought the Blackheart an audience with Zarek Yannis' master mage, Hamor-Lorn.

"You do have the aspect of the former lord of Jyotis," said the mage when Berenicis at last stood before him. "Why would you defect? Surely, you see how the prince makes a mockery of our most potent weapon?"

"The Faceless Ones? Yes, Felrad is doing well in that regard. How many has he killed?"

"Fully twenty of the demon-riders are no longer among our rank," Hamor-Lorn answered. "Valora is strong, but not that strong. Has the Prince regained the sword?"

Berenicis nodded. "It is because of that I decided to cast my allegiance with King Zarek."

Hamor-Lorn closed his eyes, letting his mind read what was not apparent in the Jyotian lord's words. "You lost the sword and fear others will reap the rewards of its return. What you do is dangerous, Blackheart. If Yannis is defeated, you will be the most-sought criminal in all Raemllyn."

"And if you quickly triumph, what reward is Yannis likely to shower upon me?" Berenicis countered.

"Jyotis?" Hamor-Lorn suggested.

"The territory from Faldin to Cahri," Berenicis replied.

"There are problems with passing control of such a large territory to you. Not the least of which is Duke Tun. His influence is great in the north."

"If I married the duke's daughter, would that not give a more legitimate claim to such territory?" asked Berenicis.

"The blonde bitch you brought with you from Rakell? My, my, Lord Berenicis, you are a man to be reckoned with. But there is more, is there not? You know our position—that much is obvious. You bring us a way of defeating Felrad and insuring yourself a full quarter of Raemllyn?"

"There is a gate still unguarded." Berenicis lightly touched his sword to indicate why Felrad was so careless in posting his men. "But this lack will soon be discovered unless you act swiftly. A score or two of Faceless Ones through this gate, coupled with a full-scale frontal assault, will rush Felrad and Rakell!"

Hamor-Lorn smirked and nodded his white-haired head. "I am sure King Yannis will be pleased to discuss this matter with you." Hamor-Lorn clapped his hands. A dozen soldiers acted as honor guard to lead Berenicis the Blackheart to his newfound ally.

chapter 22

LIJENA FARLEIGH LUNGED and drove the Faceless One back with the tip of the Sword of Kwerin Bloodhawk. Before the hissing, hell-spawned human mockery could recover, she flicked her wrist and spun the ensorcelled blade in a tight circle, bringing it high above her head. Then, with all the might she could muster, she brought the sword plummeting down.

The ancient blade struck home, slicing into the Faceless' black cowl, biting through the creature's skull—if the demon had a skull! It died without sound, greasy fingers of dark smoke escaping from its collapsing robe and twisting toward the sky.

Lijena spun about, sword leveled to meet a new attack. None came.

"The last of them." This from Davin Anane, whose arms sagged beneath the weight of the Faceless One's blade he carried. "Can it truly be that we defeat them? That mere mortals could possibly kill. . . ."

Davin's gray eyes surveyed the scene that surrounded the fortress' gate as though unable to comprehend what he saw. He staggered wearily back, supporting himself against the stone wall.

Lijena's gaze dipped to the blade she clutched, feeling no physical weariness. When Kwerin Bloodhawk's ancient sorcerer had woven his magicks into sword and sheath, he had cast spells that lightened the blade in the bearer's hand so that wielding it did not tax the strength.

"Seven, eight. . . ."

Lijena heard the giant Challing counting behind her as she replaced the sword in the sheath that restored its magic powers. Her gaze lifted to move over the battle scene. More than Faceless had died this day. At least a hundred of Felrad's green-clad soldiers lay dead—warriors who had sacrificed their lives knowing that mere steel could not stand against the demon horde.

This was courage and bravery, she realized. With their blood, these men and women had bought time for her and the sword she carried. Tears that she thought herself no longer capable of shedding rolled down her cheeks.

Davin Anane's gaze lifted to Lijena. *Magnificent* echoed in his head as he studied the swordswoman. She had fought with a cool, unwavering fury, had met and defeated every Faceless One that had ridden through the stronghold's gates.

Once he had envisioned himself as the sword bearer, now he realized that Goran One-Eye's distant prophecy had unfolded. No man, but a woman bore the Sword of Kwerin Bloodhawk to Prince Felrad.

". . . fifteen, sixteen . . ." The red-bearded Challing's voice trailed off. A pitiful cry-groan escaped Goran's trembling lips. "By Father Yehseen, no. *No!*"

Davin's head snapped around. Then he, too, saw. The blood rushed from his head, and drums pounded in his temples. The weakness in his arms and legs doubled, but he forced his body forward, trying to deny the cruel vision before him.

"Davin, what is. . . ." Lijena swallowed the rest of the question.

There at the base of the fortress' wall she saw the reason for the tears that flowed without shame down the Jyotian's dirt-and-sweat-smeared cheeks. Awendala's body lay gracelessly sprawled on the stone, unmoving, lifeless.

Knees gone liquid, body trembling, Davin Anane kept beside the oh-so-still form of the woman he lo . . .

. . . Had *loved*. Ugly reality wedged itself into the Jyotian's numbed mind. What Awendala and he had shared was gone, a thing permanently assigned to the past. Gone, stolen from him! Nor would his agile mind, quick fingers, or strong sword arm avail him now. Davin Anane, master thief of Raemllyn, reckless adventurer, daring freebooter, was helpless. "Yehseen, why? Damn you! *Why?*"

"Davin." Goran walked to his friend's side and placed a massive hand on the young Jyotian's shoulder.

As those strong fingers squeezed their sympathy, the Challing attempted to speak words of comfort. Only choked sobs passed his trembling lips. Tears flowed from his single good eye and from beneath the fox-fur patch covering the socket of his left.

"Her death wasn't in vain. She died fighting Zarek Yannis." Lijena strove to find the words that would rob Davin's loss of its painful, bitter sting . . . and failed.

To her surprise, she found that she cared that no gentle phrases of comfort would come to her, that she was lost in the sorrow of the moment. More, she discovered that Davin's suffering was her own. She knew the agony of losing one so dearly loved, knew the grief that would never pass. Her own Chal's life, love, and death remained with her always.

Davin's trembling fingers reached out and hesitantly touched the hilt of the dagger thrust with cruel force into Awendala's breast, its tip driven to pierce her gentle heart. "How? She was on the battlements with Kulonna."

The young thief turned his head to Goran One-Eye, his gaze a plea for answers. The Challing's head moved silently from side to side. "My friend, I know not how this vile . . ."

Goran's good eye flew wide with horror; his shaggy-maned head jerked about, lifting toward the ramparts. "Kulonna! Where is Kulonna!"

Davin watched the Challing dash up the stone stairs leading to the battlements three at a time. When the muscular giant stood far above, his head twisted one way, then the other, to scan the stronghold below him. A single name tore from his lips in a questioning roar, "Kulonna?"

The blonde duchess did not answer, nor was she anywhere to be seen.

"Davin!" Goran shouted from above. "She's gone! My Kulonna is gone!"

Davin's head dropped, his gaze returning to Awendala's shattered body. For once Goran would have to fend for himself.

Today, Davin Anane's life had ended here in the spilled blood of the woman he had loved.

"They were here," Goran shouted. "This is where I last saw Kulonna and Awendala."

The Challing bent to one knee and peered at the stone walkway with his right eye. "By the gods! Here, on this spot Awendala was struck. Davin, she died here."

The Jyotian's head lifted again. He saw his friend pointing to the walkway.

"Davin, come up," Goran urged. "Here is where Awendala fell."

Like a man in a trance, Davin answered the Challing's summons. With Lijena following, he climbed the stairs to the ramparts.

"Awendala fell from here. See?" Goran pointed to a damp red stain. "She was killed here, then plunged to the paving below. And it was here I last saw her and Kulonna with Berenicis."

"The Blackheart!" Davin's head snapped straight, his body going rigid.

He remembered glancing over a shoulder to see Awendala and Kulonna running up the stairs to his treacherous brother Berenicis. His body shook, sorrow replaced by hate and anger. "Not again! Not again! It can't be. Berenicis can't have robbed me again!"

"The bastard killed Awendala," Goran said. "And he's taken my Kulonna!"

"We don't know that," Lijena interjected. "What cause would he have for either act? We'll seek him."

Lijena's desire for vengeance rose once again. The Faceless Ones' attack had been met and stopped. Now she could complete the task that brought her to Rakell. Her hand dropped to the hilt of her sword. *Let the whoreson Anane join his beloved in Peyneeha's depths!*

Her hand faltered, refusing to unsheath the blade when her eyes shifted to Davin. What satisfaction was there in taking the life of a broken man? Davin Anane's death was no longer important. The Sitala had dealt him a fate far more cruel than the kiss of death.

"Davin, my friend, I am sorry. Awendala's death diminishes all of us."

A gentle voice drew Lijena's attention to the right. Nelek Kahl approached. He wore the *danne* work tunic she remembered so vividly, and had finely woven Huata lace at his cuffs and collar, but the expression on his handsome face was one of compassion unlike anything she'd expect of a slaver.

"Let her death be reason to fight even harder against Zarek Yannis." Felrad clasped Davin to him.

"The usurper is not responsible for Awendala's death." Davin stepped away from the prince. "Look to our brother. He murdered her."

Prince Felrad stared at the Jyotian as though uncertain he had heard correctly.

"Berenicis!" A feral growl rumbled from Goran's throat. "He's responsible. And he's taken Kulonna!"

"What? No, Goran, you must be wrong. Did no one see what happened?" Prince Felrad looked around.

None of those who gathered had witnessed the deadly scene. All had been too riveted by the fierce battle below, both inside and outside Rakell's gates.

"Order him found, my Prince," Davin demanded. "Berenicis should be here to advise, if nothing else."

"Very well." Felrad motioned to an aide who scuttled off to find the Blackheart. Prince Felrad turned to Lijena and stared at her, as if for the first time. "You look familiar. Who?"

"Lijena Farleigh," she said. Lijena's hand tensed on the hilt of the Sword of Kwerin. The swine didn't even remember the woman he'd sold into slavery!

"The daughter of Chesmu and Leet Farleigh," Prince Felrad replied to Lijena's surprise. "War has not been kind to you and your family."

"Not when Nelek Kahl sells me into slavery to be used by the cruelest mage in Leticia." She made no attempt to conceal her contempt and bitterness.

The expression on Felrad's face bothered her. He showed no contrition for his craven act, but neither was there any triumph at the misery he had caused. He drew a weary breath.

"I have been forced to do many things which troubled me.

Your use as assassin is certainly one of those," the Prince finally said.

"Assassin? What do you mean?" demanded Davin.

"When Amrik Tohon sold her to me, I conceived of a scheme to rid Raemllyn of the mage Masur-Kell. Lijena, do you remember anything of the trip from Bistonia to Leticia?"

"Nothing. I was drugged!"

"A special drug to remold your mind into ways beneficial to overthrowing Zarek Yannis," Felrad nodded.

"I was to kill Masur-Kell?" Lijena stared at the pretender to the Velvet Throne.

"Aye. My battle against Yannis extends even to his minions. Masur-Kell has been a staunch supporter of the usurper and is singlehandedly responsible for Leticia remaining in Zarek Yannis' camp."

Lijena simply stared, not knowing what to say.

"I take no pride in what I did to you," Prince Felrad continued, "but I do not regret it, either. I will do anything within my power to stop Zarek Yannis, even if it means slavery or death for thousands. Such a fate is less than Yannis will mete out to untold millions if he continues his tyrannical rule over Raemllyn."

"Do you truly believe that?" she asked. "Do you think that deposing Yannis is more important than any individual's death?"

"I do," the prince answered. "Even my own death."

"Then the Sword of Kwerin Bloodhawk is best carried in your hands." Lijena unstrapped the belt about her waist and passed over the magical sword and sheath to the man who would conquer a tyrant and reclaim a kingdom.

Prince Felrad accepted the weapon and held it reverently in his hands. A single tear hung at the corner of his right eye.

Reflected in that tear, Lijena saw the Sword of Kwerin Bloodhawk. From the first days of Raemllyn's written history came a hope and a chance for victory.

chapter 23

"THE PAIN, THE PAIN!" Valora shrieked.

The sorceress dropped to her knees, then fell to the ground writhing, hands clutched to her ears. Against the ebony of her robes her face, twisted in horrible agony, appeared pallid, more dead than alive.

From the corner of an eye, Davin Anane saw the expression on Goran's face. The Challing's cheek twitched uncontrollably, and the green of the fire in his good eye burned with preternatural intensity.

"Zarek Yannis!" Prince Felrad clutched the Sword of Kwerin tightly in both hands. "The usurper brings on his second wave!"

Unsheathing the ancient blade, the prince swung about and held the mystical sword high so all might see that he was now the sword bearer. "To the battlements! For Raemllyn and freedom!"

A ragged cry went up along the walkways as wary soldiers prepared to repulse the armed might that had to follow the assault of punishing magicks.

Lijena knelt beside Valora, who quaked like a leaf in a high wind. The swordswoman reached out and hesitantly touched the mage's shoulder. Valora shook the harder.

"The pressure. *I feel it!* It threatens to crush my skull. It tries to rend my limbs from my body!" the sorceress wailed, her black eyes flying wide like those of a madwoman.

"Can we help?" Lijena asked, her words as unsteady as the hand on the mage's shoulder.

"I am so alone. Hamor-Lorn has me isolated. I drift. There is no world. I am cut free and float, helpless, unable to breathe or act."

Lijena grabbed the sorceress and shook until ripples formed in Valora's cascade of raven-wing-dark hair. The mage stiffened and abruptly went limp. Like a dreamer awakening, Valora stared up into Lijena's face, seeing yet not seeing.

"Berenicis has betrayed us," Valora said, shocked. "Through Hamor-Lorn's grace, he plots with Zarek Yannis. The blonde one, Tun's daughter, she is with him, though not of her own will. Berenicis kidnapped her, and she struggles to free herself from the ropes that bind her."

Goran emitted a bull-throated roar of rage and defiance that threatened to shake the fortress' foundations. More than one of Felrad's fighters looked fearfully at the giant, grateful that he was on their side.

"I will enter Yannis' camp alone if need be!" Goran shouldered his battle-ax.

"Goran!" Davin cautioned. "The magical assault against Valora means that there will be more. We cannot go after Kulonna or Berenicis now."

Davin's pale face hardened. "After the fray is won, it will be a race, my friend, as to which of us finds the Blackheart first. For what he has done to Awendala, I claim his life. For the way he has treated me and my family, I claim his life—though I cannot deny your rightful claim, either."

"We'll take turns with the whoreson!" A bestial growl pushed from the Challing's throat. "First, I'll break every bone in his treacherous body! You may have the privilege of flaying his skin from his still-living body. Then I'll pluck out his eyes and leave him for the insects!"

The witch-fire in Goran's eye faded. Davin looked at Valora. The dark mage rose and leaned against the battlements, visibly shaken. Davin frowned. What did Zarek Yannis have to gain with such an attack? Valora had not been killed, nor did it seem that such was the intent. A diversion? For what?

"Goran!" Dread suffused the Jyotian—dread and the horrible understanding of a brother who would stop at nothing to destroy him and gain a crown for his head. "Can you sense the presence of the Faceless Ones? Do you feel them now?"

"What?" The Challing appeared lost in a world all his own. "Aye, of course I sense them. They are in front of us, in front of the gates."

The Challing lifted a hand and pointed directly ahead.

"The fortress' gates lay behind you, not ahead!" Davin said. "You point at the eastern side of the fortress."

Goran's single eye blinked, and his head straightened. He half turned, saw that his friend spoke truly, and once more faced in the direction his senses homed on. "No, there are Faceless Ones in this direction."

"My Prince!" Davin cried to the departing heir to the Velvet Throne. "A moment. It is urgent."

Prince Felrad left his aides, an expression of annoyance on his face. "There is much still to be done. What do you want, Davin?"

"Is there any way in or out of here in that direction?" The Jyotian indicated the spot where Goran sensed the Faceless Ones.

"A secret gate, yes," the Prince said. "How did you know of it?"

"Did Berenicis know of it?" demanded Goran. "If so, might he not lead in a company of the Faceless to betray us?"

"There is only one guard stationed there. More to give warning than to fight," Felrad mused aloud. "Were Felrad to fail this day, Nelek Kahl would have escaped through the gate to gather another army to stand against Zarek Yannis."

"In all likelihood, Berenicis left the stronghold through the gate, killing the sentry as he went," Goran said.

"And now leads the Faceless Ones through the same gate!" This from Lijena.

Felrad appeared torn between the waves of magical assault buffeting Valora, the need of his presence for all to see, and the possibility that Rakell's defenses had been treacherously breached, threatening the lives of all within his fortress. He decided:

"Quick! To the gate."

The Sword of Kwerin Bloodhawk in hand, the prince dashed toward the stairs. Davin, Goran and Lijena followed hard on his heels, descending the narrow staircase and rushing along the path leading to the stable where Berenicis had stolen a horse to make his escape.

"There!" cried Goran One-Eye. "There's the Blackheart's treachery!"

"They've passed through the trap-maze!" Felrad rushed forward before any could stop him, gleaming blade held high.

"So who wants to live forever?" asked Goran, giving his mighty shoulders a shrug of resignation and hefting battle-ax in both hands.

Through the trap-maze rode a line of thundering hell-riders astride steeds with hooves aflame. Neither battle cry nor war whoop passed the demon warriors' unseen lips. In unearthly silence, they charged in single file from the mouth of the trap-maze. Though he had faced and defeated the Faceless Ones twice before, an icy fist squeezed about Davin's heart.

Felrad met the attack with a mighty hacking slash that carried the Bloodhawk's blade completely through the chest of the first rider. With a quick kick, the prince sent the demon's crystalline sword spinning behind him.

Lijena stooped and hefted the sword. It wasn't Kwerin's blade, but it was a weapon. And if the Faceless carried it, the sword could kill. A howling cry tearing from her lips, she charged into the fray.

Behind her, Davin, still armed with his own blade of frozen flame, ran. Goran One-Eye followed with battle-ax readied.

Ahead, Prince Felrad ducked beneath the swipe of a Faceless and lashed out with a deadly blow that sent the third demon to enter the fortress flying from his saddle. Before the hell-creature's cloak touched the ground, its wearer had vanished in a greasy swirl of smoke.

Davin and Lijena stood their ground as the Faceless One who galloped past Felrad rode down on them. Lijena struck first, ducking beneath the hell-rider's blade and swinging her sword into the legs of the passing horse.

And Davin found himself facing a Faceless One who leaped from the saddle and alighted on the ground with sword flashing toward its human opponent's head. The Jyotian's own blade met the demon's in a shower of blue-white flames. The impact sent a bone-jarring shudder coursing through the young thief.

Again the creature struck, and again and again. Davin's own blade answered not, merely parried the hail of blows. Like it or not, the Faceless One was vastly superior in strength. And the demon fought with the advantage of height and familiarity with its weapon. As fast as Davin was, he barely managed to block the demon's strokes.

As suddenly as the Faceless One had begun the attack, it vanished. Davin thought he had been struck on the skull and dazed, but he saw Prince Felrad grinning at him. The Sword of Kwerin had a potent effect on the demon-spawns.

Returning his prince's grin, the Jyotian raced forward with Lijena to meet another rider who broke into the fortress.

As hard as he fought, Davin knew he did little more than slow the Faceless Ones' advance through the maze leading from the secret door in the stronghold's wall. One at a time they had to traverse the trap-maze, and the ones Felrad missed, Davin, Lijena and Goran had to stop.

"They can be killed!" Lijena shouted.

Her hair swung in disarray, matted and dirty, speckled with her own blood. At her feet lay a Faceless and its horse, both unstirring. The sword of crystal fire that Lijena held burned painfully bright. Nor was the swordswoman's stroke merely a lucky blow.

Goran put his prodigious power into a two-handed swing that connected his war ax with the side of one of the Faceless. The demon spilled from its mount's back, but still lived. It hit the ground, stirred, then came slowly to its feet. Goran bellowed and charged, bringing the ax down forcefully on the demon's head. The blow connected—and the Faceless monster kept fighting. A third powerful stroke also failed to destroy the demon.

"Black Qar take you!" shouted the Challing. A fourth blow separated from the wrist a skeletal hand clutching a sword. And still the Faceless One fought on.

"Don't let it touch you," warned Lijena. "Its very touch is death!"

"Brykheedah be with us!" Felrad called on the God of Warriors. "Still more come through the gateway. Warn Valora!"

Davin glanced left and right. Goran One-Eye still fought with the Faceless One who refused to yield. Lijena used her sword in a double-handed grip to hold back a pair of the hell-creatures. And in front of the Jyotian rode a demon with glowing red eyes and sword leveled to skewer a human chest.

Who was there to act as courier? The foursome was all that stood between victory and defeat! Davin leaped aside, letting the Faceless' sword slice empty air, while his blade leaped for the monster's cowled head.

"Die, damn your red-hot eyes, *die!*" Goran's muscles cracked with the effort he put into an ax blow that sent his Faceless foe reeling to the ground—but failed to kill it.

Feeling Ebil, Goddess of the Frenzy, upon him, the Challing unleashed a berserker's fury. He bellowed and swung the heavy ax as if its weight had vanished. Blow after devastating blow landed on the Faceless One. In the midst of the rain of metal death, the demon's spirit fled. Only the battered robe remained behind to give mute evidence to the demon's one-time menace.

"Goran, take its sword. Use the fire sword!" yelled Davin. His shoulders burned as if they'd been flayed. Muscles turned rubbery, and he gave way before the Faceless One bearing down on him. Simply parrying was almost more than Davin Anane could accomplish.

Goran roared and came to his aid, using the captured crystalline fire sword. The berserker fury still on him, the Challing spun and charged toward two hell-riders who escaped Prince Felrad's never ceasing blade.

The sight of the attacking red-bearded giant brought not a blink from the demons' eyes. Goran wasn't sure they knew the meaning of fear or courage. The creatures fought, seemingly without pleasure, and either won or perished, also without pleasure or fear.

Before Goran's sword struck, Lijena was at his side. Back to back, they lifted their blades of crystalline flame and swept them upward. Two Faceless died without scream or cry.

"Ho!" Goran glanced over his shoulder and winked at Lijena. "You fight well for a skinny wench!"

"And you for an over-stuffed braggart!"

Davin's two-handed blow sliced into the forelegs of his opponent's mount, bringing the steed to its knees. Again, the rider did not tumble from the saddle, but landed lightly on its feet, sword swiping out to gut the human warrior who dared oppose it.

Davin backstepped to avoid the raking tip of the weapon, then threw caution aside. He lunged, full weight behind the demon blade he carried. Like a hot iron brand burning through wood, the crystalline blade drove into the Faceless One's midriff. Then all resistance faded as the demon-spawn vanished in swirling black smoke.

"Back!" Valora's voice cried from atop the fortress wall. "Move back!"

Davin's head jerked up, and he did as the mage ordered. A heartbeat later, Goran, Lijena, and Felrad retreated—not in sudden cowardice, but to avoid the barrage of arrows that archers hailed down on the Faceless Ones. Immediately, shrill keenings rose from unearthly throats—the first sounds the demons had made in their attack!

The sorceress' hands wove in the air and her fingers danced. Her voice sang and cried, whispered and shouted, pleaded and demanded. And her magicks flowed outward, touching each of the hell-creatures who carried a shaft in its unholy body.

As with the first attack, the Faceless rocked, then tumbled from their saddles, staggering to their feet like drunkards too disoriented to know whether it was night or day.

With a shout of approval to the mage, Felrad once more hefted the Sword of Kwerin Bloodhawk and charged the demon warriors that Zarek Yannis had sent against him. Davin, Lijena, and Goran were a step behind him. And at their heels came a howling wave of green-clad soldiers who stooped and retrieved the crystal blades that had fallen from the talons of the slain hell-creatures. Those unlucky enough not to find a flame-licked sword, raised blades and spears of cold, hard steel.

Prince Felrad's gaze moved over the suddenly silent battlefield. He allowed the tip of the Sword of Kwerin Bloodhawk to droop. Amid the twisted bodies of his slain defenders, no Faceless One or hellish steed moved.

"It is over." The realization came trembling from his lips. "We've won."

"Won?" Davin blinked and stared about. He turned woozy

and weaved when he realized the magnitude of the invasion force they had met and defeated. Never since the days of Kwerin Bloodhawk himself had such a victory been won against the demons. "We slew over two dozen of them! Another score died after we were reinforced!"

"Fifty," came Goran's exact count. "We have slain fifty of the demons."

For a few seconds, utter silence descended as the impact of this announcement penetrated fatigue-dazed minds. Then Lijena shouted a cheer of triumph that was soon taken up by all who stood still.

Felrad's arms lifted, demanding silence. "You have performed a miracle this day. Yehseen has smiled upon us, but there is still a human army opposing us. Back to the walls!"

Prince Felrad stationed a small squad to watch the secret gate. None believed that Yannis would attempt a second sally through this way, but if he did, those in the squad would have ample opportunity to warn other defenders.

When Davin Anane regained the fortress' battlements, he saw that Prince Felrad was right in his appraisal of the menace facing them. After Valora had detected the threat of the Faceless Ones and sent the saving flight of arrows, she had returned to her watch, holding back the magical thrusts sent by Hamor-Lorn and his assistants.

Davin saw the weariness on Valora's handsome, cruel face. He also saw the determination. Berenicis the Blackheart might abandon Prince Felrad, but not this one. This mage fought until victory or death.

"The tides of magic abate," said Valora. "That can only mean that Yannis' generals have decided to launch a full frontal assault."

"They must know their venture behind our lines failed," said Davin. "We can hope that Zarek Yannis' anger forces him to make mistakes."

"We can hope, but not count on it," Lijena said.

Davin felt a strong hand on his shoulder. Goran pointed across the charred plain stretching in front of Rakell's gates. "They come," the Challing said simply.

Davin Anane's mouth turned to cotton. The usurper's full human army moved on the fortress. Sluggishly at first, then with gathering momentum, Zarek Yannis' troops lumbered toward the walls.

"They will die on our swords," came a penetrating voice. "They will die, and we shall triumph!"

"For Raemllyn!" Prince Felrad cried.

All eyes turned to their leader and the raised Sword of Kwerin Bloodhawk.

"For Raemllyn!" Goran answered, his voice booming through the stronghold.

And to Davin's surprise, he found himself shouting as loudly as the others when they took up the battle cry.

chapter 24

"A TRAP!" ZAREK Yannis screamed in disbelief. Foam formed at the corners of his mouth. "They were led into a trap. How else could Felrad have slain a full fifty of my Faceless Ones?"

Hamor-Lorn spread his hands in a gesture that said he was uncertain. He dared not tell his liege that more than fifty of the demons had been dispatched back to their proper dimension. The first twenty that Felrad had lured inside the walls of Rakell were also gone.

Of the hundred Faceless Ones that had been transported from the mainland, those invincible warriors that sent icy fear through any mortal facing them, only a meager thirty remained. And Hamor-Lorn worried about their efficacy against such determined defenders as Felrad's forces.

The sorcerer knew better than to speak the truth now, when the usurper raged like a madman. One slip of the tongue might mean Yannis would be seeking a new master mage.

Therefore, the white-haired wizard lied. "King Zarek, I fear that we have a traitor in our ranks. There can be no other explanation."

The mage watched the expression on his liege's face alter subtly. The anger still gave a dark tint to Yannis' features, but now cold comprehension dawned to give the answer the mage desired.

"Berenicis!"

"Who else might it be? Was he not the one who came to you with the traitorous tale of this unknown side entry? Was he not the one who promised a quick victory?" Hamor-Lorn carefully planted the seeds of doubt. He fell silent and let Yannis' natural suspicions prosper on their own.

"They do not call that whoreson Blackheart for naught!" Yannis nodded as though having come to the solution to a convoluted problem. The usurper then spun about and shouted, "Guards! Find Berenicis and bring him to me. At once!"

The four of Yannis' personal bodyguards who stood stationed near the entrance to the High King's tent bowed and hastened to comply with their master's command.

"Is it wise to commit all your forces here in Loieterland to this attack, my liege?" Hamor-Lorn asked when Yannis turned back to him. "The full twenty thousand men might fail. If, uh, seventy of the Faceless Ones are already fallen, dare we make such an assault?"

"There are only thirty of the Faceless Ones left?" Yannis' expression sagged, as if he were stunned by a blow to the back of his head. "Only thirty of a full five score?"

The High King wilted against a table littered with maps of Rakell and the surrounding terrain. "I had intended them to bear the brunt of the battle—and to pierce Felrad's defenses. We are no better off now than when we landed."

Hamor-Lorn offered no answer. They were far worse off, he knew. He and his mages had repeatedly attempted to bring Valora to her knees—and failed. The witch displayed more power and promise than Yannis' descriptions of Valora's abilities had led him to believe possible.

In spite of the danger Valora presented, the old mage admitted his admiration for her spells, her subtle skills. Rarely was such talent seen. He wished that he could have known the dark mage, could have spoken with her before this futile invasion. Together, *they* might have ruled Raemllyn instead of this pitiful worm struggling to make command decisions.

Not for the first time, Hamor-Lorn wondered exactly how Zarek Yannis had summoned the Faceless Ones.

The aging sorcerer pushed aside the question for the moment. If he stayed alert, perhaps Zarek Yannis would reveal the information in the heat of battle.

Hamor-Lorn shook his head. *The battle!* What had been a simple, decisive invasion to crush an upstart, now had all the appearances of turning into a major defeat, a fiasco. The only hope lay with the usurper, that Zarek Yannis retained enough wit to pull victory from the bowels of defeat.

Lord Berenicis the Blackheart glanced up from the maps of Rakell's fortress he drew for Yannis. He jerked around even though no one stood behind him.

"Flinching at shadows?" taunted Kulonna. She struggled futilely against the ropes binding her arms and legs securely.

"Something is amiss. I *feel* it." Berenicis believed that the Goddess of Luck often rode at his elbow and kept him alive through situations that would have sent a less fortunate man into Black Qar's embrace. When or what Jajhana would exact as payment for her grace, Berenicis didn't know or care. Whatever, the price would be small compared to continued life.

Something is wrong, terribly wrong. The dethroned ruler of Jyotis could not shake the wormy doubt awrithe at the back of his mind. Better to heed such ominous omens than foolishly lose one's head.

Berenicis shoved back from the table he worked on and walked over to Kulonna. Grasping her golden-tressed hair, he jerked her head back. To the whiteness of her vulnerably exposed throat, he pressed the blade of his dirk.

"We leave immediately. Cry out or attempt to flee, and I'll kill you on the spot."

His tone left no doubt that he was fully capable of carrying out the threat. Still, Kulonna spat, "That'd be better than what the Sitala has decreed for me!"

"Stupid bitch!"

Berenicis jerked the bound duchess to her feet. His knife flashed, not to open her graceful throat, but to sever the hobbles about her ankles. He shoved her toward the back of the tent.

"Do I dig my way under?" she continued to taunt. "With bound hands?"

The razor-edged dirk flashed again, slashing a rent in the tough fabric. Berenicis pushed his captive through. Only when she stumbled, threatening to fall on her face, did he aid her with a supporting arm.

"Not a word," he cautioned in a low whisper.

They had walked less than a hundred paces when Kulonna saw the detachment of guards striding purposefully in the direction of the tent they'd so precipitously vacated. She thought of crying out, then stopped. Zarek Yannis would kill her faster than Berenicis the Blackheart. At least the traitor had some small use for her alive.

"This way," said Berenicis, guiding her through Rakell's streets to the city's docks.

He paused and studied the abandoned vessels moored to a nearby pier. He then shoved Kulonna toward a small fishing boat. Hastily he examined the craft. It appeared sound enough, and its single sail looked new with no signs of patching. Although no sailor, he was certain he could handle the boat. After all, the Bay of Zaid was not that wide.

"In with you." Berenicis dumped Kulonna into the bottom of the small craft.

He quickly untied the mooring lines, shoved the craft from the pier, and jumped in. Within a few short minutes the Blackheart lowered the sail, letting the wind fill it. His gray eyes scanned the watery horizon before him. Their progress was slow. He would have preferred having a fisherman at the helm to carry them from Rakell's harbor, but the city's citizenry stood with Felrad in his damned fortress.

A humorless smile touched the Jyotian lord's thin lips. So secure was Zarek Yannis in his position that no vessel patrolled the harbor. Nor did Berenicis notice any sentries posted around the shore. Jajhana still smiled on him.

Or did she? Berenicis frowned. A traitor to Prince Felrad, he now deserted Zarek Yannis' army. Where in all Raemllyn could he find sanctuary? *Where?*

"Stop the arrows! Damn you, can't you see what they do? Stop them immediately!" cried Zarek Yannis.

The High King of Raemllyn stared across the battlefield and pointed toward Rakell's distant battlements indicating where Valora stood. "And Valora! Kill her! She's responsible for this. Kill the traitorous bitch!"

"Her spells are extraordinary," Hamor-Lorn said, unwilling to openly admit he and his apprentices had been unable to find a chink in the sorceress' armor of spells. "But she stands alone. Our first magical assault killed all the other mages. Soon, she must weaken. I think the time is at hand. See how few of the arrows now come from the walls?"

"What are you saying? There are still thousands showering down!"

"No, my liege, those are not the ones I mean. Among those thousands of arrows are only a few magical barbs capable of confusing your Faceless Ones. I see the difference plainly in their composition. She has ensorcelled only a few, in comparison to the hundreds that rained down on the Faceless' initial attack."

"Do you counsel I now unleash the remaining Faceless Ones?" Yannis asked, turning to eye the wizard.

"Yes." The sorcerer nodded. Hamor-Lorn tucked his hands into the loose folds of his robe. "And if they, too, fail, you can always summon more."

The expression on Zarek Yannis' face revealed to Hamor-Lorn that such was not possible. Could the Faceless Ones be brought to this dimension only at certain times? Had Yannis lost his power? Forgotten the spell? What *was* the secret of the hell-riders' summoning?

"We attack, the Faceless in the forefront. The rest of the troops will be committed to battle as quickly as they can move." Yannis summoned an aide, who took the order and ran from the camp to inform the field commanders.

The entire army stirred like a giant beast awakening from winter-long slumbers. Then it began to ponderously move forward, forty thousand feet grinding into the cinders of the plain. And at the head of the army galloped the remaining thirty Faceless Ones.

"Now, Felrad, now let's see your response," gloated Zarek Yannis.

The king's mage watched impassively as flight after flight of arrows showered from above. Dozens, sometimes hundreds struck the Faceless Ones and produced no injury. Hamor-Lorn winced when a new barrage rained down, most of these arrows ensorcelled.

One such magical arrow did little against a hell-rider, but two proved vexing and three debilitating. Some, Hamor-Lorn saw, were struck by as many as a dozen. Those unlucky demons simply vanished in black smoke, or fell, unable to rise from the ground.

"They have reached the gates!" cried Zarek Yannis with delight. "Although they are being decimated, the demons have reached the gates . . ."

The King's words trailed off to a gasp when he saw the massive wooden portal fling open. Rushing forth to do battle rode Felrad.

"He has the sword!" Hamor-Lorn silently prayed to Raemllyn's gods for aid.

Fewer than a dozen of the Faceless Ones had ridden through Valora's deadly barrage, but could any man, even one armed with the fabled Sword of Kwerin Bloodhawk, stand against ten of the powerful Faceless Ones?

Felrad did.

If he had been slain, the battle would have ended with Zarek Yannis' troops pouring into a disheartened fortress. But Felrad triumphed. Again and again the demons sliced at the Prince with their swords of crystal fire. Felrad showed more vitality than any five others. He fought—and won!

From behind him rose the cry, "For Raemllyn! For Raemllyn and freedom!"

Arrows continued to arc down on Yannis' host as they crossed the denuded plain to collide with Felrad's forces. Nor were the prince's forces ill-trained peasants and rabble, as Yannis had so often proclaimed. With sword and spear they raked into the tide of the usurper's troops, only to be slain by the black-and-white clad soldiers loyal to the holder of the Velvet Throne.

"We win!" Zarek Yannis crowed. "See how we push them back?"

Hamor-Lorn agreed. What Yannis said was true. The tide of twenty thousand fighters crushed the smaller fighting force from Rakell.

But the defenders had only to retreat behind the gates and close them, leaving Zarek Yannis' army exposed on the plain. More arrows. Pots of boiling oil. And when Felrad had the chance to regroup his forces, another sally forth from the fortress.

Again Felrad was turned back and forced to retreat, but not

before his men again extracted a bloody toll.

"The siege engines. Are the sappers finished constructing them?" Yannis glanced at his aides, who nodded. "Use them against the gates. The next time Felrad comes forth, fire the siege engines!"

Hamor-Lorn motioned to one of his assistant mages. The woman hurried off with the command.

And when Felrad again rode forth to enter the fray, the engines released their fiery, ensorcelled loads. Flaming, clinging tars burned against the walls and gates of Rakell, but few defenders were caught.

"Valora warns them of our magicks. She cannot counter us, but she can advise. We have wasted these loads." Hamor-Lorn watched another wave of green pour from the fortress.

Howling, they ran toward Yannis' troops, then abruptly stopped. A black cloud of short spears filled the air, taking a fearsome toll on those in black and white. Only when a third flight of spears had been unleashed did Felrad signal retreat.

"King Zarek, they make use of simple weapons. Those are spears with soft iron heads," Hamor-Lorn said, fearing the worst. It was only a matter of time until Felrad claimed victory. Yannis must retreat and salvage what remained of his forces.

"Do they carry a spell?" the High King asked.

"No, but . . ."

"Then have our troops pick them up and throw them back. Use their own weapons against them!"

"The points are soft iron," the mage repeated. "When they strike the ground, they bend. We would have to pound them straight to be effective."

"And," said Yannis, slumping slightly, "when they enter a body, the point also deforms, making it more difficult to pull out. Black Qar take you, Felrad!"

Both Zarek Yannis and Hamor-Lorn spun when one of their siege engines erupted in flame. Shrieks from the crew soon faded as the victims died.

"Valora!" Hamor-Lorn took a few steps forward, then stopped. The renegade mage might not have the power to oppose Hamor-Lorn and all his assistants, but she used the same tactics that Felrad employed. A quick magical strike, retreat, then a spell to confuse and disorganize. "Nyuria burn her!"

"Why can't you prevent this?" demanded Yannis.

"Why cannot your troops fight Felrad's?" countered Hamor-Lorn. "Look—and tell me if that is your victory!"

Yannis and Hamor-Lorn saw the front of the massive army sag under Felrad's onslaught. This time there was no lightning swift attack followed by retreat to regroup. Felrad's troops poured from Rakell's fortress and pursued. The huge army that had journeyed across half of Raemllyn to destroy Prince Felrad now found itself routed, fleeing before the numerically inferior defenders.

"Fight!" shouted Yannis. "You must fight!"

"They will not fight," said Hamor-Lorn. "They are in flight. You should have personally led them, as you did at Kressia. There is no way to prevent defeat now. No way. Valora's magicks are weak, but they are adequate enough to keep me from Rakell and Felrad. And the Prince's warriors show spirit yours lack."

"The Faceless Ones," moaned Yannis.

"They are gone," Hamor-Lorn said, taking some glee in tormenting Yannis with the knowledge. "Felrad has destroyed them all."

"You," said Zarek Yannis. "You are responsible. You and your mages failed me. Berenicis turned against me and betrayed my Faceless Ones to Felrad. You all conspire against me!"

"My liege, *you* have lost this battle. No one else is to blame."

Hamor-Lorn cared little for the High King's desire to place blame upon shoulders other than his own. The sorcerer had lived through other disasters, both military and magical, and survived. This time would be no different.

"We must flee," said Yannis, stunned. "A ship. Our ships! To the docks and away from the Qar-damned island!"

Hamor-Lorn motioned for his aides to begin packing what magical instruments and grimoires lay about. The mage had no desire to be remembered by history as the one presiding over such a debacle, but perhaps an accommodation could be reached with the victor. Hamor-Lorn was not above negotiating to achieve his goals.

The mage picked up his grimoire and started from the tent, when a heavy blow to the back of the head drove him to his knees; his head spun, eyes unable to focus. Even dazed, Hamor-

Lorn's fingers worked to form a ward spell.

"Valora?" he croaked, believing that the witch reached out for him with her devious spells. For an instant his vision cleared, and he looked up into the face of his assailant. The mage's eyes widened. "My liege! Don't!"

Zarek Yannis swung his scepter with all his might. The old mage's skull cracked and split in a shower of crimson and gray. Hamor-Lorn toppled over, dead. For a few seconds, Yannis stared at his victim, then he threw himself forward, his body covering that of the ancient sorcerer.

"The power, oh, the power rising, yes, oh, yes," Zarek Yannis moaned, writhing about. But all too soon the essence that had been Hamor-Lorn faded. Only a cooling corpse remained.

Yannis awkwardly rose and stared at the body. "You had little within you, mage. Not like the others."

Unsteadily, Yannis walked from the tent to find his guard. He must escape Rakell and the Isle of Loieter. The essence he had absorbed from Hamor-Lorn might not be adequate for him to summon more than one or two of the Faceless Ones from their dimension, but those and the demons who awaited on the mainland would be enough to begin anew.

The war vessel waiting for Zarek Yannis sailed, passing less than a league from the small fishing boat bearing Berenicis the Blackheart.

Following King Yannis across the waters of the Bay of Zaid came the haunting chant, "For Raemllyn! For Raemllyn and freedom!"

chapter 25

"VICTORY! VICTORY! For Raemllyn and freedom!" The cry echoed from Rakell's docks.

Davin Anane, Goran One-Eye, and Lijena Farleigh stared at the ships that fled from the city's harbor out into the Bay of Zaid. Of those that came with the invading horde of Zarek Yannis' soldiers, less than a fourth returned to the open sea. Another fourth lay afire within Rakell's harbor, while the remaining half now flew Prince Felrad's green as his followers swarmed the vessels' decks, claiming the ships for the true ruler of Raemllyn.

"Why does he stop now?" Anger growled from the snarled lips of the Challing. "We should give chase! Yannis escapes as does Berenicis. Why doesn't Felrad follow and finish what we started here today?"

"I see no sign of Felrad." Lijena's aquamarine eyes shifted from side to side, her gaze searching the harbor for the prince's banner that had flown at his side all during the long fight.

"Nor do I." Davin searched the ranks of green-clad defenders. Felrad was nowhere to be found. "Is something amiss?"

"Felrad was with us when we entered Rakell's streets, chasing the usurper's army toward the water," Goran said. "I remember seeing him, then the avenues separated us."

"Aye." This from Lijena. "'Twas the last I noticed him, too."

A fist of dread closed about Davin's chest. He refused to utter the dark thought that filled his head. "Backtrack until we find him."

Neither of his companions questioned his reasons, though their furrowed brows said that they, too, feared the worst for the prince. Wearily, bodies and souls exhausted from the day's never-ending battle, the three turned and left the cheering soldiers who watched Yannis' ships disappear over the watery horizon.

Through Rakell's corpse-littered streets they moved, fearing with each step they would find the prince lying beside his fallen banner. The plain that separated city from fortress was worse. The ground was completely covered with the bodies of the dead. To both uniforms of forest green and those of black and white was added the mutual hue of blood red.

"How many fell?" Lijena stumbled to a halt. In disbelief she sank to her knees, her eyes narrowing as she stared at the vast butchery.

"Half of Felrad's army, at least, and an equal portion of Yannis'." Goran placed a comforting hand on the swordswoman's shoulder and lightly squeezed. "It was a hard-fought and hard-won victory."

"Won," Davin mumbled, unable to accept that a victor rose from such carnage—a slaughter in which his own blade had again and again added to the numbers of the dead.

Nor was there personal victory for him. Zarek Yannis still lived, as did his half-brother, Berenicis. And as for Kulonna, he could only hope that she had not suffered the same fate as Awendala, whose body would soon lie atop the funeral pyre with all who had died this black day.

Davin glanced at the Faceless One's blade of crystalline flame that he still clutched. With a curse to the gods who so moved humankind to such horrors, he cast it from him.

"Blame not the gods for this day." Goran's good eye lifted to his friend. "Men did this to men. The gods would never be so cruel."

"Look!" Lijena pointed to where Davin had thrown the demon's blade.

The weapon crumbled to gray powder and mixed with the plain's blood and dust.

"The flame-sword dies," Davin said wearily. "As long as life grasps the Faceless Ones' swords, they burn with death. Drop it and. . . ." Davin shrugged. It mattered little to him now. He was past caring.

Both Goran and Lijena cast away their captured swords. Those weapons of frozen fire vanished, just as Yannis' army had vanished.

"Davin!" Goran pointed across the body-strewn plain. "Felrad's banner!"

The banner did fly, but not mounted beside the Prince atop his war charger. Instead it waved above a litter carried by four soldiers. Valora, the sheathed Sword of Kwerin Bloodhawk in her hands, moved in a huddled walk beside the litter, attending Felrad.

"He's wounded." Lijena pushed to her feet and hurried toward the litter. "Prince Felrad's been wounded."

Davin and Goran moved after Bistonia's daughter as fast as their weary legs could take them. Reaching the litter, they saw that Lijena's words were true. Felrad, his face a deathly hue, lay on his back. An ugly slash ran from his left shoulder down his chest to his waist.

"How did it happen?" Davin's gaze moved between the litter bearers, Valora, and the wounded prince.

"Back," Valora waved them away. "There are physicians in the fortress who will tend his wounds. He's lost far too much blood. Go, let me get . . ."

"No," Felrad's eyes fluttered open. "Davin, is that you?"

"Yes, my Prince." Davin stepped beside the litter.

"The Sitala like to play with mortals." A weak smile moved over Felrad's lips. "With the Sword of the Bloodhawk I stood against Yannis' horde of Faceless Ones without serious injury. A soldier armed but with a puny dirk did this. Jumped from an alley, struck, then raced away."

"My Prince," Davin urged, "rest. Save your strength. Valora will see that the physicians attend your wounds."

"And you attend our wounds, son of Anane," Felrad continued. "The others mustn't know of this. Not now, when victory is so sweet. Tend to the dead and wounded, and let it be known that I counsel with Valora to map our strategy for a campaign south to drive Zarek Yannis from the Velvet Throne.

Do that for me . . . my brother."

"Aye." Davin clasped the Prince's hand as it rose to him and squeezed it tightly. "I will do all that you have commanded."

With that, Davin released Felrad's hand and watched the litter bearers carry the wounded prince behind the walls of the fortress.

"Raemllyn will soon be Felrad's," Goran said as he stood beside Davin on the fortress' ramparts. "But such a price in blood will have to be paid first."

Davin didn't answer. His gaze focused on the blazing inferno that turned night into day across the barren plain separating Rakell from the fortress—a plain the survivors now called the Plain of Victory. For Davin it was a plain of weeping.

Less than an hour ago, the Jyotian had carried Awendala's cold, lifeless body from the stronghold and placed her atop the monstrous funeral pyre he had ordered built. There, among the dead from both Felrad's and Yannis' armies, he had left her, casting the first torch to set the blaze. Now a piece of hell reigned on earth, erasing Awendala's beauty and love forever.

No, Davin refused to lie to himself. Awendala still lived within his breast, as did their love, as did the pain. *By the gods, why not me rather than her?*

"Davin, I cannot stay here." Goran turned so that he faced his friend with his one good eye. "I must seek Kulonna and Berenicis. I understand you must remain with Felrad, but I can not. Not until Kulonna is safe again."

Davin's head turned slowly to the Challing. This massive giant who stood before him was not the Goran One-Eye he had wandered with for six years. The changeling's face was set like granite, nor was there a hint of jest in his voice.

"I know not what I will do," Davin answered. "My mind and heart have been with Awendala, my friend. I had forgotten your own loss."

Goran nodded. "I want to be away with the morn. I'll follow Berenicis right into Zarek Yannis' throne room in Kavindra, if that's what it takes to free Kulonna."

"I'll see about arranging passage for you to the mainland." Davin said. "And supplies. You'll also need a horse and gold. I don't think Felrad will deny you . . ."

"Davin!" Lijena Farleigh's voice called from below. "Davin Anane."

"Aye, up here," Davin shouted down.

"Quick, Felrad summons you to him," Lijena waved to the Jyotian. "And, Goran, he asked for you."

Davin and Goran hastened from the battlements and followed Lijena into the heart of Felrad's fortress. They passed by the guards outside his chamber without question. Inside, Felrad lay propped in his bed. His eyes fluttered open as the three entered. A fleeting smile touched his lips as he beckoned them to him with a weak wave of his hand.

"I'm afraid our victory this day is tainted by treachery, my friends." Felrad winced in obvious pain as he spoke. "The Sword of Kwerin Bloodhawk is gone."

"Gone?" Davin's gray eyes darted about the chamber. "But we all saw Valora carrying it . . ." He swallowed the rest of his sentence when he noticed the sorceress was nowhere to be seen. "Valora!"

"Aye," Felrad answered with a nod. "She has fled with the sword and sheath. While the physicians bound my wounds, she took a horse and rode north for Vatusia."

"The witch seeks to rejoin Berenicis, I'll wager!" Goran straightened, witch-fire sparking anew in the Challing's good eye.

"My thoughts are the same," Felrad replied.

"I'll send a whole company of men after her," Davin said. "She'll never reach Vatusia."

"Nay!" Felrad lifted a hand, halting the Jyotian as he turned to call for soldiers. "I can't risk it, Davin. Today a hard-fought victory was won. Word of it—and the Sword of Kwerin Bloodhawk—will spread across Raemllyn. Lords from the far realms will rally to me. I cannot let it be known that I have lost the only weapon capable of defeating Zarek Yannis' hordes of Faceless Ones."

"But," Davin turned back to his Prince.

"You must go after the sorceress," Felrad said. "You and

Lijena and Goran. None in my command know the witch and her powers better, or the powers inherent in the Bloodhawk's blade."

"Aye, I'll go," Goran answered. "And I'll claim the Blackheart's head while I'm at it."

Davin and Lijena nodded their acceptance of the task.

Goran looked at the weaponswoman and grinned. "Skinny one, it will be good to have your sword arm along."

Lijena answered with a smile, then looked back at Felrad. "And you, my Prince?"

"Tomorrow, I begin the campaign south to Kavindra," Felrad said. "Now I must speak to my army. Davin, help me to the balcony. They mustn't think that I've deserted them in their hour of victory."

Felrad waved away his physicians' protests and accepted Davin's arm in support as he slipped from the bed and stood. Together, prince and thief walked to the balcony. All heads below turned upward when Felrad called out:

"Defenders of Raemllyn's freedom, today you struck a mighty blow and sent the usurper and his army fleeing before your righteous strength. With the coming sun, we will board the ships that await us in the harbor and sail after the craven who has stolen the Velvet Throne. Tomorrow, Raemllyn will once again be ours!"

Joyous cheers resounded from below, and a ringing answer to Felrad's call to battle. Davin listened not. His eyes rose to the still-blazing flames of the funeral pyre burning on the plain.

Was victory truly so close, or merely an elusive dream? One battle was not a war. Zarek Yannis had suffered defeat today, but so had Felrad—half his troops and the Sword of Kwerin Bloodhawk.

Davin turned to Lijena and Goran One-Eye. Their expressions said the same thoughts moved through their minds. So much won—but so much lost. . . .

The End

Book Six: *For Crown and Kingdom*
in the *Swords of Raemllyn* series